RED ROCK BLEEDS

PART THREE OF THE RODRIGUEZ TRILOGY

GEORGE MARZOCCHI

Red Penguin
BOOKS

Red Rock Bleeds

Copyright © 2022 by George Marzocchi

All rights reserved

Published by Red Penguin Books

Bellerose Village, New York

Library of Congress Control Number: 2022914805

ISBN

Print 978-1-63777-300-0

Digital 978-1-63777-299-7

The third installment of the Rodriguez series, Red Rock Bleeds is dedicated to my wife Terry who has supported my writing career from the beginning. To our sons Damien and Julian and our four-legged sons, Maverick our Pomsky, Caribou Cody and Balkie our two cats. To our good friend and fellow author Valentina Janek who has promoted the books on social media. A big thank you to Stephanie Larkin and Red Penguin Publishing for her continued encouragement and support.

CONTENTS

PROLOGUE

Red Rock Canyon, a stone's throw from the lights and activity of Las Vegas, is a place for families to explore and marvel at the rock formations. The color of the stone changes at the whim of the sun. Reds and browns in various shades come together in a symphony of color. When the sun sets on Red Rocks, they take on a reddish glow but as darkness moves in the glow fades to black. Under the cover of that darkness, evil is emboldened and moves about. Where the lights of Sin City end, the terror begins. When night falls, Red Rock Canyon is no longer a place for families but a nightmare of shadows and twisted shapes. The rocks are no longer interesting geological structures but faces and bodies of some demonic outcroppings.

In this landscape, there is one more element of terror: a killer searching for prey in the casinos of Las Vegas. His victims lie prone on Red Rocks turning them even redder with blood. Suffocated by gambling chips jammed down their throats and playing cards nailed into their forehead. They seem to blend in with the shadows until daylight breaks. Then they become a vivid example of the previous night's terror. Sergeant Rodriguez and Agent Elizabeth McMahon hunt for the killer, dubbed Diamond Jack, in the bright lights of Las Vegas, the tunnels beneath the city, and the dark landscape of Red Rock Canyon.

CHAPTER 1
AMY AND GINO

Amy is looking in the mirror. She's hoping that the welt under her eye and the abrasion on her cheek will disappear under a layer of concealer. She was warned about the rough stuff prior to the date, but a little extra money helps dull the pain. Tonight she's dressing for a date, but it's not with some machine part salesman from Duluth or a cattle owner from Texas. Men who pay young girls like Amy to do things their wives won't do. Tonight she's meeting her boyfriend of one year, Gino Marchetti. If the girl next door had a universal representative, it would be Amy. Brown hair with sun-kissed highlights and blue eyes. Born in Nebraska, she was seven when the World Trade Center was attacked. As a child, she didn't understand what was happening. She spent many nights sleeping in her parents' bed where she felt safe from the nightmares. She came to Las Vegas at 22 years old to become a croupier but, with her looks and figure, she was offered a job as a showgirl. Her family tried to talk her out of the move, but Amy won out. One of the girls she performed with turned her on to the escort world. As she dresses, she wonders if Gino will take the next step and ask her to marry him. Gino has often asked her to reconsider her livelihood, but the needle hasn't moved. Amy calls it a temporary way to make some quick cash.

Gino always had the ability to make her laugh and help her forget the previous evening's encounters. She's hoping that tonight is one of those nights. Gino is due to arrive at seven and she checks herself one more time to make sure the concealer is working. Gino Marchetti was born in Brooklyn in 1980. His claim to fame is having known some of the local neighborhood gangsters. He wasn't part of the "crew," but he liked to imagine himself as being connected to it. In reality, he was only a paper gangster. Gino was a gambler, but he knew when to quit. He hadn't gambled in a few years, preferring to observe others while taking in the sights, sounds and smells. He did time in New York some years ago for assault. Some say he was defending himself but when your name is Marchetti in Brooklyn, it's your fault. All the talk about his gangster friends swayed the jury against him. The day he was released, he landed in Vegas. He fell into the sex-for-hire escort world for a time. That's where he met Amy. Gino never treated her rough like her other clients and assorted high rollers. The guys who think that as long as they're paying, they can do what they want. Amy was scared of these men. She carried a 22-caliber handgun in her bag, a gift from Gino. He arrives. They embrace and kiss each other passionately. The concealer wasn't quite enough, and Gino notices the bruises, but he doesn't mention them. They leave the apartment and go to the elevator arm in arm.

CHAPTER 2
RED ROCK, DEAD ROCK

The sun rises on Red Rock, bathing the vista with soft pink and red hues. Soon the sun will be over the hills to scorch the area, a typical day for Vegas. The tourists enter the park, stopping here and there for the perfect photo opportunity. A family from Anywhere U.S.A. decides to venture off the beaten path and explore areas hidden from the road. Their daughter, a young girl of 9 or 10 years old ventures further, against the wishes of her parents. She's in sight until she's not and then a scream rings out. The daughter and parents run to each other.

The daughter shouts, "There's a man over there on the rocks! He scared me!"

A father's instinct to protect his little girl from this perceived pervert forces him to run to the rocks. What he discovers when reaching the scene is not what he expected. Yes, there is a man, but this man is no more threatening to a young girl than the rock he's lying on. He's positioned on the rock as if he were part of its topography. His mouth is open and poker chips are visible. The scene is made more horrific by two playing cards nailed into his forehead. The sun is now high over the rocks, and it lights the scene showing every detail. He quickly walks his family away from the scene and calls the police as onlookers and the curious begin to swarm. Some believe it's a mannequin, part of an adolescent prank, but Agent Elizabeth McMahon knows better as she arrives accompanied by her team of investigators. For her, this is the third victim in as many weeks. She's barking orders in her usual no-nonsense way when her phone rings.

"Yeah."

"Hi, McMahon. I'm at the airport."

"Shit, Rodriguez. Bad timing. We had another one last night. Number three.

"I'm on my way. I'll rent a car and meet you. Where are you?"

"Come to Captain Steiner's office, I'll fill you in there."

Sergeant Rodriguez is from Las Vegas. He worked with McMahon as a DEA agent in her command. He was transferred to Oceanview Long Island to work on a major drug trafficking case. The transfer was to shield him from an international incident of his own doing. Oceanview at first seemed to be a slow boring town on Long Island. However, his initial observation proved wrong when a major organized crime family partnered with the biggest drug cartel in South America. The cartel wanted to use the distribution network of the DiNapoli crime family. The shipment was seized, and most of the conspirators were captured. McMahon asked him to come back to Las Vegas to assist her in trying to solve the murders in Red Rock Canyon.

Rodriguez arrives at the headquarters of Las Vegas PD. He meets Captain Steiner, and they sit down. After the usual small talk, Rodriguez asks, "So, McMahon, what do we have?"

She turns her computer screen in his direction. "They were all killed the same way."

He scrolls to look through the grisly pictures of the crime scenes. He turns the screen back around. "So we've got a serial killer loose in Las Vegas. Have all these guys been identified?"

"Except for the one this morning. The first victim was a pharmaceutical rep from New York. The second was a guy in town for an auto auction from Arizona. Oddly, they weren't robbed in spite of winning at the tables.

Rodriguez asks, "What did they play?"

McMahon responds, "Mostly Roulette. Some of the croupiers remember them at the wheel."

"The chips that were shoved in their mouths, do we know what casino they're from?"

"They're novelty chips not everybody sells them but they're available online. The first two victims had poker chips shoved into their mouths and more were scattered around the scene. Twelve in all. We haven't heard about the newest victim yet."

"Anything on the cards? Anything unusual?"

"Just that they're expensive. They're mostly used by professional players and casinos. The first victim had a seven of diamonds nailed into his forehead, the second an ace of diamonds. The victim this morning had two cards."

"Two."

"Yes, a five of diamonds and an eight of diamonds."

"Any other trauma on the body?"

"No."

"No signs of a struggle?"

Captain Steiner interjects, "the ME found traces of chloroform on the faces of the first two victims. Let's hope he was unconscious when the chips were shoved down his throat. Hell of a fucking way to die." McMahon turns to Rodriguez, "Why don't you get some sleep? We'll check with the ME tomorrow. Let's meet back here at eight. I'll have more details by then. Good afternoon, gentlemen."

CHAPTER 3
MEET AUGUSTUS

Rodriguez is driving to his hotel room when Detective Spinelli calls.

"Sergeant, how was your flight?"

"Ok, kind of rough. We had turbulence over the desert. What's going on, Marco?"

"Well, Justine Godfrey made bail. She came up with half a million dollars, and according to the condition of the bail, she has no travel restrictions."

"Let me guess, she posted the bail without hesitation."

"Yep, I didn't realize she had that much money."

"Oh yeah, she's loaded. What about the rest, Marco?"

"She's the only one who made bail."

"What about Bolton the third? He's swimming in dough."

"Apparently none of it is his and his father, Bolton the second, told him to rot in jail for a while."

"Great."

"I believe we haven't heard the last of Ms. Godfrey. I'm still not convinced that the fire that killed her parents was an accident."

"I want you to contact the authorities in Greenwich, Connecticut and ask them for everything they have on the fire at the Godfrey estate two years ago. Also, check on any arrests in the state for arson a few months before and a few months after."

"Where are we going with this, Sergeant?"

"I'm not sure. We're just rattling a few cages to see what jumps out. Let me know how it goes."

Augustus Becker was born in Cologne, Germany to wealthy parents in March of 1975. He attended the finest schools in Cologne and eventually the University of Munich. Most of the time in these institutes of learning was spent chasing coeds and dealing drugs to fellow students. During his years at the University, he established himself as a kind of campus procurer, arranging bachelor and bachelorette parties and providing the talent. He came to the United States in 2016 and met Justine Godfrey. They became lovers, and she eventually introduced him to the business. Augustus Becker is tall and handsome with a worldly and sophisticated way about him. He has an enormous ego that must be fed constantly. He uses his looks to charm and impress young men and women, mostly runaways and seekers of fame who flock to Las Vegas and Los Angeles. They're usually young and they're trafficked internationally for the sex trade or servitude. Justine is on her way to Reno to bail dear Augustus out of jail for doing something very stupid. He propositioned an undercover officer who was posing as an underage runaway. She arrives and goes to the Reno County jail. She fills out the necessary paperwork and Augustus Becker is walked out wearing a drab green jumpsuit with the letters RCF (Reno Correctional Facility) on the back.

An officer looks at Justine and bellows, "Is this Augustus Becker, Ms. Godfrey?"

"Yes, that's him."

The officer nods to the two CO's flanking him. They go back into the jail and the officer says, "Wait here. They'll bring him out. Have a seat. It's going to be a while."

After a while, Augustus Becker is brought out tanned and impeccably dressed. He picks up his belongings and fills out the necessary paperwork.

They walk toward the exit and Augustus says, "Thank you, Justine."

"Thank you my ass, Augustus. Do you have any idea what it cost me to get you out of jail?"

"The bail wasn't so much. It was a small rap."

"It's not the bail, Augustus. I had to pay off the usual assholes in the DA's office. What the fuck were you thinking?"

"Back off, Justine. How was I supposed to know she was undercover? Besides, they're trying to make an example out of me, charging me with human trafficking."

"Listen to me, Augustus, if they probe deeper, we're fucked. Luckily, my lawyer got the DA to back off. So we're ok for now. You fucked me good, Augustus. I was supposed to go to Saudi Arabia to check on dear dead mommy's oil interests that my lawyer just discovered. It's worth millions, but now I can't go 'til next year."

Augustus says, "You're jumping all over me, but what about you and that mess on Long Island. What happened there, Justine?"

"A mere misunderstanding, my dear. It was quickly straightened out, but I did meet one of the sexiest men I've ever seen. He can give you a run for your money, Augustus."

"Really? Who is he?"

"His name is Rodriguez. I'm hoping we meet again."

"This calls for a celebration, Justine. I'm flying to Vegas. Want to celebrate with me?"

"No, I don't. I'll travel to Vegas on my own. I have things to do while I'm here. Do you think I came here just to bail you out? I'm thinking of a casino investment. With you on the Gaming Commission, you could have helped me with the permits. Now they'll probably kick you off the Commission. Celebrate all you want, but don't get stupid. If you fuck up again, we won't be so merciful." Justine gives him a cold hard stare and walks away.

CHAPTER 4
THREE VICTIMS AND DIAMOND JACK

Rodriguez arrives at Captain Steiner's office and finds McMahon already at work. Captain Steiner comes in shortly after.

McMahon begins, "We've got three victims in three weeks. The first is a pharmaceutical salesman from New York. His name is Warren Schmidt. His wife said he was on a company-sponsored vacation and she chose to stay home. He was found three weeks ago in Red Rock positioned on the rocks, just like the victim last night. Apparently, a top performer with his company and also a big winner at the tables. We found a casino check for twenty-three thousand dollars in his room. A young woman was seen leaving his room at two am and about half an hour later he was drinking at the bar in his hotel. That's the last time he was seen alive."

"We're trying to find her, but it's the needle in the haystack. The only description we have is that she looked like a midwest beauty queen. The girl next door."

McMahon is reading from her computer, "The second victim is an automobile collector from Scottsdale, Arizona. His name is Peter Martin. He's famous among car collectors. He's got one of the best collections in the country. When he comes to Vegas, he always plays for big stakes. He's single and he won big at the tables. All the dealers know him and love him. Apparently, he's a big tipper. He was in Vegas for a week before his death. He went to two auctions, but he didn't purchase any cars. In his room safe, we found fifteen thousand dollars in cash and a check for thirty-seven thousand. Like victim number one, a hotel employee, who wishes to remain anonymous, said a woman asked for his room number. All he knows about her is that she's known as Amy, and she works at a few of the hotels."

"Any description?"

"Yeah, the girl next door."

"Gee, that narrows it down."

"He left the hotel around twelve-thirty and never came back. That brings us to victim number three, Horace Jenkins, a cattleman from Texas. Not married and no family. We don't know if he was here on business or vacation. He's well known to the people on the floor, and he always played the high limit tables. The dealers say he was a big whale. He left the tables close to midnight, up a few thousand dollars. Nothing in his room was touched, money, jewelry all of it was undisturbed. He's the guy we found yesterday."

Rodriguez asks, "What about him? Any woman in his room?"

"Someone saw a woman of the same description enter his room around midnight. That's all we got."

"Do we have anything else on this Amy?"

"No, and that's the problem. There's a code of silence around these escorts that work the hotels on the strip. You know, you worked here."

"Yeah, I know. We have to find Amy before she leaves town. She may be totally innocent, but she might get scared and run."

McMahon agrees, "You're right. There's something else about the bodies. They were positioned on three different sets of rocks. Together they form a straight line."

"Let's go out there and look around."

They arrive just as the sun is at its highest. Rodriguez comments, "Shit, I forgot how hot it gets out here."

"What's the matter, Rodriguez? No ocean breezes to cool you?"

The area is busy with a forensics team and LVPD. From behind police lines, the press is shouting questions at the investigators.

"Captain Steiner, can you tell us anything about the killer?"

"Do you have a name?"

"Is it a serial killer?"

"What about the chips? What do you think it means?

"Why do you think all the cards are diamonds?"

Captain Steiner turns to the press and says, "I can fill you all in at the press conference tomorrow morning. Please, let us do our job and stop shouting questions at us."

A voice booms out from behind the police line. "Hey Captain, why don't you name him Diamond Jack?"

The rest of the press shouts out the name Diamond Jack.

Rodriguez looks at McMahon, "Looks like our killer has a name, McMahon."

"Come on, Rodriguez. I'll show you where the victim was found. We have tire tracks leading to and from the scene, so we think the victim was killed elsewhere and brought here. The tire tracks indicate a heavy-duty truck or SUV something a contractor would use. The tires are common for that kind of vehicle and they match in all three locations."

Rodriguez examines the scene and observes, "There's not that much blood on the rocks."

"Not much, just a trace. That's why we think he was killed someplace else." McMahon looks up at the sun, "You're right, it's fucking hot. Let's get back. I've got to get some water. This sun is killing me."

Rodriguez responds, "Sounds like you can use an ocean breeze too. When we get back, I'll start looking for this girl Amy."

"Ok, Rodriguez, but don't get your hopes up. You worked out here. You know how it goes with all that 'what happens in Vegas' bullshit."

"I'll check some of my contacts, McMahon. See if they know anything."

CHAPTER 5
THE GAME

"So why did you call me? What's the problem, Amy? You made five hundred bucks the other night. Yeah he may have been a little rough, but he's a big fish in our pond. He'll pay anything to get what he wants. Last month he was in Germany and he paid two of our girls to curse at him in German and slap him around. The crazy part is he doesn't even speak German. He had no idea what the fuck they were even saying to him. Isn't that hysterical? Do you want to guess how much all that abuse cost him.? He paid five thousand dollars to get abused by two crazy bitches in German. The girls made one thousand dollars each for one hour. Another client paid twenty thousand dollars just to have five of our boys attend a pool party at his estate outside of Vegas. All they had to do was walk around with skimpy bathing suits and serve drinks to his friends. The arrangement was that they would serve his friends drinks while he barbecued. Do you believe that? All he did was fucking barbecue. The boys made two thousand dollars each for one afternoon and they didn't have to fuck anybody for it. These are the kind of jobs I would send you on but you're too timid. Your heart's not in it. So we start with the small stuff, a few hundred here a few hundred there. Consider it paying your dues, Amy. Stop being shy and complaining and you can make the big money. I know some of the high rollers are assholes but, for right now, you're going to have to deal with it. Now I have this rich silicon valley dude coming into town next week. His name's David Evans. He's looking for the girlfriend experience. You know 'the girl next door' and that's you. I'll call you back with the details."

……………

"Now, now. No pushback. Ok, Amy? You knew the game going in."

 ……………

"Amy, you're going to do it. So wait for my call and you better answer the phone."

……………

"I said answer the phone when I call."

……………

"That's better. See no complaining and things will be better for everybody, especially you. There's a grand in it for you."

……………

 "On your own? Did you just say you can make more on your own? Don't ever let Justine hear you say that. Ever."

……………

"I don't care what the other girls say."

……………

"Wait for the call."

Augustus Becker no sooner hangs up when Justine calls.

"So what do I tell my client? Will she be there? You know what he likes. Do you think she's up for it?"

"I just spoke to her, and I think she'll show."

"I'm not talking about showing up. I'm talking about giving this fucking ATM machine the whole experience. Dinner and all that, blah blah blah, and

then going to his hotel room and satisfying his every whim. The girls who had a date with this prick say he's a sadistic asshole. Do you think she can handle it?"

"I made it clear that she has to."

"You made it clear? What the fuck does that mean? This isn't a college course. Can she do it? Tell me the truth."

"Yes, she'll do it. I'll make sure of it."

"Your ass is on the line, Augustus. Make it happen."

"I got it, Justine."

CHAPTER 6
GINO IS IN THE CASINO

The casinos are unusually busy tonight. The coming Memorial Day holiday saw an influx of tourists to Vegas. All the tables are busy and in full swing, occupied by players of different abilities. High rollers to nervous amateurs are all included in the mix. Gino Marchetti is stopping at different tables to celebrate the winners and pity the losers. As he walks by the tables, the women turn their heads in his direction. The croupiers know Gino and they nod a greeting as he walks by their tables.

"Gambling tonight, Mr. Marchetti?"

He waves and shakes his head no. Gino is known to the pit bosses, the floor managers, and the croupiers. He gets respect because of his assumed past connection to the New York mob bosses. An assumption that he lets hang in the air as long as it benefits him. He enters the sequestered high rollers room. The croupiers acknowledge him and offer him a place at the table but he turns down all offers to participate.

The pit boss approaches him and says, "Sorry. Mr. Marchetti, if you ain't playing, you've got to leave."

"Sure, who's here tonight? Any big winners?"

"Come on, you know I can't tell you."

He gives the pit boss a nod and stands there.

The pit boss leans in and whispers, "We got an oilman winning big. He's up 85k, but you didn't hear it from me."

"Let me guess, the cowboy with the 10-gallon hat."

The pit boss just walks away. "See you, Mr. Marchetti."

He leaves the high roller area and waits by the cashier's window. After a few minutes, the big winner leaves the room and heads for the window to cash out. Gino stands behind the man looking over his shoulder at his total winnings. It seems the oilman had a great night; he won seventy-two thousand dollars minus the 60 percent lump sum payout penalty. The casino manager offers the oilman a security detail to walk him to his car.

"Shit, I don't need security when I got this." He opens his jacket and shows the manager a Colt 45 in a holster.

The cashier says, "Next time, leave the gun home, cowboy."

He smiles, "It's been a pleasure taking your money." He walks out.

Frank the casino manager walks over to Gino. "Did you see that cowboy? The guy won a little over seventy grand and gave 60 percent back to the house. Tonight, he'll get a bottle of champagne and some room service, if you know what I mean. Tomorrow, he'll give the rest back to the casino. Vegas, you've got to love it. My shift's over. Let's get a drink at the bar."

The men are sitting making small talk. Frank says, "Isn't that some shit with this guy running around killing people in Red Rock? The press named him. They call him Diamond Jack."

Gino asks, "Why do you think all the fucking assholes wind up in Vegas? Drug addicts, hookers, fucking degenerate gamblers and the list goes on and on."

"Look around you, Gino. Short of killing somebody, you can do whatever the fuck you want."

"So that's the attraction, no rules."

"Yep, you want drugs? You can get 'em if you know the right people. A girl sent to your room at two am? You can get that too. You can get a freak to do whatever you want if you're paying."

"What does that mean? A freak?"

"These broads, they'll do anything for money."

"Did you ever think that maybe their victims?"

Frank says, "Victims? Victims of what? They're not victims, it's bullshit. With the prices they charge, they ain't victims. Just a bunch of greedy whores."

Gino raises his voice and the bartender nods to a man standing nearby.

"Apologize for that, Frank."

"Apologize for what, Gino?"

"Calling them whores. It's not right."

"Ok, Gino. I'll call them hookers if it makes you feel better."

"Knock it off, Frank. Show a little respect."

"Respect for what? A bunch of hookers."

Gino grabs Frank by the collar of his shirt and raises his fist to punch him. Frank throws his hands up to cover his face when Gino is swarmed by casino security and is ushered roughly out the door.

The manager shouts, "What the fuck is wrong with you, Gino? Get him out of here!"

Gino is upset and he walks the strip to calm himself down. He calls Amy, "Hi baby. Can you meet me for a drink? Anyplace you want."

"I can't, Gino. I'm working later."

"What? Later? It's already 10:30, come on."

"I'll call you when I'm done, Gino. Sorry, I've got to go."

"I want to get married, and I want you to quit this shit."

"Can we talk about this tomorrow? Your timing sucks, Gino. And you don't propose to a girl over the phone. I've got to go."

CHAPTER 7
LOOKING FOR AMY

It's 8 am in Las Vegas and the temperature is already in the low eighties. Rodriguez is driving to a souvenir shop on the edge of the strip. He walks into the shop, and he's greeted by Freddie. Rodriguez busted Freddie some years ago for selling meth to tourists. Freddie smiles when he sees Rodriguez.

"Hi, Freddie. The last time you saw me, you weren't smiling."

"Rodriguez, how the hell are you?"

"Great, if you don't mind this fucking heat. I can't believe I actually worked out here all those years."

"Last I heard you were in New York somewhere."

"Close. I was on Long Island in a town called Oceanview. I'm a Sergeant there."

"Oceanview. It sounds interesting, like watching paint dry."

"Maybe, but I love it there and I can't wait to get back."

"So, what brings you to Vegas?"

"I'm on loan from Oceanview. I'm here helping McMahon."

"Oh yeah. Are you working the Diamond Jack case? That's some crazy shit. Why did you come see me?"

"Well there's a girl that was seen around a few of the victim's rooms. Her name is Amy and I'm trying to find her."

"I wish I could help you, but all that shit is behind me now. The drugs, the girls. I got this little shop and I make a decent amount of money selling this shit to tourists. Tell you the truth, I don't even gamble anymore. Besides, these girls change their names once a week. Today, it's Amy. Tomorrow, it's Vicky."

"I know. Freddie. If you hear of anything, can you give me a heads up?"

"You got a description?"

"Yeah. 'Girl next door', that's all they said.

Freddie smiles, "Beauty queen gets freaky, I get it."

"Somebody's got to know something."

Freddie gets closer and says, "I ain't supposed to tell you this, but there's a guy who hangs out at the Metropolitan Hotel. You can talk to him. His name is Andy. He's a real piece of work, kind of a go between. Ask for Manny at the desk. He knows him. He was one of my contacts back in the day."

"Did you say the Metropolitan? Has it changed or is it still a shit show?"

"What do you think?"

"Thanks, Freddie. If you hear anything, get in touch."

"Wait, before I go, do you sell these chips?"

"No, I don't sell those but I got a ton of others."

"Thanks, again."

Rodriguez arrives at the Metropolitan Hotel, and he goes to the concierge desk.

"Are you Manny?"

"Yeah."

"I'm looking for Andy. Is he around?"

Manny answers, "Andy? Did you say Andy? I haven't seen him in a while."

Rodriguez shows his badge, "What about now? Have you seen him?" Manny looks to the side and a man sitting nearby gets up and hurriedly walks to the doors and runs down the street.

Rodriguez sees him, "I guess that was Andy."

He chases the man and catches him a few blocks away. He grabs him by the arm and holds him in place.

"What do you want? I didn't do nothing."

"I'm Sergeant Rodriguez. Why did you run, Andy? I just want to ask you a few questions."

"I got nothing to say."

"I'm looking for a girl named Amy. Do you know her? I just want to ask her a few questions."

"Why are you looking for her?"

"I can't tell you. Do you know where I can find her?"

"She goes from casino to casino. Nobody knows."

"That's not what I heard, Andy. I was told you can set it up."

Andy gets closer and says, "If they know I'm talking to you, I'm a dead man."

"Are you in danger?"

"If I talk to you, I will be. Now, I'm leaving. I can't be seen talking to you so let me go."

"Take my card. My numbers on the back. We can talk privately." Rodriguez loosens his grip and Andy quickly walks away and he calls Manny and tells him that the police are looking for Amy.

Hours later Andy is walking on the strip when he's grabbed by two men and pushed into a limousine. Augustus Becker is sitting in the back wearing an expensive suit and quite full of himself. The two men sit alongside him.

Augustus is the first to speak, "So, Andy, how are you today?"

Andy doesn't answer and looks straight ahead at the two men.

There's silence then Augustus asks, "I understand you had a visitor earlier. Manny said he was a cop and I assume he told you his name."

"No, he didn't tell me his name."

"What did he want to know?"

"He was asking about Amy."

"Amy, really? Did he say why?"

"No, he said he wanted to ask her a few questions."

"Questions about what, Andy? Our little arrangement?"

"No, I cut the conversation short. I didn't tell him anything."

"So he chases you down the street and doesn't tell you why he wants to talk to her?"

"I swear he didn't tell me."

"I see. Tell me his name, Andy. Don't lie to me and I'll let you out."

"Ok. He said his name is Rodriguez."

"Rodriguez, would that be Sergeant Rodriguez?"

"Yeah, he gave me his card and said he's a Sergeant. Can I get out now?"

"Let me see the card."

Andy gives him the card.

Augustus says, "Sergeant Rodriguez is in Vegas. Justine is going to love this." Augustus gives him back the card.

"Tell me, Andy, what did he look like?"

"What?"

"I asked you what he looked like."

"He was tall and built, like he worked out a lot. He had dark hair and dark eyes."

Augustus pauses and looks out of the window. Then he asks, "Do you think he's better looking than me?"

"What?"

"Is he?"

"Why are you asking me that?"

"Tell me the truth. Is he better looking?"

"No, you are. Now, can I get out?"

Augustus motions to the driver to stop. He nods at the two enforcers, and they pin Andy to the seat. Augustus says to the driver,," let's go to the tunnels, I don't believe him."

Justine Godfrey is at an all-male strip club just outside the strip, drinking cheap champagne and stuffing twenty-dollar bills into G-strings. Money can't buy you class. Her phone rings.

"Hello, Augustus. How did it go?"

"Well, he didn't tell us much. But you'll never believe who's in Vegas. Where are you, Justine? I can hardly hear you. Are you in a club?"

"You might say that. So tell me who's in Vegas? Brittany Spears?"

"Very funny. It's Rodriguez."

"No fucking way. How do you know?"

"He was the cop asking questions about Amy."

"I had a feeling we'd meet again. What about Amy? What makes her so important? Do you think he's looking into our business?"

"Maybe, but Andy said he didn't say much."

"Don't underestimate this cop. If he gets close to Amy, you may have to use your powers of persuasion on her. Stay on top of it, Augustus. Let's see where it leads. What about Andy? Where is he?"

"They took him to the tunnels to the room with the chair."

"Why the tunnels, Augustus? We should have kept an eye on him. Now we'll never know what's going on. Sometimes you don't think. You don't use your fucking head!"

He responds, "I'm not going down there. Besides, it's probably too late. I left Rodriguez's card on him to send a message. Before they took him to the tunnels he said that I was better looking than this Rodriguez. What do you think about that?"

"I think you're a fucking asshole, Augustus. Bye."

She waves her glass at the waiter, "More champagne, please."

CHAPTER 8
THE TUNNELS

Hidden from the bright lights of the Casinos and the lure of the jackpot lies an underground labyrinth of tunnels. These tunnels were built as storm drains to protect the city from flash floods. Built in the 80s and 90s, they slowly became a refuge and shelter for Vegas' homeless, some dealing with drug addiction and mental issues. As many as 2,000 people at one time or another have lived in the tunnels. This system of tunnels, stretching a total of two hundred miles in all directions under the city, have also been used for nefarious purposes. Human traffickers, drug traffickers and various criminals have all eluded the police by moving through these tunnels. During periods of heavy rain, the tunnels flood causing the occupants to grab whatever belongings they can and move to higher ground. Some more industrious inhabitants have found ways to elevate their possessions so that they're not affected by the rising waters. It's in this dark and mold ridden system of musty passageways, occupied by not just the homeless but scorpions and spiders, that human traffickers like Augustus Becker and Justine Godfrey dispose of their victims. Deep in the undiscovered sections of the tunnels where nobody goes are the ghosts of the unfortunate who have been forgotten by the revelers above ground. Here is where they bury the dead and torture the living in the room with the chair.

Occasionally brave explorers, mostly young people, will venture into the dark recesses. With spray paint in hand and skateboards under foot, they seek the adrenalin rush. With flashlights strapped to their helmets, they go into a world few people above ground see. There's graffiti adorned walls no one will see in the dark. There's worn couches, dirt laden pillows and an old barbecue grill indicating that at one time someone called this small part of the tunnels home. The "mole people", as they're called, shun the outside world, coming out at night to see what money they can scrounge up at the casinos, perhaps enough for a few meals. A voucher dropped on the floor, money left in the slots, a drunk dropping some of his winnings or chips left behind could mean food or an article of clothing. The heat outside drives an adventurous group of skateboarders into the coolness of the tunnels. With artificial lights mounted to their helmets, they branch off and venture into the unknown areas. A trio of skateboarders breaks off from the rest of the group. After a while they come across a figure against the wall of the tunnel. It appears he's asleep in a sitting position. As they get closer they notice a red halo behind the figure's head. In this case, it's not graffiti. It's a halo of blood. A grate on the street above allows enough light to pass through and it shines on the sitting figure. In this light, the extent of cruelty endured by this person shocks the skateboarders as they shout to their friends.

Rodriguez is driving to his hotel when he gets the call from McMahon.

"We have a body, Rodriguez."

He asks, "Diamond Jack?"

"No, this one's in the tunnels. It's pretty bad."

"Any ID?"

"No but he had your card in his pocket. Does it ring a bell?"

"Shit, that's probably a guy named Andy."

"Why does he have your card?"

"I was told he knows where I could find Amy, but he was afraid to talk to me. He said he feared for his life. Do you need me to come out there?"

"No, we're wrapping it up here but I need you to identify what's left of him."

"Left of him?"

"Yeah, he was beaten really badly. He's got some other marks on him. Looks like he was here a while, the spiders and whatever the fuck else had their way with him. When did you see him last?"

"About four or five days ago."

"Yeah, it looks that way."

There's silence and then Rodriguez says, "I'll be in touch."

He does a u-turn with tires screeching and drives to the Metropolitan Hotel. He fast-walks through the front doors. Manny sees him and bolts for the exit with Rodriguez in pursuit. He has a head start and he eludes Rodriguez by hiding in a maintenance closet. Rodriguez loses sight of him and searches the area but abandons the hunt and returns to his car.

CHAPTER 9
THE GIRLFRIEND EXPERIENCE

The private plane touched down on time as usual. David Evans demands that everyone and everything be on schedule. He owns a big piece of Silicon Valley, not the businesses but the land the businesses occupy. He gouges the businesses with exorbitant land lease and rental rates, making him one of the richest men in the Valley who doesn't own a technology company. His father invested in the land before it became the technology capital of the world. The land passed to him when his father died. Augustus greets him as he steps off the plane accompanied by his secretary.

"Hello, Mr. Evans. How was your flight?"

"It sucked, Becker. We got caught up in the desert air currents that Vegas is famous for. Made the ride bumpy as fuck."

"I'm sorry to hear that, Mr. Evans."

"Why are you apologizing, Becker? You didn't make the desert, the guy upstairs did. This is my secretary, Susan Harris."

After the introductions Evans pulls Augustus to the side, "Is everything set for my stay?"

"Yes, it's all arranged, Mr. Evans. I've reserved a suite for you at the Cosmopolitan. There's champagne and lunch waiting for you whenever you're ready."

"Good job, Becker. I'll need fifty grand in chips and send a tailor to my suite in about an hour."

"Yes, Mr. Evans."

"Make sure Ms. Harris is waited on hand and foot. I trust you put her in a different hotel."

"Yes, I did, Mr. Evans. She's at the Stratosphere."

"Good. Now what about that other thing? Was that arranged?"

"Yes it's taken care of."

"What's her name?"

"Amy, her name is Amy."

"I hope you and Justine have a deep bullpen. If she's not as advertised, I'm going to want a stand in."

"Don't worry, Mr. Evans. She'll be fine."

"I'm looking for better than fine, Becker. I can get fine at the Metropolitan. Tomorrow night at seven in my suite would be perfect. Ask her to wear black."

Amy is exercising in the gym when Augustus calls, "David Evans just got in. He's at the Cosmopolitan and he's expecting you tomorrow night at seven in his suite. He's in the Penthouse Suite #2. It's on the left when you get off the elevator. There's only two on the floor. Ask for Chris at the front desk. He'll take you up. Wear something sexy and black but not trashy. Remember, you're his girlfriend, not some hooker he picked up on the strip. The hotel dicks are working overtime this weekend so keep it low-key. I'm sure you'll look gorgeous. This guy pays us a lot of money so treat him right. Remember our talk."

"I don't want to get hurt again, Augustus."

"Listen, Amy. We're paying you a thousand bucks, so make sure Mr. Evans is happy. Deal with the fucking pain, Amy. Just deal with it. My ass is on the line. Remember Amy, it's the girlfriend experience. Until he gets tired of you."

Amy hesitates then calls Gino, and he answers, "Hi baby, I can't wait to see you tomorrow night."

"I can't, Gino. That's why I'm calling. There's some big shot in town and he wants me to spend some time with him."

Gino is angry, "Who's the big shot, Amy? Anybody we know?"

"I don't know. I only know he spends a lot of money, and he wants me to be his date around Vegas."

"Yeah, I get it. The girlfriend experience. "What are you getting paid for that Amy?"

"I'd rather not tell you, Gino. You're angry."

"I'll bet they're going to make a ton of money on this guy."

"What about you, Gino? Remember, you used to be a client. You knew what I did."

"Yeah but I never figured I'd fall in love with you."

Amy is quiet, "I've got to go and shop for some clothes. This guy wants me to wear black."

"Yeah, ok, go ahead. I'm going down to the casino."

"Gino, if you see me tomorrow night, please don't make a scene. I'll get in trouble if you do."

Gino angrily replies, "Sure, baby. You got it."

CHAPTER 10
WHERE'S MANNY?

Rodriguez is driving to Captain Steiner's office when McMahon calls him.

"Where are you?"

"I'm on the way to the office."

"Make a U-turn and meet me at the Medical Examiner's."

"Ok, I'm on my way."

Rodriguez arrives at the Medical Examiner's office, and McMahon comes out to greet him.

"We need you to make a positive ID. Make sure it's the same guy you gave your card to. It's pretty nasty so brace yourself."

Rodriguez is looking at Andy's body. "Shit, what a fucking mess, McMahon. Yeah, that's the guy. His name is Andy."

"See the marks on his wrists? Looks like rope marks. He was tied to a wooden chair, or something made out of wood, there's bits of wood fibers and splinters on his wrists. There's these welts and abrasions on his chest."

"Did you find anything on him?"

"The only thing we found was your card. He had no ID, no jewelry, nothing. Just your card."

"Where was he found?"

"A couple of skateboarders found him propped up against a wall. Whoever left him there tortured him somewhere else and finished him off with a round to the head."

"What part of the tunnels is that, McMahon?"

"It's less than a hundred feet from The Metropolitan Hotel."

"I want to go into that tunnel, see if I can find anything."

"Not a good idea, Rodriguez. Leave it to Steiner's men. Now tell me about Andy."

"One of my contacts gave me a tip that he could help us find Amy. He said if they knew he was talking to me, he'd be in danger."

"Who is 'they', Rodriguez?"

"I don't know but I think the concierge at the Metropolitan Hotel knows how we can find Amy. I went to see if I could talk to him, but he took off on me. I'd love to find his address and break his fucking door down."

"Come on, Rodriguez. You know better. We'll find him sooner or later."

He asks, "what about Diamond Jack's victims? Anything new on them?"

"Yeah, the ME found traces of chloroform on the face of our last victim. Just like the previous two."

"What about the cards? Did we find out where they were purchased?"

"They're called Arista. You can buy them online for about forty dollars a deck."

"So, McMahon, let's assume there's a message in the cards." Rodriguez takes a pen and paper and writes. "For the first victim, it was a seven of diamonds, the second an ace of diamonds and the third victim had two cards, a five of diamonds and an eight of diamonds. Maybe a number code? Not numbers but letters of the alphabet. Seven equals G, Ace is A and Five plus Eight is M. GAM, the first three letters in gamble or gambling. He's trying to tell us something with these cards."

Manny is hiding out at his girlfriend's house outside of Las Vegas and he calls Augustus Becker.

Becker answers, "Manny, where are you? I came by to see you at the Metropolitan."

"I'm not going back there, Augustus. There's a cop asking questions about Amy."

"What did you say to him?"

"Nothing. He came looking for me, but I got away from him. I'm trying to call Andy and he ain't picking up, so I don't know what the fuck is going on."

Augustus says, "Let me come to your place and talk about it. What do you say?"

"Don't bother, I'm not at my place. Why is everybody looking for Amy?"

"Take it easy. We're trying to find out what's going on."

"Where are you, Manny? I can pick you up. You can stay at Justine's hotel for a while."

"I want to talk to Andy first. I want to know he's ok."

"Do you remember this cop's name, Manny?"

"Yeah, Rodriguez. He said his name is Rodriguez. You think they busted Andy?"

"No, I don't think so, Manny. He's probably hiding out like you. So tell me where you are and I'll come get you."

"No thanks, Augustus. After I talk to Andy to make sure he's ok, I'll call you."

"Wait, Manny. Don't hang up, Manny. Manny, dammit."

Augustus calls Justine, "So where's Manny? Did you find him?"

"I spoke to him, but he wouldn't tell me where he is. He confirmed that Rodriguez is looking for Amy.

"We need to find him before Rodriguez does. You better get on it, Augustus. It's your ass. Our people aren't happy. Find this fucking guy and make it soon."

Rodriguez gets a call from Captain Steiner.

"We got an address. His full name is Manuel Alvarado. He's got an apartment on Mountain Drive just outside of the city in the Mountain View apartments. Are you familiar?"

"Mountain View. Yeah, I know where that is. Any apartment number?"

"Yeah he's in 5G. The entrance is around the back."

"Is McMahon in your office, Captain?"

"Yep, she said she'll meet you there in half an hour. She wants to make sure you don't kick the door in."

"Very funny. I'll see her there."

They arrive at Manny's apartment and find there's nobody there. They locate the superintendent who tells them Manny hasn't been there for almost a week. He doesn't know where he is.

"Well, Rodriguez, another dead end."

"Yeah, I'm starting to get used to it."

CHAPTER 11
THE METROPOLITAN HOTEL

The Metropolitan Hotel was, at one time, a luxury hotel catering to movie stars, politicians and visiting dignitaries. Due to poor management and neglect, it went from one of the top hotels in Vegas to around the bottom of sought-after accommodations. Rodriguez arrives and walks into the hotel past the concierge desk and through the kitchen. He thinks it strange that security or an employee didn't stop him or ask who he was. At the end of a long corridor that leads to the street, he finds a rusted and locked metal door. He approaches one of the kitchen staff and quickly flashes his badge and tells her he's the fire inspector. "My name's Roberts. That door at the end of the hall, the one on the right, where does that go?"

"I don't know Inspector Roberts, nobody does."

"Does anybody have a key?"

"No, just Manny the concierge and this guy who comes around from time to time."

"What guy? I need to see what's back there in case there's a fire hazard, you understand."

"Sure, but I don't know his name. He was around here with a couple of guys not too long ago."

"Was it four or five days ago?"

"Yes, I think so. He was here for a few minutes, and he left and then a few hours later, two other guys came out and locked the door."

"What did these guys look like?"

"I don't know. They kinda looked like bouncers, you know, big and brawny."

"What about the guy who was here for a few minutes? What did he look like?"

"He was tall like you, good looking but thinner like he doesn't work out as much as you do. Oh, and there was something else when the two guys came out. It looked like their clothes were wet."

"Wet?"

"Yeah the two guys and they were dirty too."

"Thanks for your help."

"You're not really a fire inspector, are you Mr. Roberts."

Rodriguez changes the subject, "what do you do in the kitchen Ms.........."

"Corrales, Maria Corrales I'm the head baker."

"Well Maria, maybe I'll come back and sample your baking. Thanks again Maria."

She smiles and watches him leave. On the way out he passes hotel security who approaches Maria and asks her, "who was that guy?"

"He's the fire inspector."

"Fire inspector? He's not the usual guy, and he wasn't wearing a uniform. What did he say to you?"

"He said there's a fire hazard behind that door at the end of the hall. I've got to check my cookies, excuse me."

44

"Fire hazard?" The security guard stands there not knowing what to do.

Rodriguez is in Captain Steiner's office with McMahon. "I was at the Metropolitan Hotel today where Manny works. There was no sign of Manny, but there's a door at the end of a corridor behind the kitchen just before the exit. I get a feeling this door leads to the tunnels. I spoke to an employee who works in the kitchen, and she told me the only one with a key is Manny and some guy who comes around from time to time. Four or five days ago, she saw three men, one was there for a short period of time and the other two came out of that door about two hours later. I think the two guys are the ones that tortured and killed Andy. She said they looked wet, and their clothes were dirty."

"What about the other guy, Rodriguez?"

"I don't know, and I'm trying to figure out how all this ties into Diamond Jack. Nobody seems to know who Amy is, Andy gets killed for talking to me and Manny runs away from me and disappears. I want to go into the tunnel where they found Andy's body and look around."

"What are you looking for? The detectives already checked it."

"I want to see how far that door is from where Andy's body was found."

"Ok but take one of Captain Steiner's men with you and go in the morning. You may get some daylight down there and be careful." "I'll try to get some information on this guy Manny. I just hope he doesn't turn up like Andy.

CHAPTER 12
FIGHT THROUGH
THE PAIN

Amy is dressed in a black dress designed to show off her fit body. A string of pearls, jewelry and black heels finish off the outfit. She takes a deep breath and rings the bell to Penthouse 2. The door opens, and David Evans is standing in the doorway. He's 6ft. tall and 45 years old and in good shape thanks to a lineup of personal trainers. Dark hair, brown eyes and dressed all in black he welcomes Amy in. "Come in, you must be Amy. I'm David Evans."

"Hi Mr. Evans."

"Please call me David. Would you like a drink?"

"No, I'm ok, maybe later."

"Mind if I do?" Amy is telling herself so far he seems like a gentleman. "Are you hungry Amy? We have reservations at the Skyline Club."

"The Skyline, that's a very nice restaurant."

"So I've heard. Are you sure you don't want a drink?"

"Yes, I'm sure I'll have one at dinner."

"OK I'll wait too so if you're ready we can go."

They leave the room and go to dinner. At dinner, they make small talk and Amy reveals a little bit about herself as does he. Amy is distracted, thinking about what might happen later in the evening. She's been with men who seem pleasant and charming at first but as the evening wears on, and after a few drinks, they change. He talks about his business in Silicon Valley and how his family made their fortune in land deals in California, Arizona, and Nevada. Amy thinks to herself, 'he doesn't seem so bad.' A man seated at a table across from them catches Amy's eye. He's with two other men, and they're drinking heavily. She tries to ignore him ,but he's staring at her, making her nervous.

"Amy, are you ok?"

"I think so, but that man keeps staring at me."

"Do you know him? Is he someone from your past?"

"You mean a client?"

"I didn't say that, Amy. If he makes you uncomfortable, we can leave or change seats so he can stare at me for a while. He might like that."

Amy laughs, "No, it's ok." Halfway through dinner, one of the men approaches the table. He begins to berate and insult Amy calling her a whore and saying he didn't get his money's worth. Evans warns the man, but he continues. Finally Evans jumps up and punches the man in the face, knocking him to the ground. The man is cursing, and he threatens Evans. Apologizing to them, the management unceremoniously throws the man into the street. His friends get up and stagger out of the restaurant.

"Are you ok," he asks her.

"Yeah I'm alright."

"I apologize for the violence I don't usually get like that. All of a sudden I'm not that hungry anymore. Come on, let's go to my suite, have a drink and relax." As they leave the restaurant, they're not aware they're being followed by the man and two of his friends. When they get to the suite, the three men are waiting in the shadows. As Evans opens the door to Penthouse 2, they strike. Evans valiantly tries to fight them off, but they overpower him, and pistol whip him into unconsciousness. They drag him into the room and close the door. Amy is now at the mercy of the men, and she tries to scream but a hand covers her mouth. The last thing she sees is Evans on the floor and the two men leering at her, then the room goes black.

The sun is rising in Vegas, signaling another oppressively sweltering day. Gino is leaving the bar, thinking about Amy and hoping she's ok. The strip is unusually quiet for the Independence Day weekend. Red, white, and blue decorations are everywhere and old glory is proudly displayed. The quiet is pierced by the sounds of police sirens and ambulances as they whiz past Gino and stop in front of the Cosmopolitan. Gino picks up the pace, the sun now in his eyes. A small crowd gathers as the paramedics and police rush in. Gino recognizes one of the officers in the group, and he walks over to speak to him. "Hey Robbie, what's going on?"

"What's up Gino? Not really sure yet. It seems the maid found a couple beat up pretty bad in one of the penthouse suites, that's all we know right now."

"Did you say the penthouse?" He remembers Amy saying she had a date with a high roller." "Shit Robbie, can I hang out for a while?"

"Sure Gino, but stay behind the lines in case my boss shows up. He can be a hard ass." Gino waits and the first stretcher comes down with Evans, who is still in and out of consciousness. A while later, Amy is brought down her face partially wrapped in bandages.

Gino recognizes her and attempts to run through the police lines, "Robbie, Robbie, that's Amy."

"What are you talking about Gino? You know her."

Gino is beside himself, "I have to ride to the hospital with her. Robbie, let me get in the ambulance with her."

"Are you sure Gino, maybe it ain't her." The house dick thinks she's one of the girls that works the hotels."

"I know that's her, that's my Amy. You've got to let me ride with her please Robbie."

"Ok, ok Gino go ahead." Gino gets into the ambulance over the protestations of the EMS crew. Robbie sticks his head in, "it's ok fellas he's family."

Gino takes Amy's hand and whispers to her, "fight baby, fight through the pain."

CHAPTER 13
MEDITERRANEAN BONES

Justine is getting a massage from a masseur. She always felt that a woman could never massage her with the strength and endurance of a man. This massage happens to be one of the better ones. The fact that she's lying half naked on a table while being massaged by a young man adds to the experience. She's about to roll over when her phone rings. She thinks to herself, "great fucking timing." She answers brusquely, "yeah what is it?"

"Hello Justine, am I interrupting something intimate?"

"No, Mr. Rinaldo. I'm getting a massage."

"A massage, well, that's intimate isn't it? So Justine, how are things going? Is everything under control?"

"Not quite, it seems we're having a problem with a certain cop from my past. He's in Vegas, and we're trying to find out why."

"That could be a problem. Do you suppose it's about our business Justine?"

"Maybe Mr. Rinaldo, but there's a serial killer loose, maybe he's investigating that."

"Oh yes that Diamond Jack fellow."

"Yeah that's him."

"Well at any rate, Justine, I'm coming to Vegas. I'll be there in a few days. I'll notify you of the exact time I will need you to pick me up. I'll be arriving at night, you know how I hate the sun. I'll need a suite at the Luxor. I'm very comfortable surrounded by Egyptian artifacts, fake as they may be."

"Would you like some company, Mr. Rinaldo? I can arrange it."

"Justine, please don't insult me with your whores. This is what I want, Justine. I want a black limousine waiting for me with a bottle of Bollinger 2006 chilled to between 47 and 50 degrees. If it's any colder, it numbs the taste buds and definitely not warmer. I expect you and Augustus to be in the limousine to greet me. In that case, make it 2 bottles, Justine."

Justine replies, "two bottles that's over 2 thousand dollars."

"Yes I know."

"Wait Mr. Rinaldo, if you don't mind my asking, why are you coming to Vegas?"

"The truth is that since the last time we spoke nothing has changed and things are not going well, and now there's a cop in the mix. Sounds like you need an adult in the room. I'll be in touch, good bye Justine."

Achille Rinaldo is from Sicily, and at one time, was on Interpol's most wanted list. He had ties to the Santino crime family and the Sicilian mafia and was hunted by the authorities and fellow mobsters during the crackdown of 2016 and 2018. He had a falling out with his boss Vincenzo Santino and was forced to flee to Malta. While in Malta, he and Justine Godfrey oversaw a vast international sex trafficking ring. He had numerous surgeries on his face to alter his appearance and he was able to hide from the Maltese authorities. These surgeries have caused hyper sensitivity to the sun. He was nicknamed "Il Vampiro" (the vampire) by those who know him. His tall gaunt figure and pale skin add to his vampire like appearance. He has a penchant for dark women and sadomasochism. Tonight, he's flying on one of his private jets and as he approaches the city, the lights of Vegas light up the horizon. Accompanying him are three bodyguards who fled with him to Malta and who he trusts without question. The desert air currents jostle the plane as it approaches the runway at McCarran Airport. The plane touches down a little after midnight and proceeds to a private hangar. A limousine is waiting with Justine and Augustus inside. Rinaldo and his bodyguards sit across from them. They ride in silence for a while and then Rinaldo asks, "So, Augustus, I heard you had some trouble with the authorities in Reno and Justine had to post bail." He leans forward and turns to Justine. "How much was that?"

She answers, "it would have been more, but I have a few connections in the DA's office."

"I understand you propositioned an undercover officer. How absolutely stupid, Becker. By now you should be able to spot them, isn't that right Justine?" Justine is silent. "If something like this happens again, we won't be discussing it in the back of a limousine while waiting for the champagne to chill, isn't that right, Paolo?" Paolo grunts, nods his head, and flashes a big smile while staring at Augustus. "What about this cop, Justine. Do you think he knows anything about our business?"

"No I don't think so."

"But how can you be sure? You don't even know why he's in Vegas." Rinaldo turns his attention to Augustus. "Augustus, what do you think?"

"I think he's investigating the Diamond Jack killer."

"In that case, we have nothing to worry about, right?"

"Yes I think so, Mr. Rinaldo."

"You think so? No, Augustus. You must be sure do you have any idea what the penalty for human trafficking is? It's twenty years to life isn't it Justine?" Justine nods in the affirmative. "So, tell me who the players are in this drama. There's the cop and who else?"

Justine says, "There's Amy. She's one of our girls, and Manny."

"You forgot about Andy, what about him?"

Augustus replies, "he's dead." The bodyguards sit stone faced with no expression.

Rinaldo pauses and sits forward in his seat and says, "Let me tell you a story about how I wound up in Malta that I don't tell too often. Two years ago, I was forced to run from my beloved Sicily because my life was threatened by some lowlife gangster named Vincenzo Santino. I made him a lot of money, you know drugs, gambling, the usual, but I got bored." The bodyguards laugh and look at each other. "I decided to branch out on my own, and I began a very profitable human trafficking business. Apparently, he didn't like the way I made my living, and he wanted me to stop. I wouldn't, so he had his bodyguards torture and beat me as a warning, but fuck him. I was making too much money. I tried to recruit one of his daughters, but she refused and before I left Sicily, I made sure she would never forget me." He winks at his bodyguards, and they smile. "He's been trying to find me to get his revenge, but I've changed my appearance over the years."

Justine and Augustus are uneasy listening to this.

"From this beautiful island of Malta, I built this business, and we're international and prosperous because of me and my contacts. Yes Justine, I know you also have a growing network, but compared to me you're a neophyte. It's my contacts and my organization that supports the way we live. In running this vast network, I sometimes had to resort to violence to get my message across. The message is simply this: I don't tolerate fools, and I definitely don't want them around me." The bodyguards smile again when they hear this. "In fact, Malta is littered with Mediterranean Bones, the bones of foolish people who do foolish things. I'll be in Vegas for a little over one week. Then I fly to

Istanbul to meet with my contacts there. Straighten all this out, and find out why this cop is in Vegas, and find this fellow Manny before the cop does, and kill him. Don't be fools doing foolish things or you'll both become Mediterranean Bones." The bodyguards are still smiling, and Rinaldo says, "Now, let's have that champagne. The temperature is 47 degrees and perfect."

CHAPTER 14
VICTIM NUMBER FOUR

Augustus Becker is trying to call David Evans to ask about his evening with Amy. He gets no response, so he tries to call Amy and again, no answer. He's on his way to the Cosmopolitan when his phone rings. It's David Evans, "David how did it go?"

"Not well Becker, we got jumped by three men in front of my suite. They fucked me up pretty good."

"And Amy, what about Amy?"

"They hurt her real bad, Becker. She's in Vegas General with me, and she's in bad shape. One guy started the whole thing at dinner. He was with a bunch of assholes. He called her a whore and some other names, so I punched him in his face. When we got upstairs they were waiting for us, the three of them. I tried to fight them off, but I was outnumbered. The maid found us and called the cops. They just left. They questioned me for a long time."

Augustus asks, "what did you tell them? You didn't mention my name did you?"

"Relax Becker I kept you and the fucking princess Justine out of it. Here comes the nurse with some meds. I've got to go."

Justine is shopping when her phone rings. "Amy's in the hospital Justine."

She replies," If Evans put her there, I'm going to cut his fucking balls off."

"No, that's not what happened. They were attacked by three men outside his suite. I think one of them may have been one of her clients from the past."

"What about Evans?"

"They fucked him up, but he was able to talk to me. He said that she was in bad shape."

"Shit, what are we going to do? Are the police involved?"

"What the fuck do you think? Of course they are; the maid found them."

"Do you think Evans told them about us?"

"No, he said he kept us out of it. I'm going to find out who did it and take care of it, Justine."

"What are you going to do?"

"Leave it to me. Nobody messes with our merchandise and gets away with it."

Gino is at Amy's bedside when a team of Doctors comes into the room. The doctor in charge greets Gino, "good morning I'm Doctor Beasley and you are?"

"I'm Gino Marchetti. Amy is my girlfriend. We're going to get married soon."

Doctor Beasley pauses, then she tells the other doctors present, "would you excuse us for a few minutes. Have a seat, Mr. Marchetti. Right now Amy is in a medically induced coma. She was beaten badly, and she suffered some internal injuries. It may be too soon to tell, but all indications are that she may not be able to bear a child; we'll know more as time goes on." Gino buries his head in his hands. "You just spoke about marriage, and I wanted to be up front with you."

Gino asks, "is she going to live?"

"Yes as of now it appears her injuries are not life threatening she'll survive. We'll take it one day at a time, Mr. Marchetti."

The Cosmopolitan is having a busy night. It's vacation season and the rooms are full of tourists trying their luck. The room is loud and teeming with action at the gaming tables. The sound of roulette wheels and chips being swept off the table fill the air. One table is especially loud, and it overpowers the sounds in the room. Foul language and expletives are thrown about at the tables surrounding them as the alcohol flows. The floor manager walks to the table and asks them to keep it down "If you continue, we'll have to remove you like we did the other night now keep it down."

The man looks around, "Speaking of the other night, where's that whore, is she here? Oh that's right. She's not feeling too good."

The other men laugh, and the manager speaks up again. "I'm sorry, but you have to leave. If you refuse, I'll get security." They respond with a few more expletives aimed at him. He motions for casino security, and the men soon find themselves surrounded by three large men. The floor manager says,"get them out of here."

One of the men responds, "fuck you we're leaving anyway this place sucks."

The floor manager tells security, "gentlemen, make sure they leave the casino grounds, thank you."

The men leave followed by the security guards. This entire scenario was observed by a man standing nearby, who also follows the group outside. The man, who's dressed all in black, is walking close behind the men, blending in with the crowd on the strip. A few blocks ahead, the men separate. The figure in black following them now focuses on one man and continues to walk behind him. The man enters the parking lot of another casino on the strip and walks to his car. In the dark, he fumbles for his key and finally opens the driver's side door. The man in black waits till he's almost inside, and then he strikes. Running from the shadows, he attacks the man before he has a chance to close the door. The driver tries to fight him off, but chloroform infused cotton in the man's hand covers the driver's face, and he ceases to struggle, the chloroform putting an end to the fight. He pushes him into the passenger seat and drives out of the lot and into Red Rock Canyon. He approaches from the opposite side through an entrance not open to tourists. He zip ties the man's hands and ankles together, turns off the headlights and waits. He sees lights on the other side of the park, the headlights of police cars patrolling the area. The man is beginning to shake off the effects of the chloroform, and he looks around and realizes he's being restrained." What the fuck is going on? Why am I tied up and who the fuck are you?"

"What's your name?" The man struggles to free himself and the driver tells him, "don't. I'll just make them tighter. I asked you your name."

"It's Steve. What do you want?"

The driver stares ahead, "I'm going to ask you one question, Steve. Do you know a girl named Amy?"

"No, I don't know any Amy."

"I think you do. A few nights ago, she was with a man and a group of…….

"I don't know what you're talking about."

"I don't believe you." He takes a zip tie and puts it around the man's neck and says, "if I tighten this one click at a time, you'll die a very slow death. In fact, I could keep you alive for an agonizing hour, slowly suffocating you. Now tell me the truth. One click, two click, three click. It's getting tighter, isn't it."

"Ok, ok. Amy, the girl from the other night, are you talking about her?"

"Yes, her, the girl from the other night."

"Listen, I didn't do nothing. I just watched; I swear I didn't touch her."

"You just watched, that's kind of sick, isn't it?" The man continues to stare straight ahead, "you watched a young girl get tortured, and you didn't do anything. I wonder how many other girls did you and your friends torture."

"I never did that before. I just watched, I swear." He tightens the zip tie one more time, click. "I swear, I swear. I just watched. I got no reason to lie." The man is wheezing as the zip ties are beginning to cut off oxygen.

"Ok, I believe you. Now give me names. There were three of you, correct? Give me their names and I'll cut the zip ties."

"They're friends of mine. I can't tell you."

"Do you want to hear the sound of the zip ties again? Click, click, click."

"No, please don't tighten it anymore."

"Ok, I won't if you give me their names." The man names the other two men, and the driver writes them down." "Did you rape her? Which one of you was the first one with Amy that night?"

"It wasn't me."

"Then who?"

"It was Billy. It was Billy Powers. Now will you let me go?"

"Addresses please."

"No, these guys have families. I can't tell you." The man pauses,

"Ok, ok. I'll have to find them on my own. I'll start with this Billy guy. Are you sure you've been truthful, Steve?"

"Yes. Please let me go please, I gave you a name."

"Thank you, you've been helpful. I have one more question: do you know who I am?" The man shakes his head no and is visibly trembling. "Well, allow me to introduce myself. I'm Diamond Jack." The man screams, and the cotton covers his face again, and the night is quiet except for the clicking of the zip ties as Steve slowly suffocates.

CHAPTER 15
ALL HELL IS BREAKING LOOSE

Augustus Becker arrives at Vegas General. He walks past the front desk and rides the elevator to the ICU floor. He is stopped by a nurse at the ICU desk and asked who he's there to see. "I'm here to see Amy, Amy Styles."

"I'm sorry, sir. Only immediate family allowed."

"I'm like family to her. I've known her since she came here from Nebraska. Please, can I see her just for a minute? We're very close."

"She's not able to speak. She's in a medically induced coma. The best I could do is to let you see her through the glass, but you can't go into the room."

"Ok, through the glass is ok, but when do you think I could see her?"

"I can't tell you that's up to Doctor Beasley. Come on, she's over here."

Augustus looks through the glass and sees Gino sitting by her bedside." "Who's that guy in there with her?"

"It's her fiancé."

"She's engaged?"

"You said you were like family, and you didn't know she was engaged. I'm going to ask you to leave." Gino turns and looks at Augustus and turns back to Amy.

"What's her fiancé's name?"

"I can't tell you that." The nurse says, "May I ask you your name?" Augustus pushes past her and fast-walks to the exit. Gino leaves Amy's side and asks the nurse, "that guy who just left, who is he?"

"I don't know, Mr. Marchetti. He said he was a friend since she got here from Nebraska. When I asked him his name, he stormed out. Do you know him?"

Gino just says, "thanks."

"Good morning Rodriguez. I just got a call from Steiner a few minutes ago. A couple of hikers found another one in Red Rock. I'm heading there now. Come in by the ranger trail on the south side. The body is about a hundred yards in. I'll meet you there."

"Ok, I'm on my way." Rodriguez arrives on the scene and finds the body positioned on the rocks as with past victims. He does a quick investigation of the body and the area. The hikers who found the body are standing off to the side. Captain Steiner and his men are securing the scene when McMahon arrives. Rodriguez briefs her, "this couple was camping on the ridge up there, and they found the body hiking down this morning. Let's see if they can tell us anything."

"Good morning I'm Agent McMahon and this is Sergeant Rodriguez. First of all, you do realize this part of the park is off limits to everyone except park rangers." The couple nods yes. "Do you know why?" The couple is silent. "There's coyotes, flash floods and a few years ago, a pack of wolves killed a hiker on that same ridge." The couple glance at each other. "There's an eight-foot fence that separates the rest of the park from that area for a reason. Did you climb the fence?" The hikers are silent. "That's what I thought. So, you were camped up there all night. Did you hear or see anything?"

One of the hikers speaks. "We saw headlights at around midnight stopped just after the trail. We thought it was a ranger but after a few minutes, they went out."

Rodriguez asks, "can you tell what kind of car it was, small, large, SUV?"

"It looked like a regular car, not a van or anything."

"How long was the car there?"

"About a half hour, and then we heard a scream. We thought it was an animal."

"It was only one scream, how long did it last?"

"Just a few seconds, and then the headlights came on and the car moved, and the lights went out again."

"Did the car move further into the park?"

"Yes and about ten minutes later, they came on again, and the car left the park."

"Thanks, give your contact information to Captain Steiner in case we need to ask you more questions. He's the bald handsome guy with the suit." Rodriguez and McMahon walk toward the body and as they approach Rodriguez says, "Diamond Jack broke the pattern. This is the other side of the park."

"Yeah, he must have known the other side was under surveillance."

Rodriguez crouches down and asks, "Look at these tracks. They were made by a smaller vehicle than the one at the other crime scene." "Look at the amount of blood compared to the others this guy was killed here, the others were killed elsewhere and dumped in the park?" Rodriguez looks over the body, "I think he was alive when the card was nailed into his head that would account for all the blood. When the heart stops pumping, well, you know the rest."

"That's rather macabre Rodriguez."

"It is, but it's true. There's a lot more blood here and look at the marks on his neck. He was strangled."

"It looks like a thin piece of wire."McMahon picks up a piece of the ziptie, "Or a zip tie."

"He was unconscious but still breathing." "There's traces of cotton around his face."

"The two of diamonds, McMahon. That's the letter B."

McMahon says, "Except for the cards and the chips, this one looks like it was ad libbed. Do you think it's a copycat?"

"No, it's not the same as the others, but I think it's the same killer."

David Evans is released from the hospital, and he calls Augustus," I'm heading to the airport, Becker. I've had enough of Vegas for a while. I hope Amy gets better. She's a class act. The cops questioned me for a couple of hours a few nights ago, and they told me when I was better, I could leave Vegas. I hope they catch these fuckers. I'll be in touch, Becker."

Augustus says, "I hope you don't let this keep you from visiting us again Mr. Evans."

"Stop sucking up, Becker. You sound like a fucking travel agent, and if there's anything Amy needs medicine, doctors, anything let me know, and make sure you take good care of her."

"Yes Mr. Evans."

McMahon gets a call from Captain Steiner, "I think we found your Amy. Her full name is Amy Styles. She's in Vegas General Hospital in a medically induced coma. She and a guy named David Evans were attacked outside of his suite. He said they were having dinner and some guys at another table began insulting Styles. He got up and punched one guy in the face and when they got up to his suite, they were waiting for them."

"They?"

"Yeah, he said there were three of them."

"Where's Evans now?"

"He checked out of the hospital last night after he was questioned by the local cops and released."

"What's the story on this guy Evans?"

Steiner responds, "He's a big shot in Silicon Valley; it just happens that his family owns most of the land these tech. companies are on. His family controls all the leases and sales in most of the Valley."

"Any description of the men who attacked them?"

"Not really, just the one he hit. According to Evans, he had dark hair, chubby and not too tall. He didn't pay much attention to the others since this guy seemed to be the ringleader."

McMahon says, "it's not the victim we found in Red Rock, this guy was tall and thin and almost bald."

"So you think Diamond Jack strikes again."

"Yeah, looks like it but we can't be sure it feels like all hell is breaking loose."

"I'll get Rodriguez to go to the hospital and see what he can find out."

CHAPTER 16
THE DICK AT THE METROPOLITAN

Hotels in Las Vegas have house detectives sarcastically called house dicks. They're job is to patrol the lobbies and the halls in an effort to keep out prostitutes and drug dealers that work the strip. The hotels don't want such riff raff walking their lobbies unless they're approved by the management. The Metropolitan Hotel is no exception to the rule. As rundown as it is, it still has to put its best foot forward. However, the detectives in this hotel are on Augustus Becker and Justine Godfrey's payroll. One of these detectives witnessed Maria Corrales, the bakery chef, speaking with Rodriguez. He thinks it's important to let Augustus know about the visit.

Augustus is having a hard time at the blackjack table. He's down about two thousand dollars and he's in the middle of what looks like a possible winning hand when his phone rings. The croupier points to a sign that says no cellphones at the tables. Augustus mumbles something and leaves the table to the delight of the other players. Angrily he answers, "Yeah what is it."

"Mr. Becker, it's me, Carl the security guard over at the Metropolitan."

"I know who it is, Carl. What do you want, and it better be important. I had a winning hand."

"Last week a man was here asking about the door in the back by the exit."

Becker calms down. "Really, who did he talk to?"

"He spoke to Maria she's our baker you know she makes the cakes and-"

Becker interrupts, "I know what a fucking baker does, Carl. Did she say what he was looking for?"

"That's the funny part, Mr. Becker. He told her he's the fire inspector and there may be a fire hazard behind the door."

"Fire hazard, what are you talking about?"

"That's what he said. There's a fire hazard."

"What did he look like?"

"I saw the guy as he was leaving. He was big with dark hair and dark eyes, looked like he worked out a lot."

"That sounds like Rodriguez."

"No, Mr. Becker. He said his name was Roberts."

"His name is not Roberts, it's Rodriguez. How did he get all the way to the back without one of you morons stopping him?"

"I don't know, Mr. Becker. I was upstairs. When I came down, he was just leaving."

"This Maria, the baker, keep an eye on her and if he comes back, call me right away and let me know if he talks to her again. Maybe a visit to the tunnels is in this cops future."

"Alright Mr. Becker, I'll do that."

"Wait before you go, was this guy good looking?"

"What?"

"Was he good looking? It's a simple question."

"I don't know Mr. Becker, I'm not gay."

"I didn't ask you if you were fucking gay. I asked you if he was good looking, was he?"

"I guess so."

"Better looking than me?"

Carl pauses, "I don't think so, maybe but I'm not sure."

"Fuck you Carl." Augustus returns to the table to find that his hand is gone, and the game has moved on. He asks the croupier, "where's my cards?"

"Your cards, are you kidding? You left the table as far as I'm concerned. You were out, we don't reserve seats once you leave you forfeit."

"But I had a winning hand. What the fuck."

"Cry me a river. What are the rest of the players supposed to do? Wait for you to finish your call? In the first place you're not supposed to have cell phones at the table, and once you leave, you're out. So do you want to leave or play another hand?"

Angrily he responds, "I'll play."

A voice comes from Augustus's left side, "I want in."

The croupier states. "Two players in if no one objects." The other players are silent. "Fresh deck coming out." And the croupier opens a fresh deck. Augustus turns to his left and it's Gino Marchetti. Augustus looks at Gino suspiciously.

Gino asks," is the table hot?"

Augustus replies, "Not for me." Augustus looks back at Gino. "Haven't I seen you somewhere before?"

"I don't know, probably at the casinos." Gino extends his hand. "My name's Gino."

Augustus reluctantly extends his hand. "Augustus." Gino says, "Good luck, hope your horse comes in Augustus." He looks at Gino then turns and faces the croupier.

CHAPTER 17
ISABELLA

"Rinaldo is talking to Augustus, " So who do you have to replace Amy? It seems she will be in the hospital for a while,"

"Yeah I know I'm working on it."

"Work harder. I don't want a deficit in the stable 'cause it affects our bottom line, so replace her immediately. Are we on the same page?"

"Yeah."

"And get in touch with Justine. She must have someone who can stand in. I want all this straightened out."

Augustus hangs up the phone, and he says to no one in particular, "What a fucking asshole." He calls Justine. "So Rinaldo wants me to replace Amy, do you know how she's doing?"

"How the fuck should I know I'm not her doctor."

Augustus asks, "Do you have anybody who can replace her?"

"I may have somebody in Reno, drop dead gorgeous but a real fucking diva. I'll let you know."

"Can you make it sooner rather than later Justine? Rinaldo is up my ass."

She answers sarcastically, "Sure Augustus, anything else?"

Rodriguez is driving to the hospital to try and interview Amy. When he arrives, Dr. Beasley is there to greet him. She tells him that although her condition is improving, she is not able to answer questions. Rodriguez asks, "Has anyone been in to see her?"

And the doctor answers, "Yes, her fiancé is in there with her now. He comes to see her every day."

"Her fiancé, I didn't realize she was engaged. May I have a few words with him?"

"Of course, but not in the room. I'll ask him to come out."

"Thank you doctor."

Gino exits the room and Rodriguez identifies himself. "Hello Sergeant, I'm Gino Marchetti."

"Hi Mr. Marchetti, the doctor tells me your fiancé is doing better."

"Yes, but I have to make a confession, Sergeant. We're not engaged. I told them that so they would let me stay with her."

"So, what is your relationship with Ms. Styles?"

"We're dating, and I was going to ask her to marry me."

"I see. Don't worry, I won't say anything. Mr. Marchetti, are you aware of what happened that night?"

"From what the police told me, Amy and her date were jumped by three men. I know what Amy does for a living, Sergeant and since we're being honest, I was a client when she first got here, and then I fell in love with her."

Rodriguez says, "The person she was with tried to fight them off, but there were three of them. Do you have any idea who the three men might be?"

"No Sergeant, I don't. It's Vegas, these pieces of shit come and go."

"Yeah I guess you're right, Mr. Marchetti. Have you lived in Vegas a longtime?"

"No, just a few years. I'm from New York Brooklyn to be exact. Listen, I know you're probably going to check me out so I'm going to come clean. I did time for assault in New York. I did a few years. It was a fight in a bar, and I didn't start it, but because of the people I hung out with in Brooklyn, well you know it was guilt by association. Find these guys Sergeant. I want them to pay for what they did."

"We'll do our best. I appreciate your honesty Mr. Marchetti."

"When Amy gets better she can give the police more information, right Sergeant?"

"Ok Mr. Marchetti, I'll let you get back to your fiancé. Oh by the way, are you a gambling man?"

"Not anymore. I used to be, why?"

"'Cause I've been noticing your cufflinks. They're nice, something a gambling man would wear."

"Thanks Sergeant."

"I hope it all works out Mr. Marchetti, I'll be in touch."

As he's leaving the hospital, a voice calls him back. It's Dr. Beasley, "I misspoke earlier, Sergeant. There was someone else in to see her. The duty nurse Janet Paterson said a man wanted to see her, but he stormed out after a few minutes."

"Really, when was he here?"

"A few days ago."

"What did he look like?"

"He was tall with dark hair and brown eyes, about 40 or 45, good looking and well dressed."

"Did he identify himself?"

"No, he told her he was a friend of Amy's, but Nurse Paterson said something about him just wasn't right. When she questioned him, he stormed out."

"Thank you. If I need to ask any more questions, can I find her here?"

"Yes, her name is Janet Paterson. Today she'll be here at four."

On the way back from the hospital, Rodriguez calls McMahon. "Amy's not well enough to speak to us. I just came from the hospital. She has a visitor, a guy named Gino Marchetti. The nurse said he's been at her bedside the whole time. He claimed to be her fiancé so he could be with her. He was going to ask her to marry him and then this happened. The nurse said there was a strange guy that wanted to see Amy, and he made her uncomfortable. When she pressed him, he bolted."

McMahon asks, "Should I run a check on this guy Gino?

"No, he told me he did time for assault in a bar fight. He said it wasn't his fault. I believe him, so I would leave it alone for now."

The limousine from the airport arrives in the middle of a rainstorm. Inside is Isabella Joia, one of Justine's girls. Justine considers her a star in the escort world and Augustus is there to greet her. The door to the limousine opens and Augustus is star struck. Isabella is from Italy with dark hair and green eyes, a real stunner. Augustus stands there with umbrella in hand, frozen in place. A voice from inside the limousine says, "Are you going to stand there 'till it stops raining or are you going to open the umbrella?" Spoken in the sexiest accent he's ever heard. He fumbles with the umbrella and finally opens it. He extends his hand and helps her out of the limousine.

"I'm Augustus, Justine's partner."

"I'm Isabella, have someone come out for my luggage please." Augustus hands her the room card. "Thank you. I hope it's exactly what I asked for. Justine knows what I want and speaking of Justine, where is she? I thought she was meeting me also."

"No, she had other business."

"Tell her I need to speak with her after I've had a warm bath and some rest say around nine tonight."

"Sure Isabella, I'll let her know here's the paperwork you'll need to check in and be incognito as much as you can. Did Justine tell you you're Mrs. Ayad and your husband will be-"

She cuts him off, "joining me in a few days blah blah I know." She looks at him and smiles. "Thank you, Augustus. Justine said you were a handsome man. I see she was right. Remember nine not before."

Augustus calls Justine to tell her of Isabella's arrival. "She just got here. She's on her way to the room. Did you tell her I was handsome?"

"Come on, Augustus. Don't let it go to your head. I have to call Rinaldo, and then I'll call Isabella."

"Wait she said not to call her before nine. She's resting."

Rinaldo is anxious to meet Isabella and he calls Justine. "So when can I meet this Isabella?"

"After nine tonight Mr. Rinaldo, she's resting."

"She's resting really? Justine, how far is it from Reno to Las Vegas by plane and then from the airport to her hotel room?"

"All together?"

"Yes all together."

"Figure the flight is an hour and a half, and a twenty-minute limo ride, about two hours."

"Two hours on the plane in first class I assume and a short limousine ride while sipping champagne and she needs to rest. I want this whore on her back tomorrow night and making money, Justine. I don't like divas."

"Ok Mr. Rinaldo, I'll see to it."

"Mansour Ayad is my, shall we say, business partner, and he's used to having things done a certain way. Let's see if she's all you say she is."

CHAPTER 18
NEW STILETTOS

The funeral for the latest victim of Diamond Jack was held in a small chapel in Las Vegas. You can get buried or married in the same chapel on the same day. The circle of friends is small and congregated on one side of the room. The outsider, the one nobody knows, is off to the side and slowly makes his way to the group of men. He introduces himself. "Hi, I'm Arthur Baker. It's terrible what happened to Steve."

One of the group asks, "How do you know Steve?"

The stranger, having done his homework, replies, "I worked with Steve at the MGM Grand."

"Nice to meet you Mr. Baker. My name is Dennis, and this is Billy, Tony and Craig." The men exchange pleasantries and then Billy asks, "Did the cops talk to you yet Mr. Baker?"

"No not yet and you can call me Arthur."

"Well, they're probably going to talk to you about Steve. We got questioned by these two cops, Rodriguez and McMahon. The bartender ratted us out. He knows us since we go there a lot. So get ready. They might talk to you too."

"Shit, I don't know too much. I just worked with the guy."

"He never mentioned you. How long did you guys work together?"

"Well, I was on a different shift, and we'd talk shit when I relieved him. You know sports, girls, guy shit.

Billy says, "Well, nice to meet you Arthur."

Dennis continues, "So, I got questioned by these two cops. They questioned me for two hours about the fight I had with some fucking john."

"Fight?"

"Yeah, me, Billy and Steve got into a beef with some guy who was sitting with one of the whores at the Cosmopolitan. We were drunk and acting stupid when the guy pops Billy in the face for no reason."

"He hit you for no reason?"

"Yeah, the fucking asshole. Hey Billy, show him your lip."

"Yeah, I see it's still swollen. So, what happened after that?"

"They threw us out of the joint and I didn't have a chance to finish my drink."

Baker asks, "What happened to the guy?"

The men glance at each other and smirk. "We taught them a lesson."

Baker asks,"Them?"

Billy looks at Dennis and shakes his head.

"Do you think the guy killed Steve?"

"No, I think the guy was in the hospital when Steve was killed. Besides, the cops suspect it was that serial killer, Diamond Jack."

"Wow, you put the guy in the hospital?"

"Well it wasn't just me. Let's leave it at that."

"So this cop Rodriguez, what's he like?"

"He's a big dude with no sense of humor. He questioned me for over an hour trying to wear me down."

"What about this guy McMahon? What's his story?"

"McMahon's a she and just as fucking tough. They kept going over and over the same shit trying to pin it on me and Billy."

Arthur asks, "You guys want to get a drink? I'm about ready to leave."

"Sure, we can head out in a few minutes." The men are having drinks and alcohol makes for a perfect truth serum. After the third round, the subject turns back to the events of that night, and the real story begins to emerge. Arthur Baker is listening intently to the details. "So Billy, what was this hooker's name?"

"Her name is Amy. The worst ever. Avoid her."

"Oh yeah? What does she look like?"

"Like Miss America but stiff as a board awful. If hookers are your thing, stay away from her if you can."

"Ok Billy, I'll keep it in mind. So what happened to the guy and this whore?"

Billy looks at Dennis and says, "Let's just say we taught them both a lesson and had some fun at the same time."

Arthur looks at his watch and says, "Well, I gotta go. It was nice meeting you guys. I'm sure we'll see each other soon. I got this round," and he puts the money on the bar.

It's nine 'o' clock and Isabella is ordering room service for her dinner after resting from her Reno trip. She gets a call from Justine. "Hello Isabella, I hope you got your beauty sleep, because you're on tomorrow night. Mr. Rinaldo has a special friend coming into town."

"Rinaldo's in Vegas since when?"

"A few days ago. I told him all about you. It seems this friend from the middle east has special tastes."

"Special tastes?"

"Yes, he has a thing for strippers in stiletto heels, and he wants you to wear stiletto heels when you're with him."

"Come on, Justine. Did you ever try walking in those fucking things? Even strippers who wear them on the job have a tough time. I ain't wearing them. What other special tastes does he have?"

"Sorry Isabella, the heels are non-negotiable. Rinaldo insists."

"Justine, I work for you, not Rinaldo."

"Well Isabella, I work for Rinaldo. It sucks, but that's how it is."

"I don't even own a pair of those fucking things."

"Don't worry, he's bringing a few pairs for you. I told him your shoe size."

"Jesus Christ Justine, what the fuck. What other special tastes does this guy have?"

"I don't know, just go with it. Don't be a fucking diva."

"My price just went up, Justine. Fuck Rinaldo."

CHAPTER 19
THE WHEEL OF MISFORTUNE

Billy Powers is leaving his job at the Las Vegas Water Commission. He's employed as an engineer and is paid handsomely. He lives in the affluent suburb of Summerlin North about ten miles outside of Las Vegas. The sun is setting as he walks through the parking lot to his car. The seven am to seven pm shift just ended. Billy works that shift three days a week, which allows him extra time for gambling and prostitutes. It's Wednesday, his night to meet friends and hang out in the casinos and do some gambling. If he gets lucky and wins, he may give part of it to a hooker for services rendered. This is Billy's life. His marriage has been on the rocks for a long time and as long as he provides for their two children, all the animosity stays below the radar. As he walks to his car in the darkening parking lot, the sound of his footsteps merge with footsteps that keep getting closer and closer. As he gets to his car, he turns and behind him is Arthur Baker. "Shit you scared me. What are you doing here?"

"Tell me about Amy again, Billy."

"What about her? I'm done talking about that bitch."

Arthur is quiet and he looks around the parking lot. "Did you guys take turns with her? Who was first, you?

"What the fuck is wrong with you Arthur? Get away from me, or I'm calling the cops."

Arthur produces a gun and commands, "Get in the car or I'll shoot you right here."

"What the fuck are you doing?"

"You're driving, I'll tell you where."

The men are in the car and Billy asks, "What are you going to do?"

"Shut up and drive." Baker's voice breaks the silence, "So, who was pulling the strings that night, Billy? Was it you?"

"What are you talking about, what strings?"

"You know what I'm talking about, Billy. I'm talking about Amy. Your buddy Steve told me you were the boss. You told everybody what to do and you admitted to being there, remember."

"Steve told you but that means…." Billy's getting agitated. "Are you Diamond Jack? Are you going to kill me?"

The car veers and almost goes off the road as Billy tries to reach for the gun, and he gets hit in the face. "Drive the fucking car Billy I'll tell you where." The Wheel of Misfortune was for a long-time part of the Vegas underground. The wheel is located in Henderson about fifteen miles from Vegas but just three miles from where Billy works. The wheel is actually a circular shallow pit that was used to manufacture pulp for a manganese mine that was abandoned in 1961. In one of the circular pits, a renegade artist painted his own version of the game show Wheel of Fortune in 2012. This wheel however is anything but fortunate. Its spaces are painted with sayings like "lose all Hope, lose a Job, lose a Home, Bank owned," etc. As if that wasn't unlucky enough, the area is toxic due to the mining waste buried there. The wheel is about two hundred- and fifty-feet wide and painting it must have been quite a feat. The men arrive at the wheel as nightfall begins to set in. Arthur says, "let's wait a while, Billy. I want you to tell me about Amy."

"I told you, I don't know anything about her. We were drunk, and we fucked up."

"You sure did, Billy." Baker is quietly staring out the window when he asks, "You got kids?"

"Yeah two."

"Girls?"

"One girl."

"So let me ask you, Billy, how would you feel if someone did that to your little girl?"

Billy thinks for a minute and answers, "I'd want to kill him."

Arthur pauses for a minute and then he explains, pointing with the gun. "You ever been here before Billy?" Billy shakes his head no. "Let me fill you in about this place. It used to be an old mine. This circle we're in was used in the production of manganese. It's very toxic, but I don't give a fuck, do you Billy? This circle is two hundred fifty feet across. I'm going to give you a break. Get out and start running. If you can outrun this car, I'll let you go, and if you try and climb the wall, I'll shoot you. Now get out."

Billy is scared and begging. "I can't outrun this car."

"I know, Billy, so I'll give you a head start. Now get the fuck out." Billy begins to run as Arthur goes to the driver's side. He guns the car with the horn blowing and as he gets close to Billy, he turns the wheel to taunt him. "Run Billy run, you piece of shit." This continues with Arthur taunting and coming close to Billy and at the last minute, turns the wheel. Billy tries running in the opposite direction, but the driver is relentless. Around they go, the driver constantly taunting as Billy begs for mercy. Billy is getting tired, and he's slowing down, and finally Arthur ends the cat and mouse game. The Wheel of Misfortune lives up to its name as Billy is dragged beneath the car for almost an entire revolution of the wheel. The car finally releases its prey and his body lands on the space painted Lose all Hope. Arthur leaves the car and walks down the hill to where he parked earlier in the day and drives off. A figure who saw the entire incident comes out of the shadows and using a cane to help him walk, he slowly makes his way to Billy Power's body. As he gets closer he notices that the car's engine is still running. He reaches the mutilated body and realizes there's nothing anybody can do for him. He hobbles down the hill to a convenience store where he's found shelter at times during those cold desert nights and reports what he saw.

Captain Steiner is on the scene when Rodriguez and McMahon arrive. "Who called it in, Captain?"

"That guy over there with the cane. He claims he saw the whole thing, told the clerk at the convenience store and he called it in. He's over there talking to my men. His name is Rudy, but he can't remember his last name."

Rodriguez exclaims sarcastically, "great" and walks over to Rudy. "Hey Rudy, how're you doing? I'm Sergeant Rodriguez. Want to put the bottle down and tell me what you saw?"

Rudy is a veteran that was overlooked by the system and suffering from PTSD. He took to drugs and the bottle, and now he calls the wheel home. Rudy takes one more drink from the bottle. "I saw a monster dragging this poor guy around the wheel, and then he spit him out, and there was fire." Rudy's eyes widen and he points to the monster. "It's still there, see it?"

Rodriguez, shaking his head, points to the car. "Is this the monster you saw, Rudy?"

"Yes that's it. Don't get too close, or it'll kill you too."

"Was somebody riding the monster, or was somebody inside the monster?"

"Somebody came out from inside the monster."

"Can you tell me what he looked like?"

"He was big, real big, bigger than you and twice as wide with red eyes-"

Rodriguez cuts him off, "Ok, thanks Rudy you've been helpful."

McMahon looks at Rodriguez. "Well."

"Forget it, McMahon."

"Come over here Rodriguez. Does this guy look familiar to you?"

Rodriguez looks at the body. "Yeah, considering that half his face is scraped off, a positive ID is a little tough, but if I were to guess, I would say that's Billy Powers, one of the guys we questioned about Amy Styles."

"Good call, Rodriguez. First Steve Owens in Red Rock, and now this guy."

"McMahon, what was the third guy's name? Wasn't it Dennis something?"

"Yeah Dennis McCarthy."

Rodriguez says, "I'll bet Mr. McCarthy shows up soon wanting protection."

"Why would he do that? He said they had nothing to do with what happened to Amy."

"And we all know that's bullshit, don't we? Give it a few days. He'll come in begging for protection, and he'll tell us everything."

"We really need to talk to Amy."

"Not anytime soon, McMahon. She's still in bad shape. Do me a favor, McMahon. Run Gino Marchetti with two t's. It's time we checked him out."

"A few days ago you asked me not to."

"That was a few days ago."

Rodriguez is walking to his car and McMahon shouts," Where the hell are you going?"

"Can you wrap it up here? I'm going to try my luck."

CHAPTER 20
VINO WITH GINO

Rodriguez gets to his hotel room, changes his clothes and drives to the strip. When he worked in Vegas, the Cosmopolitan was his casino of choice when he wanted some excitement and tonight is no exception. The atmosphere is vibrant, young, and alive, and women give him the eye as he walks through the room. He goes to one of the many bars and he notices a man sitting alone enjoying a glass of wine. It's Gino Marchetti, and he approaches and asks, "Is this seat taken Mr. Marchetti?"

Gino turns and recognizes him, "It depends, Sergeant. Are you off or on duty?"

Rodriguez puts up his hands and says, "I hung up my badge a few hours ago I swear."

"I'm only breaking your balls, Sergeant. Sure, sit down. Let me buy you a drink. What's your poison?"

"I usually drink Scotch, but tonight I'll have what you're having, a glass of red."

Gino says, "I used to drink Bourbon, but I gave up the hard shit a long time ago." Gino motions to the bartender and he brings the drink. "Put it on my tab."

"Sure Mr. Marchetti."

And Gino throws the bartender a twenty. "So Sergeant, are you a gambler?"

"I play once in a while."

"Oh yeah? What's your game?"

"Blackjack. It's got the best odds for the player."

"I guess, but when I was playing, I played the wheel."

"So you were a roulette player."

"Yeah, roulette with some blackjack thrown in."

Rodriguez takes a sip of his wine and looks at Gino. "How's Amy doing, Gino?"

Gino takes a sip. "About the same. The Doc says it's going to be a while. She's got something going on in her head."

"Sorry to hear that."

Gino says, "I wish I could get my hands on these motherfuckers. The guy that was found in Red Rock three or four days ago, wasn't he a suspect?"

"You mean Steve Owens?"

"Yeah, I didn't know his name."

"We questioned him and two other guys, but we couldn't hold them." There's silence and then Rodriguez asks, "You told me you stopped gambling, when was that?"

"I quit a few years ago. It was getting too expensive."

Rodriguez asks, "How did you do it? GA?"

"You mean Gamblers Anonymous? No, I did it on my own. I looked into that GA, but it was too much work for me, all the meetings, the steps and all that. I'm probably a bigger wino than I am a gambling addict."

The men laugh and then Rodriguez asks, "What did you mean by steps?"

"Steps, oh yeah. They got these steps, twelve of 'em. It's almost like a religion."

"I hear it works for a lot of people." Rodriguez is sipping the wine listening to Gino.

"Back in Brooklyn, if the fellas knew you were doing that, they would laugh you right off the block." Gino takes a sip and asks, "So Sergeant, do you think you're close to finding this Diamond Jack?"

"I shouldn't be telling you, but I got some leads we're chasing but nothing solid yet." As the men are talking, all heads turn and people are whispering to each other at the sight of Achille Rinaldo. He's walking through the casino with two bodyguards, and people stop what they're doing to look at him. Some just turn away and others snicker at his strange appearance.

Gino says, "What the fuck. Check this guy out, Sergeant. You better cover your throat before he takes a bite."

Rodriguez looks and says, "Do you know who he is, Gino? Did you ever see him before?"

"Me, fuck no. Somebody better get him some of that sunshine vitamin, and did you see those two fucking mooks with him? Holy shit."

Rodriguez isn't laughing. "I'll be right back, Gino. I've got to take a leak." He follows the men and watches as they get into an elevator and go to the Penthouse. He returns to the bar to continue his conversation with Gino. "That was quick."

"Yeah, turns out I didn't have to go."

"You know what I think?"

"No Gino, what do you think?"

"I think you followed those mooks, and if you ask me, there's your Diamond Jack."

Rodriguez smiles and takes another sip of his wine.

CHAPTER 21
THE DAME'S STILETTOS

Rinaldo and his bodyguards go to the Penthouse floor to meet Isabella and make sure everything is perfect for his guest. He arrives and instructs his bodyguards to wait outside. Augustus and Justine are there having drinks. Isabella is sitting and reading Italian Vogue, wearing a bathrobe and with her hair wrapped in a towel. Rinaldo approaches her and introduces himself. "I'm Achille Rinaldo from Malta."

"Isabella Joia from Napoli."

"Che bello, siamo Italiani."

Augustus asks, "What did you say?"

"I said how nice, we're Italian." Rinaldo turns to Justine, "Why isn't she dressed, Justine?"

Isabella answers, "Why don't you ask me?"

"Ok I will. Why aren't you dressed? Mr. Ayad will be here in an hour. He's from Saudi Arabia, worth billions and he demands promptness."

"Saudi Arabia, they really know how to treat women there, don't they?"

Augustus moves closer to Isabella, "You better show some respect."

She replies, "Get away from me. You stink of cheap cologne. Now, all of you get out so I can get dressed."

Rinaldo says, "Let's go and let the young lady get dressed." He moves closer and whispers in her ear. "Don't forget the stilettos, Isabella. He's paying a lot of money for the stilettos."

They get into the elevator and Becker says, "What a fucking bitch." Rinaldo turns and gives him a cold stare.

Justine asks, "So Mr. Rinaldo, what do you think of Isabella?"

"Well Justine, you're right. She's beautiful. I might even say she's stunning, but then everybody says that, don't they? Do you have any idea how much Mr. Ayad is paying for two nights of bliss?"

"No, Mr. Rinaldo, how much?"

"Well, if you factor in our private security, a full-time driver and fully stocked limousine 24/7 to take him wherever he wants to go, plus Isabella's servicing his every whim, it comes close to one hundred thousand dollars in 2 days, not to mention future business from him and his associates. All that money for two days of bliss. I hope everything's perfect for Mr. Ayad. I'm sure you and Augustus have seen to it. Now, what about this cop Rodriguez? Why is he in Vegas and have we found Manny and killed him yet?" There's silence and the bodyguards are staring at them. "I'm extending my stay in Las Vegas, but you better have answers soon."

Mr. Ayad is on time and Isabella opens the door and invites him into the suite. He's older than she expected and not at all attractive. Paunchy and pale, she wonders how someone who lives in that part of the world can be so pale. She laughs to herself, maybe all of Rinaldo's friends look like he does. He enters and looks around. "This is a very nice suite." He introduces himself, "I'm Mansour Ayad."

"Nice to meet you. I'm Isabella." On a table overlooking the strip, there's chilled champagne, lobster tails and an assortment of fruit and expensive cognac. "Would you like some champagne, Mr. Ayad?"

"No I'm afraid my religion doesn't permit it, but I have a gift for you, actually two gifts." From a Christian Louboutin bag, he removes two pairs of stiletto heels. "Here, try these on. I hope you don't mind. I got your size from Justine. I wasn't sure, so I brought a pair in red and a pair in black."

"I like the red ones. I'll try them on." Isabella forces her foot into the shoes. "They're a little tight. It's been a long time since I've worn stilettos."

"You'll get used to them again. Look how they accentuate your legs. All women should wear them."

"I guess you want all women to suffer."

Ayad lets out a laugh. "Come, let's go to dinner."

"May I change my shoes? I'll wear these later if it makes you happy."

"No you'll wear them till I tell you to take them off. Let's go, I'm hungry."

Isabella says to herself, "Fucking asshole."

They return from dinner and Ayad tells his security to leave them. When they enter the suite, she begins to remove the stilettos. "I'm sorry Mr. Ayad, but I have to take these off and give my feet a break."

"But they're your size. Justine told me, and I told you to leave them on." Isabella pours herself a glass of champagne and sits down and begins to take the stilettos off. "What are you doing? I said leave them on and do not defy me."

Isabella is getting agitated. "Listen, they're too small. If I don't take them off, I won't be able to wear them tomorrow night. Please just for a little while. I'll put them back on in bed if that's what turns you on."

"I said leave them on and dance for me now."

"Dance? I'm having a hard time walking, Mansour.

"It's Mr. Ayad, never call me by my first name again. You are my property until I release you. If you can't walk, it's because you drank too much at dinner."

"I had one drink. It loosens me up." She moves closer to him and says, "Let me take these off. You won't be disappointed."

"Dance, I'm paying for you to dance with the shoes on. Do it now, or I'll call Rinaldo," and he pushes her away.

"Come on Mr. Ayad, they're killing my feet. Let me take them off. I promise I'll wear them to bed."

"Leave them on, or I'll call my friend Achille and let him know how disappointed I am in the whore he sent me."

Isabella says angrily, "That's right, I'm a whore and fuck you. I'm not wearing them."

Ayad slaps her and she defiantly stares at him. He shouts angrily, "What did you say to me?"

"I said fuck you."

"You American women think you can talk to a man anyway you want."

"I'm not American, I'm Italian."

He raises his hand to slap her again as Isabella reaches for the other pair of stilettos still on the bed. As Ayad's hand goes up, the stiletto heel hits him on the side of the head. He stands there in disbelief. Afterall, he's Mansour Ayad, a very important man, and a prostitute dares to strike him. He grabs her by the throat and pushes her against the door and tightens his grip. "I could kill you whore, and nobody would care."

"Don't call me a whore,, you motherfucker." The heel comes down again and a trickle of blood runs down his face. He's stunned, and he tightens his grip, and Isabella can't breathe. He's staring at her wildly, and Isabella's legs are getting weak. The next blow goes into his eye and part of the heel is embedded in his skull. He begins to scream, and he's flailing his arms. He grabs her again with the heel still embedded in his skull, but she fights him off. Blood is spurting from what's left of his eye. He attempts to remove it, and she punches the shoe further into his skull, and he falls to the floor rolling around and begging for her to call for help. He attempts to pull the shoe out of his eye, but she walks over and slams her foot on the shoe. When she does, the heel snaps off and Ayad stops moving. She's breathing heavily, and her hands are trembling. She goes to the bathroom and throws cold water on her face. She slowly looks back and sees Ayad's body in the last throes of life; he lets out a low-pitched gurgle and stops moving.

Moments later, Isabella sits on the bed trying to compose herself. She looks down at the body as a small pool of blood begins to form. She grabs the champagne and drinks straight from the bottle. After a while, she feels calmer and goes to one of her bags and removes a gun and slips it into a garter she has attached to her thigh. She calls Justine. "You need to come. Something terrible just happened."

"What the fuck are you talking about, Isabella?"

"Something happened to Ayad. You should come right away. I'm in the penthouse." She hangs up and drinks again from the bottle. She removes the stilettos and throws them across the room. After a while, there's frantic knocks on the door. She lets them in and sits on the edge of the couch, looking at the body. Justine and Augustus storm into the room and freeze in their tracks when they see Ayad lying on the ground with one lifeless eye staring at them and dried blood forming a semi-circle around his head.

Augustus is staring at the body. "What the fuck."

Isabella gets up and walks over to Justine and says, "I told you the stilettos were a bad idea." Justine is standing there, not believing what she is seeing. Augustus charges Isabella and slams her into the wall with his hand squeezing her throat. She pulls the gun from her garter and puts it against his crotch. He looks down and softens his grip. "That's a Beretta M9 pressed against your little balls. It has quite a kick. Do you want to feel it, you fucking pimp."

Augustus puts his hands up and backs away. "Where the fuck did you get a gun?"

"A friend met me at the Vegas airport. He's Italian ex-military. Do you think I trust you fucking people."

Justine asks, "So, what do we do now?"

Isabella answers, "Now we wait for Rinaldo. Call him, Justine."

CHAPTER 22
MADAME ISABELLA

Rinaldo arrives at the Penthouse with his bodyguards. He enters and Isabella has Justine and Augustus against the wall with the Beretta pointed at them. He pauses and looks down at the body of Ayad. "What the fuck happened here? Justine, do you have anything to say?" One of his bodyguards slides his hand into his coat as if reaching for a gun.

"Ask me, Mr. Rinaldo. Justine wasn't here, and you Mr. Bodyguard, if your hand moves another inch, I'll shoot your boss, and I'll keep firing till I run out of bullets. Then we can stand around waiting for the police and explain what the fuck we're doing here."

Rinaldo motions to the bodyguard. "Ok Isabella, tell me why one of my associates is lying on the floor with a heel sticking out of his fucking eye." As he speaks, his voice does a crescendo until he's screaming.

Isabella answers, "He wanted me to wear these stilettos, and I did all through dinner. Do you have any idea how hard it is to walk on these things? It's like walking on a straw. I told him I would wear them to bed if that's what excites him, because they were hurting my feet. He said no, and he wanted me to dance in them, and I told him no. I told him to go fuck himself, and he slapped me. But that wasn't enough for him, and he began choking me. Nobody puts their hands on me unless I want them to, and that's when I gave him his fucking stiletto in the eye."

Rinaldo is looking down at Ayad's body. "Do you realize what you've done? Ayad is my contact in the middle east, and everyone knows he's in Vegas. When he doesn't return, people will be asking questions."

"I'm sorry. He gave me no choice. He was trying to kill me, and I defended myself. Besides, if I break an ankle, what good am I to you? I saw it in his eyes. He would have fucking killed me. He told me I was just a whore and nobody would care, so fuck him. And these fucking stilettos are not made for dancing or walking. They're made for S&M."

Rinaldo's eyes light up and he says, "Sadomasochism?"

"No, standing and modeling." There's silence and then Rinaldo begins to laugh, and it gets louder.

Augustus asks, "What the hell is so funny?"

"Oh, Augustus, you have no sense of humor," and he continues to laugh. He composes himself and he says, "Ok, Isabella. Put the gun down and let's talk."

"What do you want to talk about?"

Augustus says, "Shouldn't we get rid of the body?"

"Shut up, Augustus. All in good time. I'm speaking to the lady. I have an offer for you Isabella."

"Offer, what kind of offer?"

"Perhaps you could work for me, no more on your back."

Justine says, "What the fuck are you talking about? We can't afford another partner."

"Partner? Who said anything about a partner? From now on, she reports directly to me, which would make her your boss as well as yours, Augustus."

Augustus is not happy, and he shouts, "Bullshit. No way am I working for this bitch."

"Well, you can work for her or go back to Reno. The same goes for you, Justine. So, what's it going to be?"

Augustus asks, "What about your contacts in the Middle East? What're you going to tell them?"

"Leave that to me, Augustus. I'll figure it out. Ayad had enemies, maybe one of them got to him. So Isabella, what's it going to be?"

She pauses and says, "Have your men wait outside, and I'll lower my weapon." Rinaldo motions to them and they leave the room. "Augustus, do we have a deal? Justine, what about you?"

There's silence and then Augustus asks, "Why her? I've been with you longer, and she just killed one of your contacts."

"I'll tell you why, because you fuck up a lot, like the latest adventure in Reno where Justine had to pay off a bunch of officials to keep them away from us. And to be honest, what she did here tonight proves that she's got bigger balls than you. So, are we on board?" They glance at each other and reluctantly nod yes, and Rinaldo says, "Great, now we have a more pressing problem. Getting rid of this body. Isabella, I've been admiring that large trunk. It seems you've packed a lot of clothes for just two nights in Vegas."

Isabella says, "Nobody spends just two nights in Vegas. I was planning on an extended vacation. Why not make as much money as I can while I'm in Sin City."

Rinaldo lets out a laugh, "Splendid, well said. So here's what we're going to do. I'll call my men back inside, they'll put the body in the trunk and take him to the desert, and just like that, he's gone. Augustus, unpack her clothes and hang them up."

"What? No fucking way I'm doing that."

"It's ok, I can unpack my own clothes."

"No Isabella, I insist that you start thinking like a person in charge, so Augustus, please unpack her trunk. Justine, help him. I'll have a new trunk here within the hour to repack everything. I have a suite at the Luxor. You can stay there."

"The Luxor, I don't like that place. Why the Luxor?"

Rinaldo glares at Isabella. "It's the Luxor or the desert. You choose. Tomorrow you and I will discuss the terms of your employment. See you around noon, yes? Augustus, get that bloodstain out of the rug unless you want to explain how it got there. Make sure you clean the room. Everything must be out. Justine, help him. Until then, I bid you all good night."

CHAPTER 23
PENTHOUSE #1

Rodriguez walks into the lobby of the Cosmopolitan and is greeted by some of the staff. He goes to the concierge desk, and Nicky the manager welcomes him. "Rodriguez, how've you been? Are you back in town for good?"

"No, I'm just helping McMahon. Listen, Nicky, I need you to do me a favor. I want to know who's in the Penthouses."

Nicky looks around and motions for them to move to the end of the counter. He goes to the computer and brings up the Penthouse guest list. "What do you want to know?"

"Who checked in a few days ago, say two or three?"

Nicky checks the guestlist. "I got a couple from New York on their honeymoon in #2 and a Mr. and Mrs. Ayad in #1."

"The others are empty."

Rodriguez asks, "Have you seen any of the new guests?"

"Yes I see the honeymoon couple go out at night and come back early the next day."

"What about Mr. and Mrs. Ayad, have you seen them?"

"Briefly."

"Can you describe them, Nicky?"

"Yeah, she's European looking with long dark hair. She was wearing sunglasses and a hat, but I could see her hair. Let's just say she was hot. About five-foot seven, great body."

"I get it, what about him?"

"Him, I couldn't figure out why they were together. He was short, almost bald, on the heavy side. Don't know what she saw in him. They checked out this morning."

"Did they say anything when they left?"

"No, I didn't even see them. Their assistant did all the paperwork. They left before my shift. I was told it was a woman."

Rodriguez pauses for a minute. "Has the room been cleaned yet?"

"Not yet. It's been rented for the weekend starting tomorrow night. I haven't even changed the key code yet."

"I need to get into that room. Nicky, can I have the key?" Nicky reaches under the counter and slides the key across to him. "Thanks, I'll keep it between us."

"One more thing Nicky, I saw this guy last night walking through the casino. He had two big guys with him." He was creepy looking tall and pale like he doesn't get much sun." I followed them to the elevators and they went to the Penthouse any ideas on who it might be."

"Tall, creepy and pale sounds like Rinaldo, Achille Rinaldo he's in the fashion business from Italy he used to stay here when he was in town but he hasn't stayed here for a while." "Really strange dude."

"Thanks Nicky."

Rodriguez enters the suite. The first thing he notices is the half bottle of champagne and the untouched food from the night before. He puts on a pair of gloves and checks the room. He opens the closets and checks the shelves, and everything seems normal. He looks out over the large suite, and he notices a section of the rug that's slightly darker than the surrounding area. For a moment, he thinks it could be a shadow being cast from the outside. He moves his hand in front of the open blinds to make sure. The area doesn't change shape or color and it's definitely darker. He feels the spot, and it feels damp. He notices the bed hasn't been slept in, but it seems someone was lying on the top sheet and there's two towels on the floor. He opens the dresser drawers and they're empty. He moves to the other side of the room and sees a shopping bag labeled Christian Louboutin stuffed into a garbage can. He examines the bag and notices reddish brown droplets on one side of the bag. He's been to enough crime scenes to know that's blood on the bag and the dark stain is the result of someone attempting to get blood out of the rug. If the maid had gotten there before he did, the suite would have been scrubbed clean. He makes his way through the suite and into the bathroom. He notices a clump of hair caught in the shower drain. It's dark and long. He looks under the bed and he sees an object that looks like the heel of a shoe. He reaches under and removes it. It's a black patent leather section of a heel about two inches long. On the heel are reddish brown smudges and what appears to be skin or human tissue on the end. The opposite end of the heel looks like it broke off from a larger piece.

He calls McMahon and she answers, "Where are you?"

"I'm at the Cosmopolitan in Penthouse one."

"What's going on there, Rodriguez?"

"I've got a shopping bag with blood droplets on it and part of the heel of a shoe with blood and what looks like skin or tissue on it. Something happened here last night and whatever it was, somebody tried to wash a bloodstain out of the rug."

"How did you get into that suite, and why are you there?"

"Call it a hunch McMahon."

"A hunch. Well congratulations, Rodriguez. None of that can be used as evidence since you didn't have a search warrant."

"Do me a favor, McMahon and run a check on a guy named Achille Rinaldo, an Italian businessman and get back to me."

"Why."

"'Cause I got a bad feeling about this guy. Let me know what you find out."

"What is it, Rodriguez? Another hunch?"

"Yeah, something like that." He continues to search the room when he hears the door open, and housekeeping enters the room. He quickly removes his gloves.

"I'm sorry sir they told me you had checked out."

"Well my boss did. I'm just making sure he left nothing behind. Would you mind coming back in an hour or so? Oh, and would you happen to have a few small plastic bags that I can have?" Thank you. Another hour, and I'll be gone."

He closes the door behind her and goes to the bathroom. He takes the hair from the drain and puts it in one of the bags. McMahon calls him back with news of Rinaldo. "Ok Rodriguez, here goes. Achille Rinaldo is an Italian national, born in Sicily in 1975. According to the Italian authorities, he was a member of the Santino crime family in Sicily. He left Sicily about two years ago and wasn't heard from since."

"What about warrants? Is there anything outstanding in this country or Italy?"

"No Rodriguez, nothing. I think his record was sealed by the authorities in Italy."

"If he was part of the Santino family there must be court records or arrest records."

"Nothing in the Italian courts. Zero."

"Shit."

"Yeah exactly, Rodriguez. You need to leave the suite. We can't prove he was even there."

"Sure McMahon, I'll shut it down." Rodriguez puts the heel in one of the bags. He then takes a knife and cuts some of the carpet fibers and puts them in a different bag. As he leaves the hotel, he signals Nicky, and he nods back.

Someone working the front with Nicky leaves the desk and makes a call. "The cop just left."

CHAPTER 24
THE CHAIR

Rodriguez walks into McMahon's Office and puts the items he found on her desk. "What are these?" she asks.

"I took these from the penthouse."

"I thought we agreed to leave it alone, Rodriguez."

"No, I agreed to leave the suite."

McMahon leans back in her seat and sighs. "Ok talk to me. What did you find?"

Rodriguez reaches into his pocket and pulls out the section of bag with the blood splatters on it. He hands it to McMahon and points to spots on the bag "That's blood, isn't it? There and there."

"It sure as hell looks like it, but at the risk of repeating myself, we didn't have a warrant."

"I know, but I have a few friends in the ME's office. I'm going to pay them a visit and have this stuff checked."

"Off the record, Rodriguez?"

"Yeah, exactly. By the way McMahon, the name on the bag is Christian Louboutin. I looked them up. You want to know what they're famous for?"

McMahon picks up the bag with the broken heel and looking at it says, "Stiletto heels. Looks like somebody was on the receiving end of this pair." McMahon pauses, "Go ahead, Rodriguez, use your contacts in the ME's office. If you get pushback, have them call me. I got friends over there too."

"I will, but first things first, I'm going to see if this Achille Rinaldo is still in Vegas. Can you hang on to these for me?"

He walks the strip canvassing the hotels he has no luck with the first ones he tries. As he's walking into the Bellagio, two men walk alongside of him and one puts a gun to his side. "Make a left into the garage. There's a car waiting for us." Rodriguez sizes up the situation and realizes there's too many people in the lobby to make a move. They get to the garage, and he's forced into the back seat as he's getting in he's struck in the back of the head, and everything goes black. He wakes up in a room built in a section of the underground tunnels. He's handcuffed to a wooden chair that's been bolted to the floor. The chair is old, and the wood is beginning to splinter. There's stains on the arms of the chair that appear to be blood. The room is cold and damp and smelling of mold. As things come into focus, he sees three men wearing hoods.

One of the men, who appears to be the leader, says, "Welcome back, Rodriguez. Do you know where you are?"

Rodriguez looks at the men. "KKK rally."

The men chuckle, but not the leader. He says, "Very funny. Laugh now, but soon there'll be tears."

"Why, are you gonna take the hood off?"

The men laugh again, and the leader turns and angrily shouts, "Stop laughing you fucking idiots. I understand you were curious about the tunnels and now you'll get a closer look." He turns to his men and says, "Go get the damn thing." One of the men wheels out a large power washer and places it near Rodriguez. The leader asks, "Do you know what this is, cop?"

"Yeah, it's a power washer. Is that the one you used on Andy?"

"Oh yes, too bad about Andy. So, let me tell you about this particular machine. It has five adjustable nozzles that control the water pressure. The pressure of the water is three thousand pounds per square inch. At the highest-pressure setting…"

Rodriguez cuts him off, "I know how it works asshole."

"Good, did you see Andy's body? And that was half way. Imagine what would happen if I aimed this at your eyes. So, I'm going to start at the lowest level and ask you some questions, and you better answer, or I'll gradually increase the power. Your friend Andy made it to three out of five, but I get the feeling you'll get past that."

One of the men rips his shirt open and Rodriguez says, "You owe me a shirt asshole." The man walks back and punches him in the face. Rodriguez spits out the blood and says, "I'm gonna kill the three of you."

The leader laughs and says, "I really don't see how. So, let's begin." Rodriguez looks around the room and notices electrical wires hanging haphazardly and running down to a circuit breaker box. The water line to the power washer is hooked up to a slop sink in one corner of the room. The leader brings the power washer even closer and turns it on. The machine makes a loud whirring sound that echoes through the empty room, and the man says, "So Rodriguez, let's see what low feels like," and he aims a stream of water at his chest.

The water is cold, and it causes Rodriguez to flinch, and he shouts, "Fuck you."

"So, here comes question number one. Why are you looking for Amy?"

Rodriguez replies, "Amy who?"

"Wrong answer, Rodriguez," and the man sprays him again. "Now, I'll change the nozzle and we turn it up a notch. Tell me about Amy. Why are you looking for her?"

"I told you I don't know anybody named Amy." The pressure is increased, and he's sprayed again. "Fuck, that's cold. I think I'll kill you first."

"You're going to kill me first. How does this feel?" This time the man keeps it there longer. Rodriguez doesn't want to give them the satisfaction of screaming, but he's beginning to feel the pain. The leader speaks again. "You see, first it's very cold and when it stops, it feels hot and as I turn up the pressure, the skin begins to break down. Just ask Andy. So tell me why are you in Vegas?"

"I thought I'd gamble a little and maybe get laid."

"Wrong answer." The leader sprays him again. He grits his teeth not wanting to show weakness. The hooded leader says, "In a little while, if I don't get answers, I'll pour drain cleaner into the reservoir, and then the fun starts." The door opens and Rodriguez hears the sound of high heels hitting the concrete floor. A woman walks in and stands in the background watching. Rodriguez tries to see her face, but she's standing in the shadows. The leader asks again, "Amy, tell me about her. Why are you looking for her and why are you in Vegas?"

"I told you I don't know shit about Amy."

"Let's turn it up a notch. What do you say?"

He changes the head on the machine and sprays him again and he keeps spraying until Rodriguez shouts, "Ok, ok I'll tell you about Amy."

"Good, I knew you'd come around. So tell me."

"See, it's like this. It started in high school behind the gym. I was about fifteen, and she was sixteen, and you know boy meets girl."

The leader shouts, "Tell me what I want to know," and he sprays again and continues spraying. Rodriguez is feeling the pain, and welts are beginning to form where the spray is hitting the skin. "Let me ask you again with more pressure this time. Amy, why is she so important to the police? Why do you want to speak to her?"

"Fuck you." The leader sprays him again and Rodriguez struggles against the cuffs as he moves closer to him. He feigns unconsciousness, but the man continues to spray him.

The hooded man shouts, "Wake up, Rodriguez. Wake up, I'm not done." He continues to spray and finally gives up. "Let's get the fuck out of here. I'm freezing. We'll come back in the morning." They leave, locking the door behind them.

Rodriguez is in pain, and his chest is covered in welts and it's burning from the spray. The room is cold and he begins to shiver. He tries to move the chair, but it's firmly bolted to the ground, and his wrists are swollen from the cuffs. He looks at the floor, and he sees rats scurrying around. There's fluorescent lights hanging around the room, but only one bank is lit, the others having burned out a long time ago. He attempts to loosen one of the arms of the chair, and it feels like it might come apart. Suddenly, he hears a noise behind him and to his left. It's the sound of someone moving around. He hears footsteps getting closer, but he's unable to turn around completely. Suddenly from the left side, he hears a voice. "Hey, are you alright?"

"Rodriguez answers, "Come to the front so I can see you." A boy of about fifteen or sixteen walks around the chair, and Rodriguez asks, "What are you doing down here?"

"We live down here, me and my pop."

"You live down here."

"Yeah, for a while. You see, my father lost his job, and my mother was an alcoholic, and she died a few years ago. We moved down here when we got kicked out of our house. We fixed it up ok." It ain't that bad, and it's higher than the other tunnels, so it don't flood. I heard some screaming, so I came to see what was going on. Sometimes, I hear shit like screaming and people arguing down here, but my dad says we should mind our own business. I think he's kind of pissed off about what happened to us."

"That's too bad, kid, but right now I gotta get these cuffs off before they come back. Do you think your father has something to cut me out of these cuffs?" Suddenly, a voice comes from behind, "What are you doing in here, boy? I told you never to come in here." The man sees Rodriguez and asks, "What the hell is going on here? Who are you?"

"My name is Rodriguez. I'm a cop. Some guys with hoods want to kill me."

"Kill you, why?"

"It's about a case I'm working on."

"Did you say your name's Rodriguez? Why does that sound familiar?" The boys' father thinks for a while and says, "Wait, you're the guy from the newspaper."

"Newspaper?"

"The same Rodriguez that went off Sky Jump about a year ago, right?"

"Yeah, the same."

"Well goddam, Rodriguez. I'm Charlie, and this is my son Mark. All of Vegas was talking about that for months." The man leans in and says, "I heard it started some international shit." Rodriguez just nods. "Let's get you out of those cuffs. Mark, go get my bolt cutters." Mark runs back through the hole and returns moments later with a pair of bolt cutters. After a brief struggle with the cuffs, the cutters work and he's free of the chair.

Rodriguez asks, "You wouldn't happen to have a gun."

"Down here you need at least one. I got four. I'll bring them. Mark, you stay here." The man returns with the firepower. "Here they are. I like the 9mm. What about you?"

"I'll take the 9 if that's ok."

"Sure, whatever you want. I got an extra clip for that one. I'll get it."

The man returns and Rodriguez says, "No matter what you hear, do not come back into this room. Promise me, especially you, Mark."

"What if those guys want to finish the job? You're gonna need help."

"Promise me, Mark, do not come back in."

"Ok, I won't."

"Can I get to the street through that hole?"

"Sure, just make a left and keep going till you see daylight.

"Thanks for the help and the gun. Get going, I'll put the board back."

CHAPTER 25
CHAMPAGNE AND OTHER DELIGHTS

Classical music is playing in the background as Achille Rinaldo and Isabella are sipping champagne in his suite at the Luxor. "So, did the cop say anything, Isabella?"

"No, not while I was there. The cop passed out, and we left."

"Fucking Augustus. He's useless. Tomorrow we'll question him again, and then I'll kill him myself in the most painful way. It should send quite a message. Care to join me?"

"Of course."

"You know Isabella, since that first night I saw you in the suite, I wondered why a woman of your beauty and wits would turn to prostitution. You could have been anything you wanted."

"I had no choice. It's in the genes."

"The genes?"

"Yes, my mother was a prostitute in Naples, forced into it by the Camorra crime family, and the same with my aunt. They killed my mother when she rebelled and sent some men to kidnap me, but I stabbed one to death and I was able to escape. I ran to the United

States and swore that if I were going to make my living on my back, I would set the price and pick the customer."

Rinaldo begins to laugh. "Wonderful, you and I are going to make a lot of money, and you don't have to be on your back." He lowers his voice and asks, "I've been noticing your beautifully manicured hands. I love a woman's hands. I want you to rake those nails across my back. How much will that cost me, Isabella?"

"I'm not sure I could do that. Wouldn't that hurt you?"

"No, Isabella. That's not the right answer. Start thinking like a business woman. You need to charge no matter the customer. So, tell me your price, one thousand, two, three."

"One thousand. It'll cost you one thousand."

"See how easy that was? All you have to do is ask." Rinaldo removes his shirt and lies face down on the bed. Isabella is appalled by his pale skin." She straddles him and begins. He says, "Harder, Isabella. I want to feel pain." She exerts more pressure. "That's better, but increase the pressure even more. I want to feel those nails raking across my back."

Isabella takes a drink. "If I do it harder, I'll break the skin."

"Yes, yes Isabella. Harder. Press down."

Isabella can't continue. "I'm sorry I can't keep going. It's just not my thing."

"It'll get easier as we go along. You see, part of me not killing you was that now you must cater to my every whim." Isabella gets off the bed, "what do you mean?"

"It means that occasionally, I'll call upon you to satisfy an urge I may have."

"So, I'm a prostitute again. Is that what you're saying?"

"No, you're a madam, and I expect you to act accordingly. I want you to recruit for our business since Becker and Justine aren't stepping up. Vegas is a good place to start, but unfortunately we can't stay much longer. The authorities will eventually figure it all out, but by that time, we'll be long gone. I feel over time, we'll be rid of Augustus and Justine, and you'll be wealthy beyond your dreams. The only person you'll be, shall we say servicing, is me." Rinaldo picks up a glass of champagne and says, "Saluti." Isabella reluctantly picks up her glass.

Rodriguez is fighting sleep and he struggles to formulate a plan. He sees the hanging wires and checks the circuit breakers. This room may have been an engineering room at one time when the tunnels were dug. He notices the lines are two hundred and twenty volts, which is enough electricity to kill. Daybreak hits and the hooded men return to the tunnels. Rodriguez is sitting in the chair with the gun in hand. Earlier he turned the power washer on, and it's spraying gallons of water on the floor. He hears the clicks of the door locks, and the men enter. The leader, seeing the water on the floor, says, "Did you assholes leave this thing running all night?"

Rodriguez is now standing on the chair with the gun trained on the men. He says, "No, I did. Stay where you are. You're all under arrest." The leader, realizing what's happening, pushes his way to the door and escapes. One of the men attempts to reach for his gun, but it's too late. Rodriguez fires the bullets severing the connection, and the live wires drop into the water. They scream and their bodies jerk and spasm as the electricity passes through them. Their bodies begin to smoke as they twitch and continue screaming. Rodriguez, showing mercy, shoots them both. The smell of burnt flesh, and the sight of their bodies is nauseating, and he vomits. He turns off the power, and he goes out through the hole and pulls the board back in place. He makes it to the street, and he flags down a patrol car. He identifies himself. "I'm Sergeant Rodriguez. I'm working with Captain Steiner. Can you call him?"

The driver says, "I'll call him."

The officer in the passenger seat turns and looks at him. "What the hell happened to you?"

"I got power washed. Don't ask."

The driver says, "It's the Captain. He wants to talk to you."

"Hi Captain."

"Rodriguez where the fuck you been?"

"I've been busy. There's two bodies in the tunnels not far from the Metropolitan in a small room. You might want to send the coroner and a team down there.

"What're you talking about? McMahon's been trying to reach you."

"A couple of goons grabbed me. They were looking for information on Amy."

"Amy, why is everybody so interested in this Amy woman."

"I get the feeling this ain't about Diamond Jack anymore. I'm coming in. I'll explain when I get there. Is McMahon around?"

"She stepped out. She'll be here when you get here."

"Remember Captain, in the tunnels, there's two bodies there."

"I'll send some men down."

The captain hangs up and Rodriguez asks the officers, "Anybody got a shirt I could borrow?"

The officers look at each other and one says, "Yeah, in the trunk, but it probably won't fit you."

"It's ok I'll live with it."

"So Rodriguez, what's this about bodies in the tunnels?"

"Yeah they tried to power wash me, so I fried them. Thanks for the shirt."

As he gets out of the car the driver looks at him and says, "Hey Rodriguez, ain't you the Sky Jump guy?"

"Yeah that's me."

"Goddam, the Sky Jump guy in my car. Wait till I tell the wife. By the way, you can keep the shirt."

Rodriguez walks into Steiner's office. When McMahon sees him, she exclaims, "What the hell are you wearing? Is that shirt from high school?"

"Very funny, it was the best I could do under the circumstances."

"So tell me, what happened?"

Captain Steiner returns with a shirt. "Here, put this on. It belongs to Officer Connelly. He looks about your size. So, talk to me. What happened?"

"Well, I was canvassing some of the hotels on the strip when a couple of guys stuck a gun in my ribs and forced me into a car."

"Did you get a look at these guys?"

"Not really. By the time I got into the car, they slugged me, and I was out. I woke up cuffed to a chair, and they hit me with a power washer. I couldn't see their faces. They were wearing hoods.

McMahon says, "Hoods, those motherfuckers. You said they used a power washer. That explains what happened to Andy."

"At one point, a woman came in and stood in the back of the room."

"Was the bitch wearing a hood too?"

"No, but she made sure to stay in the shadows."

At that moment, Captain Steiner gets a call. "They found the bodies in that room. My officers say it's bad. What the fuck happened to those guys?"

"Electricity, two hundred and twenty volts, but the guy giving the orders got away. This isn't about Diamond Jack. There's more going on here. Somebody doesn't want us to talk to Amy. I think we should put an officer outside her room."

McMahon and Steiner look at each other. Rodriguez begins to change his shirt and McMahon sees the welts on his chest and neck. "What do you think is going on?"

"I think it's human trafficking."

McMahon is staring at the injuries, and she exclaims, "Jesus Christ. You're a mess. Go and get some rest, Rodriguez. I'll canvas the rest of the hotels."

"Thanks McMahon, but I've got to find this guy Rinaldo. There's a few more to check. I'm going to stick with it. I'm going to take a shower and change my clothes, and then I'm going out again."

"Ok, if you insist I'm going with you. Let's go."

CHAPTER 26
AUGUSTUS'S WALK OF SHAME

Rinaldo is pacing back and forth. He pours himself a drink and shouts, "He killed two of your men and got away. How could you let that happen, you incompetent idiot."

Augustus hangs his head. "Maybe somebody helped him."

Rinaldo yells, "He was handcuffed to a chair in a goddam tunnel."

"We can grab him again and…"

Rinaldo throws his glass across the room. He puts his finger in Augustus's face and says, "Quiet Becker, no we can't just grab him again. This time he'll be ready for us. We have to back off for a while. I should put you in that chair, Augustus, and where the fuck is Justine? I'll bet she's at some strip club. Get her on the phone."

Justine is shopping when Augustus contacts her. "So, what's going on with Rodriguez? You didn't hurt him too much, did you?"

"Rinaldo wants you at the Luxor now. Rodriguez got away and killed two of my men."

There's silence and then Justine begins," Only two. What did I tell you? Too bad about your men, but I warned you about him, didn't I? But you wouldn't listen. I'm on the way."

"So, where was our socialite, Ms. Godfrey? Was she at a strip club, shopping, fucking?"

"I don't know, Mr. Rinaldo, but she'll be here soon."

"Good, I'm behind on my other business matters, and I can't stay in Vegas forever to make sure that you two do your jobs. My patience is wearing thin." There's a knock on the door and Justine enters the room carrying shopping bags from her spree. "Justine, how nice of you to stop by. I see you've been shopping while this cop is making us look like fools. I don't like looking like a fool, Justine. Have a seat next to Augustus." Rinaldo pulls up a chair and moves closer to them and he says," Do you remember the story about Malta I told you when you picked me up at the airport?"

Augustus glances at Justine. "You mean about the bones?"

"Yes, Augustus. The Mediterranean bones." Rinaldo's eyes are darting between the two of them. Finally he says, "I feel we're going about this all wrong. I have to think about how to proceed from now on. You two don't make a move without talking to me first. Augustus, did you know that Rodriguez was in the Penthouse suite the morning after Mr. Ayad met his demise at the hands of Isabella?" Augustus is quiet and he looks at Justine. "You two work for me. So, why do I have to find out from a bellman at the front desk? I hope for both of your sakes that you cleaned the room thoroughly. Now get out. All of you."

Rodriguez and McMahon arrive at the Luxor Hotel and McMahon asks, "I wonder who's on duty tonight. I guess we'll find out soon."

Rodriguez replies, "Good news, it's Stella."

Stella is the night manager who was in an abusive relationship, and it was Agent McMahon who helped her get out of it when the local authorities did nothing. She lights up when she sees them. "Hi Agent McMahon. We miss you in Vegas. It's nice to see you."

"Thanks, I hope you're doing well. Do you remember Agent Rodriguez, now Sergeant Rodriguez?"

"Hi Sergeant, we haven't seen you in a while. Where have you been?"

"I've been working on the east coast."

"You're working in New York. I always wanted to visit."

"Not New York, but in Long Island, a town called Oceanview. It's beautiful, you'd love it."

"Are you coming back to Vegas?"

"No, I'm just helping out on a case."

"I see so how can I help you?"

Rodriguez gets closer. "We're looking for a guy named Achille Rinaldo. Do you know if he's staying here?"

"Let me check." She checks her computer. "There's someone by that name staying in Penthouse 4."

"What does he look like, Stella?"

Stella thinks for a minute, "Well, he's scary."

"Scary? What's scary about him?" McMahon asks.

Stella gets closer and answers, "He's tall, pale with dark hair and dark eyes, and he always has 2 big guys with him. He's just creepy."

Rodriguez looks at McMahon, "That's him. That's the guy I saw."

Stella says, "He showed an Italian passport when he checked in. He was supposed to leave a few days ago, but he extended his stay till next week."

McMahon asks, "Have you seen him recently?"

"Yes, once or twice at night. I don't think he likes the sun."

"Thank you, Stella."

"You're welcome. It was nice seeing you again Agent, and you Sergeant Rodriguez." She smiles at Rodriguez and says, "Bye Sergeant, maybe we'll see you again soon."

Rodriguez responds, "Bye Stella."

. . .

They're walking to their car and McMahon asks, "So, what's on your mind when it comes to this guy?"

Rodriguez says, "Like you said, everything I found in the Cosmopolitan penthouse is inadmissible, and we can't even prove he was there, but he was. Trust me."

"If he's here on business, why does he mostly go out at night?"

"Come on McMahon, let me buy you dinner."

"Ok Rodriguez, as long as it's not a buffet." Halfway through dinner McMahon asks, "So, you never told me how you escaped from the tunnels. How the hell did you get out?"

He begins, "A father and son who live down there helped me. I was tied to a wooden chair in a room that was probably used as some kind of an engineering office when the tunnels were being built. The son found me first. There's wires hanging all over the place, a slop sink and the chair bolted to the floor. The leader used an industrial strength power washer on me, the same one they used on Andy. After a while, a woman entered the room, and she stayed in the shadows, but I could see her outline. I faked passing out, and they locked me in the room. The father and son freed me, and the father gave me a gun, and I was able to escape."

McMahon says," Those tunnels have always been a thorn in the side of law enforcement, but they're under Federal jurisdiction. We can't do shit about them." McMahon asks, "You said they were electrocuted?"

"Yeah, I flooded the floor and when they came back in the morning, I shot the hanging wires, and they fell into the water. The voltage is 220. Nobody could survive that." There's silence and Rodriguez says, "You know McMahon, I've worked for you for a while, and I don't know too much about you."

"Yeah right, this from a guy that doesn't want anybody to know his first name is Humphrey." They both laugh and McMahon leans back in her chair. "Ok, I'll give you the summary of my life. I became a cop in the late 90's. I was married for 6 years from 2006 to 2012, and we were going to have a baby, a boy. I had a problem with the pregnancy, and we lost the baby. My husband couldn't handle it, and he blamed the job, you know, long hours, stress, whatever, but I think in his mind he blamed me. He started drinking heavily, and he drank himself to death. I tried everything to save him, but he began to get abusive. There were days when I wanted to blow his fucking head off. Therapy, interventions, doctors, nothing worked, and he died from a combination of drugs and alcohol in 2012. So, there's my story. If our son would have lived, he would have been 11 years old. The last thing I want from anybody is sympathy, you hear me, Rodriguez?"

"Sure."

"That's it. So, let's talk about this guy Rinaldo. What are we going to do? I trust your instincts, and we both know that something happened in that room."

"I think somebody died."

"The penthouse was registered to a guy named Mansour Ayad, and I'll bet he doesn't wear stiletto heels."

"You said the people that tortured you and probably killed Andy were wearing hoods, and you said one of them was calling the shots. Could it be this guy Rinaldo?"

"No, McMahon. It wasn't him. I'd like to pay this guy Rinaldo a visit to see what he knows."

"Not a good idea, not yet."

CHAPTER 27
OLD STILETTOS

The waters surrounding Sicily are a bright blue with shades of emerald green where the water is close to the shore. Lorenzo Carazzo and Richie DiNapoli sit on the veranda of Carazzo's villa in Catania overlooking this vista with Mt. Aetna in the distance. Richie DiNapoli fled to the villa of his boss Carazzo after the drug deal with the Delacruz family fell apart. The Carazzo crime family controls most of the organized crime on the east side of the island. In the early days before the massive crackdowns on the Sicilian Mafia, his family, under the leadership of his father Gianni Carazzo, carved out a big piece of Sicily for themselves in the early 1930's. If this crime family were a corporation, Richie would be the C.E.O., and Lorenzo Carazzo, not only the Chairman of the Board, but the entire board.

Lorenzo looks in the direction of Mount Aetna. "Look how beautiful the mountain looks today. It's hard to imagine how much damage it can do if it blows it's fucking top, right Richie?"

"Yeah, but I don't think about it much." Richie looks around suspiciously. "Where's your wife and the rest of the family?"

"You noticed it's quiet. I gave them a couple thousand euros each and sent them shopping. No yakkity yak and nobody making noise in the pool."

Lorenzo is looking out over his vineyard. "Richie, I'm going to ask you something and don't get pissed off, ok? Hold your temper. You and I are going to take a ride."

"Where Lorenzo?"

"Go change your clothes. There's a car picking us up in one hour." "Where are we going, Lorenzo? Level with me, Mr. Carazzo. What's going on?"

"Ok, but don't lose your fucking mind. Promise me, Richie."

"Ok, I promise. Go ahead."

"We're going to have a sit down with Vincenzo Santino."

Richie looks at Carazzo in disbelief. "Santino? That cocksucker. No fucking way. If I get close to that wop prick, I'll beat him to death with my bare hands. Don't ask me to do this, with all respect."

"Did you call him a wop? Easy Ricardo, there's that fucking temper again. Can I explain? Let me fucking explain. Ok, shut up a minute, Richie. Now the boss is talking." Richie calms down and Lorenzo says, "Ok, you ready to listen?"

"Yeah, I apologize Mr. Carazzo."

"Achille Rinaldo, does that name ring a bell?"

"Yeah, there's another sack of shit I'd love to strangle, but how does he fit in with Santino?"

'While you were in the states, it seems Rinaldo made a move on Santino's daughter."

"A move? What does that mean?"

"Go change, Richie. The car will be here soon. Please don't push back. Trust me on this, we're going to bring Vittorio and Giovanni, two of my best men, just in case. Now, go change."

The car arrives at the villa of Vincenzo Santino, and the men exit the car. Santino comes down the stairs of his villa accompanied by two bodyguards. Carazzo extends his hand and Santino kisses the ring given by the organization to the heads of the families. Vincenzo Santino is the underboss to the Giuseppe Scotto family. The Carazzo and the Scotto family have had an unsteady truce for a number of years. Santino is a sadistic and unforgiving underboss who has eyes on his boss Giuseppe Scotto's throne. Santino started as an enforcer in the Scotto family. His cruelty and sadistic approach to the job was legendary in Sicily. Santino extends his hand to Richie, and he's ignored. Santino looks at Carazzo.

"Richie, we're guests, show respect."

Richie reluctantly shakes his hand. Santino says smugly, "So, Richie, I heard you couldn't cross the finish line on that Long Island deal."

Richie looks at Carazzo and back at Santino, and he says, "Say another fucking word and…"

Carazzo shouts, "-Knock it off. We came here to talk business. Let's talk business, or we're leaving."

Santino says, "Ok, ok, let's go inside. My chef prepared a feast for us, and we can break through the ice. What'd you say, Richie?"

"Yeah, sure." The men go inside, followed by their crew. They sit at a long table flanked by their bodyguards and advisors.

"So, Mr. Santino, tell Richie why you called this meeting."

The room is silent and then Santino speaks, "It's about this fucking mook Rinaldo. This guy thinks he's smarter than everybody in the room. He was part of my crew, but he hurt one of my children."

Richie looks at Carazzo and back at Santino. "What did he do?"

Santino ignores the question. "Let's not kid ourselves. We know what we do, how we pay for our lifestyle. The villas, the cars, jets, all of it. We're no fucking angels, but one thing I'll never do is traffic humans, and there's a ton of dough to be made. I got two daughters, and I just won't do it, and I forbid anybody in my crew to get involved in that shit. Unfortunately, Rinaldo didn't see it my way, and he started his own little trafficking ring under my fucking nose."

Richie sits up in his chair. "Maybe you should learn how to control your family."

Carazzo shouts, "Come on, Riccardo. Abbastanza (enough)."

Santino says, "I heard recently that he's in Vegas. I don't know why he's there, but he's got millions, and he can move around anywhere he wants. He's got plenty of protection and an international network that can hide him out. If I don't get him while he's in Vegas, he'll disappear."

Richie says, "So, what's that got to do with me?"

"I want you to go to Vegas and kill him for me."

Richie looks at Carazzo and back at Santino. "Why me? Can't you do it, or send a couple of these goons you got hanging around, why me?"

"Because, I can't leave Sicily. If I do, I'll get arrested, and this time they won't be so understanding, and if I go to prison, there's men in there that would love to see me dead."

Richie looks at Santino and says, "I wonder why."

Santino looks at Carazzo. "I'll pay you one hundred thousand dollars, DiNapoli, if you do this for me, and maybe our families can find some peace."

Richie is angry and he says, "In the first place, I don't do wet work anymore, and a hundred thousand dollars is insulting."

Carazzo interjects, "Come on Richie, he's not insulting you. Hear him out."

Richie is quiet, then he says, "I'll let you know what I want if I decide to do it, but a hundred grand is fucking insulting."

Santino says, "Mr. Carazzo, he's out of line."

"I'm out of line? You offer a hundred grand, and I'm out of line? I'm leaving." Richie is on his feet and ready to leave.

Carazzo glares at him, "Sit down." Richie looks back at Carazzo who says, "It's the boss talking, now sit." Richie sits and Carazzo speaks. "Alright, let's everybody calm down."

Richie says, "It's risky for me to go to Vegas. There's a cop, her name is McMahon, and she's looking for me. The last I heard she was transferred to Los Angeles, but if she goes to Vegas and spots me I'm fucked. Why do you want this guy so bad?"

Santino's eyes dart between the men. "Before he left Sicily as a parting shot to me, he tried to recruit one of my daughters who was sixteen at the time. That's why. He hurt her and made sure I found out about it. I want this fucking animal dead. I can't send my men 'cause they're like bulls in a China shop. In half an hour, every cop in Vegas will know they're there. It has to be you, Richie. You're smart."

Carazzo says, "Give us a few days to figure it out, Vincenzo." "Richie says, "you're asking me to risk going to prison for some fucking mook that didn't do shit to me." 'I get it's your daughter and if I were in your shoes I'd want the guy dead too but you're asking a lot." "A hundred grand ain't going to cut it let's go." Carazzo turns to Santino, "we'll let you know in a few days."

CHAPTER 28
THE CASTLE IN TUSCANY

The sun is setting on Sicily, and the Carazzo family of seven is having dinner. Lorenzo Carazzo is at the head of the table with Richie DiNapoli seated to his right. He's staring at the sunset, and he says, "I've traveled the world, Richie, but the best sunsets I've ever seen are right here in our beloved Sicilia."

Richie turns his head towards the sunset and turns back. "Yeah, sure, it's nice." He reaches into his pocket and puts a photo of a Tuscan castle in front of Carazzo. "You see that Mr. Carazzo? Tell Santino that's what I want, and I'll do the job 'cause he ain't got the balls."

Carazzo cuts him off, "Richie, not in front of my family. We don't talk that way at the table."

"My apologies, Mr. Carazzo. I meant no disrespect."

"So, tell me Richie, what's this? It looks like some kinda castle."

"That's right. It's a castle in Tuscany, and it's going to be for sale in two months. That's what I want, and I'll hand him Rinaldo's fucking head."

Carazzo is agitated. "Richie, come on. We're going to eat soon. Please, the language."

"Tell Santino that's what I want."

"A castle. You want a castle in Tuscany," and he begins to laugh. "Listen Richie, a hundred grand is a lot of money. Santino's being generous." He lowers his voice. "Who's going to give you that kind of money to put some fucking mook to sleep? nobody, that's who."

"I'm worth more than that, Mr. Carazzo. With all due respect, I'm not some fucking punk off the street looking to make his bones."

Carazzo's wife says, "Lorenzo, I thought we don't discuss business at the table in front of the children."

"Did you say children? Theresa, they're not children anymore. Go check the pasta. I think it's been cooking too long." She walks towards the kitchen muttering under her breath, followed by two of their daughters.

Carazzo leans in to Richie, "How much?"

"It's going for half a million, plus another hundred and fifty thousand for some renovations."

Carazzo says, "Are you out of your fuck….." He catches himself and looks around the table. "Richie, he's never going to go for it."

"That's up to him, but if there's no castle, he can go kill the cocksucker himself, sorry about the language."

Carazzo's sons at the table look at each other and snicker. Teresa, helped by the daughters, brings out the food. "My wonderful Teresa was up all-night making sauce, the best in Sicily. Look at this food Richie, where are you going to get food like this? Artichokes from the garden, veal pizzaiola, chicken with sundried tomatoes fresh from the garden, stuffed zucchini. you got everything you want right here in Sicily. What more could you ask for?"

Richie looks at Carazzo with a smile on his face. "A Tuscan castle."

Carazzo changes the subject, "Richie, I think you should say the prayer tonight."

Richie is surprised. "Me? Nah, I ain't good at that."

Carazzo is taken aback, and he asks, "What's the matter? You don't believe in God?"

Teresa looks at Richie. "Please Ricardo, it would be a good example for the children."

Carazzo says, "Teresa they're not children. The boys are in their twenties, and the girls are ready for college. They're not children. Jesus Christ." He pauses. "I'm sorry, go-ahead Richie." Richie awkwardly gets through the pre-dinner prayer. Carazzo opens a bottle of wine. "Is this castle negotiable? Maybe a smaller one."

"No, present it to Santino the way I presented it to you: no changes and no negotiation."

"So there's no wiggle room.... nothing."

"Please, Mr. Carazzo, present it the way I told it to you."

Teresa comes over with the bowl of pasta. "Ricardo un po di pasta per te." (Richard, some pasta for you).

"Si, Gracie Teresa."

Carazzo pours Richie a glass of wine with a scowl, "I ain't got a castle, but I got a vineyard. After dinner, walk with me. I'll show you the latest batch of grapes for my Moscato. It's the first year for this grape, and it promises to be a good batch."

"You want to talk about grapes after we were disrespected by Santino?"

"Richie, not everything in life has to be a battle. After dinner we'll take a walk, ok? Don't be so fucking stubborn."

Teresa interrupts, "Lorenzo, guarda la tua lingua," (watch your tongue).

Lorenzo sighs and says, "See, Richie? We fight every day, but I love her to death, and she makes the best sauce in all of Sicily. After dinner, we're going to take a walk. Now it's the boss talking, you got it?"

"Yeah, sure Mr. Carazzo, whatever you say." The men are walking in the vineyard, and they stop at a section that's abundant in large white grapes. "See these grapes? I had them shipped from Siracusa and Noto. They produce a nice muscatel wine, just the right amount of sweet without being sugary. I've got a secret way of fermenting the grapes." Carazzo whispers, "I mix in some pinot noir grapes."

Richie says, "Nice, Mr. Carazzo, but we didn't come here to talk about wine, did we?"

"Come on, Richie, let's sit down. Let me tell you a story, Riccardo. A lot of years ago, maybe forty, I built an empire in New York, actually a big piece of the east coast. I had a guy there working for me who I trusted, but slowly he started making moves on his own. His name was Tony Diamante, a real piece of shit. He was a hot head, killed a lot of guys sometimes for no reason. I found out he was skimming off the top, and that's my money, and nobody fucks with my money. I kept hearing stories about this sadistic fuck, and finally I said enough is enough, and I sent a couple of guys to New York to put a stop to it, know what I mean? When my crew got there, somebody had already done the job. They found him in some junkyard in Queens." Carazzo spits on the floor. "Fuck him, the sfacim. The point is, when you came to me after that thing on Long Island, I gave you refuge, and I would do it again anytime. This bad blood between you and Santino has got to stop or people are going to get killed. Take it from a 76-year-old man. These things never end well unless you make peace. I'll present your Tuscan castle idea to Santino, and I'll tell him, and this is me talking, that he's got to put down half up front to hold it for you. I'll make sure he does it. Go take care of this prick Rinaldo and when you get back, we'll go castle shopping."

Richie looks at him surprised. "You're going to do that?"

"Yeah, you're family, he ain't. I'll do it if you tell me you're going to make peace when you get back. But here's one thing you've got to know, Richie. If you don't get this guy, don't come back to Sicily, 'cause I won't be able to save you from this fucking Santino." Carazzo looks at Richie. "I got contacts in Vegas. How many men are you going to need?

"I don't need anybody, just fifty grand."

"Fifty grand for what?"

Richie puts a grape in his mouth and stares ahead. "I may have to pick up a few things. I'll be in and out. Nobody'll know I was there. I'll leave as soon as I can get my papers together. Talk to Santino, and let me know what he says. Don't tell that prick about my travel plans, not a word ok Mr. Carazzo."" By the way, these grapes are going to make a perfect Muscatel."

Carazzo smiles. "Give me a few days Richie, I'll talk to this prick Santino. If he goes for it, I'll get your travel documents in order. I assume you'll be traveling under a different name."

"I'll be traveling as Richard DiNapoli. I don't need another name."

"What about the cops? Ain't they looking for you?"

"Like I said, I'll be in and out. The cops won't even know I was there."

"Ok, Richie, whatever you say. I'll have a limo pick you up at the airport. It's the least I can do. Come on, let's get back. Teresa made a special dessert. She breaks my balls, but she's a good woman."

"You're a lucky man, Mr. Carazzo."

CHAPTER 29
WHO IS MANSOUR AYAD?

McMahon calls Rodriguez. "Come see me. I have some information for you." Rodriguez arrives a short time later. "I had Captain Steiner run a check on this guy Mansour Ayad and what we found is interesting. Ayad is a Saudi national, and he's been investigated for human trafficking, kidnapping and soliciting. He made a reservation, but he didn't check in until a few days later. The concierge said a woman took the room a day before he showed up and claimed to be his wife. The concierge said she was wearing a hat and dark glasses. He didn't get a good look at her."

"A woman checked in before he did. I guess that explains the stilettos, doesn't it, McMahon?"

"No, it doesn't. Do you have any idea how hard it is to walk on those things? No my friend, they were a prop, a fetish item, and things got out of hand."

Rodriguez says, "So, you don't think it was his wife."

McMahon replies, "I don't think so. According to the front desk, he had two large gentlemen with him who we have to assume were his bodyguards, but his reservation was made with an American Express Black card under his name for a single seat in first class."

"A black card, shit. Did you know you can buy a Ferrari with that card and drive it out of the showroom?"

"Dream on Rodriguez. What do you think? Maybe his bodyguards flew coach."

"If you're in first class, and your bodyguards are in coach, you have no bodyguards, McMahon. I think he hired them here, or they were on loan."

"On loan from who?"

"Nicky, the concierge, said that his assistant checked them out of the hotel."

"What about the woman? Was she with him?"

"Nobody knows. We assume they left the hotel together."

"Call Steiner, see if he can find out if Mr. Ayad ever left Vegas. For all we know, he could still be here."

"What did you hear from the ME, McMahon?"

"The stuff on the heel was human blood and tissue, and the rug had blood in the fibers."

Even a DNA test won't help us if we don't have a suspect or a victim."

 "The problem, Rodriguez, is that the evidence was obtained illegally, but let's see if there's a workaround. I'll talk to the District Attorney."

Rodriguez says, "I had a hunch, and I checked it out. If the maid had gotten in there first, she would have trashed it and thought nothing of it. After all, this is Vegas. I'm sure maids clean up bodily fluids all the time. It's par for the course."

One of Captain Steiner's men enters the room. "There's a Dennis McCarthy out here. He wants to speak to Sergeant Rodriguez or you, Agent McMahon."

Rodriguez looks at McMahon and she says, "You were right." She tells the officer, "Send him in." Dennis McCarthy enters the room with head bowed accompanied by an officer McMahon asks, "So, what's on your mind Mr. McCarthy?"

"I want to tell you what happened that night with that girl. All of it."

"Have a seat, Mr. McCarthy." Rodriguez moves closer to him, and he's startled. Rodriguez says, "The only reason you're here is because two of your buddies were killed by Diamond Jack, otherwise you would be home with the wife and kiddies like nothing happened. Unfortunately, David Evans, the guy you beat up, refuses to press charges because he doesn't want to get caught up in this fucking mess. If you would have stepped up the first time, your friends would be alive now."

Dennis McCarthy begins to sob. McMahon gives Rodriguez a look and motions for him to sit down. "So, tell us what happened Mr. McCarthy."

McCarthy takes a deep breath and pulls a tissue from a box on McMahon's desk, and he begins, "That night was Billy's birthday, and we were going to get him you know."

Rodriguez fills in the blank. "Laid."

"Yeah, so we went to the bar at the Cosmopolitan, and we had a few drinks."

Rodriguez interrupts again, "A few. That's not the way I heard it. You were trashed. All three of you assholes, and you were annoying the rest of the people in the room."

McMahon interrupts, "Take it easy, Rodriguez."

"Ok, Mr. McCarthy, go-ahead then. What happened?"

"We were having a good time and then Billy spots this girl sitting at another table with this guy."

Rodriguez asks, "You mean Amy?"

"Yeah, it was Amy. So, he starts getting agitated, and he's cursing, and we're trying to calm him down, but it didn't work. Next thing we know, he jumps up and goes over to the table and starts yelling at her and cursing, calling her a lousy fuck and a whore who ripped him off."

Rodriguez says, "I guess this guy Billy wasn't such a classy guy."

McCarthy hangs his head. "He gets like that when he's had a lot to drink."

McMahon says, "A lot? A few minutes ago you told me you had a few."

 "This guy's full of shit, McMahon. I'll bet you he blames the whole thing on Billy and the other dead guy. So, what happened when you got to the Penthouse floor?"

"We waited for them to get off the elevator and we jumped them. He put up a fight, but there were three of us."

"How did you get into the suite?"

"Right after he opened the door, we made our move and we pushed them inside. I wasn't the one that hit her. It was Billy, and he kept on hitting her. We couldn't stop him."

McMahon asks, "Which one of you sexually assaulted her first?"

"It wasn't me. It was Billy and Steve, I swear."

McMahon leans in and says, "So, you didn't do anything. You just watched. Is that your statement?" McCarthy nods. "Well, the fact that you were there makes you an accessory to everything that happened. You're under arrest. Get Captain Steiner in here and have him read him his rights." Dennis McCarthy, sobbing, is led away in cuffs.

Across the street from the police station, a man sits in a car. He was watching as Dennis McCarthy walked into the precinct. He's angry that McCarthy eluded him, and he slams his fist against the steering wheel and drives away. Diamond Jack will bide his time, give it a few days, and follow the story in the news. If he's out of his reach, he'll choose another victim from the casinos, perhaps a high roller, and he'll send a message to Dennis McCarthy.

CHAPTER 30
ACHILLE SPEAKS

"Good morning, Augustus. I want you and Justine in my suite in an hour. We'll be waiting for you."

"We?"

"Yes, Isabella and I. Like I said, in an hour." They arrive, and Justine is barely awake, having spent the night involved in some form of debauchery or another. "Give your breakfast orders to Augustus. It's time we discuss a plan to rid ourselves of these pests."

Augustus glares at Rinaldo. "Do I look like fucking room service to you?"

Achille glares back, "You've been in Vegas almost two weeks now, and you've accomplished nothing. In fact, you've set us back by killing Andy, a real stupid move, and you let Rodriguez get away and lost two men in the process. So, you'll order breakfast and go pick it up if I ask you to." They eat breakfast in silence. Finally, Achille takes a sip of his chamomile tea and looks at Justine and Augustus, his eyes darting between them. "There are people that need to be disposed of." Augustus looks at Justine, and Achille continues. "Don't worry, it's nobody in this room. Although I've been tempted. Does anybody have an idea who I'm talking about?"

Isabella stands up and walks back and forth in front of them. "Let me guess, this person named Manny whoever he is," and sarcastically she says, "The poor girl in the hospital Amy, and last but not least, this nosey fucking cop."

Nobody says a word, and all eyes are on Rinaldo, and he slowly claps his hands. "Brava, brava, brava Isabella. I see I've made a good choice."

Augustus interrupts, "But we don't know where Manny is."

"Yes we do, Augustus. I found out he has a girlfriend, and she has a small place just outside of Vegas in Boulder City about 25 miles from here. See? I did your job for you." He hands Augustus a piece of paper with the address on it. "Do you think you can take two of my men, go there and find out if he told Rodriguez anything?"

Augustus looks nervous, and he looks to Justine. "What about his girlfriend?"

Rinaldo just gives him a look. "Find out what Rodriguez knows, and after that, it's your call. And you Isabella, since I met you, I've wondered how you would look in a nurse's outfit. Find one and then go to the hospital, and kill Amy with this," and he hands her a small syringe filled with a liquid. "It's a poison, undetectable, and it mimics cardiac arrest. It slowly wears down the heart muscle until it can no longer function. It could take 24 to 36 hours to kill. You'll be long gone before then. I don't care how you do it, get it done."

The room is silent again then Augustus asks, "What about Rodriguez? Shouldn't we kill him first?"

"No, he doesn't know anything. The people that can hurt us the most are the first we have to eliminate. As these corpses show up, he'll be busy, and if he begins to get close, then we'll kill him. For now, let him chase his tail. We have to move fast before Amy is able to talk to the police."

CHAPTER 31
THE DOUBLE CROSS

"So, Mr. Carazzo, is our pigeon on the way to Vegas?"

"Yeah he left this morning."

"What name is he using?"

"He's using his own name, the stupid fuck. He should be in Vegas tonight."

"I've got a couple of guys in Vegas. They'll keep an eye on him. After he kills Rinaldo, he's done. Can I ask you a question, Mr. Carazzo?"

"Yeah go ahead."

"Why do you want Richie dead? I know it's none of my business, and tell me if I'm out of line."

"I got twenty million reasons why. Besides, he's lost the edge. He's been here almost a year, and I told him to go back to New York to take back what's his, what's ours. Instead, he lays around here drinking my wine and eating my food. My family's crazy about him, so this Vegas thing works out good. You know, out of sight out of mind."

"When he doesn't come back, what are you going to tell them?"

"My family knows what we do. When he doesn't come back, they won't question it. Guess what he wants as payment for killing this guy."

"What?"

"A castle, a fucking castle in Tuscany. I told him you were going to put down half a deposit on his castle to hold it till he gets back. Ain't that some shit, and he believed me, the stupid fuck. Make sure he don't come back." Vincenzo Santino laughs, and Carazzo laughs along with him. There's a pause and then he says, *"It's time to put this guy, Riccardo Giuseppe DiNapoli, to bed once and for all."*

"I'll let you know when it's done."

"Let me tell you something, Santino. Tell these guys they better be sharp. I know Richie, and maybe he got a little soft, but he's still a fucking lunatic. Smart but nuts.

"Don't worry, Mr. Carazzo. He don't stand a chance against these guys. When Rinaldo is dead, they'll finish DiNapoli."

"I told him there's a limo picking him up at the airport. The driver works for me

"That's good, Mr. Carazzo. Like they say, una mano lava l'altra." (one hand washes the other.)

Richie arrives in Vegas and is going through processing, and he hands his passport to the customs agent. The agent looks at the passport and back at Richie and gestures for him to remove his sunglasses. "Your name is Richard Diamante?" Richie nods yes. "What brings you to Vegas, Mr. Diamante?"

"Taking a break from business."

"And what is your business?"

He replies, "Oil."

"You mean crude oil, fuel."

Richie smiles and says, "No, olive oil. I import and export it along with a few other things."

The agent looks over his glasses. "Other things?"

"Yeah, you know olives, vinegar, stuff like that."

"Are you traveling alone?"

Richie looks from side to side, "Yeah."

The sarcasm doesn't go unnoticed, and the agent asks, "Going to do some gambling?"

"Some, but I prefer sure things."

"How long will you be in Las Vegas, Mr. Diamante?"

"I'm not sure, maybe a week, maybe two. Depends on the business."

"Where are you staying?"

"With friends."

The agent looks through the passport. "How's Italy this time of the year, Mr. Diamante?"

"Italy's always beautiful. Are you Italian?"

"Yeah, on my mother's side, but it's been a while since I've been there."

Richie puts his sunglasses back on. "You should go visit. Are we done?"

The agent continues to look at Richie and he stamps the passport. "Ok, Mr. Diamante. Have a good time in Vegas."

"Thank you." Richie picks up his bags and mingles among the crowd. As he heads for the exit, he sees a driver holding a sign that says DiNapoli. He also notices the man is wearing a thousand-dollar suit with an obvious bulge in his jacket. He walks past and looks out onto the street in front of the airport. He notices two men waiting in a car not far behind the limousine and his instincts take over. Richie walks to the other side of the airport, exits and flags down a taxi. "I want to go to the Metropolitan Hotel."

The driver looks in the rearview mirror. "The Metropolitan it is."

Richie leans closer and asks, "How far is the hotel from the strip?"

"It's about twenty minutes without traffic."

"Can I rent a car near there?"

"Yeah, right across the street." He checks in and goes to the front desk. "Do you have a landline in the hotel?"

"Yeah, probably the only one left in Vegas." "It's behind you to the right." Richie makes a call, "Hey Aldo, it's Richie DiNapoli, how's it going?"

"Holy shit, Richie. Where the fuck you been? Last I heard you were laying low, what happened?"

"Long story, but I'm in Vegas now, and I need some help. Are you still with Mancini's crew?"

"Yeah, but he's inside for a few years."

"No shit, what happened?"

"It's an assault rap. He always was a hot head, kind of like you, Richie."

"Yeah sure, just like me. I need a favor from you."

"Sure, Richie. Anything."

"I need someone to watch my back while I'm here."

"Why are you here?"

"I got something to take care of. You got a couple of guys?"

"Yeah, two guys just got in from Chi-town."

Richie replies, "Don't give me mooks and rookies. I want old school guys, you know old stilettos, the type of guys I can trust. I don't want them to follow me around. I'll let them know when I need them. I won't be here for more than a week, maybe 2."

"I get it, what are you paying?"

"I'll give them twenty-five grand each. How much time will you need to reach out?"

"These guys are in town. I'll let you know tomorrow."

"Good, I'm going to grab a phone. I'll call you tomorrow. I hope these guys know how to keep a secret. Don't send me loud mouths. Like I said, old school."

"Don't worry, Richie. For twenty-five grand, they'll keep their mouths shut."

"I'll need a piece while I'm here. I'm thinking a 38. You got any? I'll pick it up tomorrow."

"I got more powerful, Richie, if you want it."

"No, a 38 is fine, easy to hide."

Lorenzo Carazzo is having dinner with his family when his phone rings. Caller id tells him it's Santino. He looks around the table, "yeah go ahead."

"My guys in Vegas tell me DiNapoli never got off the plane."

Carazzo throws his napkin down and says loudly, "Are you fucking kidding me, Santino."

He leaves the table as his wife says, "Lorenzo, e ora di mangiare." (it's time to eat).

He answers angrily, "Teresa, per favore chiudi quella cazzo di bocca." (please shut the fuck up). He goes into a sitting room and the conversation continues. "Are they sure? How long did they wait?"

"Mr. Carazzo, I don't know what to tell you. They waited for him a long time, and he never showed."

"Do you think he's still in Sicily?" "Listen Mr. Carazzo the flight was booked solid not an empty seat I

think he's in Vegas."

"So, he's running around Vegas, and we don't know where he is. Shit, do you think he's on to us?"

"So, what if he is? He can't hurt us."

"You don't know him like I do. If he knows we set him up, he'll kill Rinaldo, and then he'll come back to Sicily and cut our throats while we sleep."

Santino asks," Do you think he's got the balls to come back to Sicily?"

There's silence and then Carazzo tells him, "Get more men to watch your back. You're going to need them." Carazzo hangs up and turns to his bodyguard. "Tell the men to stay alert and keep their eyes open. We may have some trouble."

CHAPTER 32
THE VISIT

Achille Rinaldo is having dinner with Isabella and Justine at a five-star restaurant on the strip. Isabella puts her fork down. "I went to the hospital today."

Rinaldo looks at Justine and back at Isabella. "Really, why?"

"I wanted to get a feel for the place."

"Did you get a feel, and what did you find out while you were there?"

"Amy has a police guard outside her door."

Achille stops and takes a sip of wine. "That's a major complication. That means there's somebody there twenty-four hours. Any ideas, Justine?" Justine sits quietly and looks at her plate. Rinaldo says, "Of course not. Why would you have any fucking ideas?" Rinaldo puts his head in his hands. "We waited too long."

"There was someone in the room with her, a man."

Rinaldo looks up. "Really? A relative or perhaps a friend?"

"I don't know, but he was holding her hand as if they were close, really close."

"I think we should find out who this man is and befriend him. He could be our way in, a way to get to Amy. Isabella, I think you should find out who this man is, introduce yourself, and tell him you're a friend of Amy. Call Augustus. He can tell you all about her. Go to the hospital tomorrow and see if he's there. If the nurses see you on a regular basis, they'll be comfortable with letting you into the room. Bring flowers for Amy and perhaps a bouquet for the nurses. They like that. Go there in the morning and introduce yourself. Like I said, we need to move fast. And here I was so looking forward to seeing you in a nurse's uniform. Perhaps I still can," and he smiles.

Justine seems taken aback and asks, "What do you want me to do, Mr. Rinaldo?"

"Nothing for now, Justine." He shoves a forkful of food into his mouth and exclaims, "This ossobuco is the best in Vegas." Justine glares at Isabella, who smiles and continues eating her dinner.

Gino is with Amy in the hospital when Isabella walks to the desk and asks to be let in to visit with Amy. Gino sees Isabella gesturing towards the room and comes out. "Hi, my name is Gino Marchetti, and you are?"

"My name is Isabella, Amy and I worked together."

"Worked together doing what?"

"You know, Mr. Marchetti."

"No, I don't suppose you tell me." Isabella nervously looks at the nurse and back at Gino, hoping he would let it go. "How come she never mentioned you?"

"I don't know why, Mr. Marchetti."

"Call me Gino. I'm still wondering why she never mentioned you."

Isabella changes the subject. "I bought flowers for her room, you know, to cheer her up."

"I appreciate it, but she can't see them. She's in a coma." Isabella is obviously uncomfortable. Gino says, "I'm sorry I know you're trying to be nice." He asks, "Do you know what happened to her?"

"Only what I read in the papers."

"How long have you known Amy?"

"About a year, Gino." The nurse approaches Gino and asks if it's ok if she visits. Gino pauses and says, "Yeah, it's ok."

They both go into the room and sit at Amy's bedside. Isabella is visibly uneasy, and she asks, "How do you know Amy?"

"She's my girlfriend, and we were supposed to get married."

"I'm sorry, Gino. What do the doctors say?"

"Well, it's been a little over 2 weeks since the attack, and she hasn't progressed much so it's day by day." Gino is still curious about Isabella's relationship with Amy, and he asks, "So, how did you meet Amy?"

"We met about a year ago on the strip. Usually people in our line of work don't socialize with each other, but I liked her right away."

"That accent is familiar, are you Italian?"

"Yes, I'm from Naples."

"Naples, I heard it's beautiful there."

"Yes it is."

Gino says, "My family's from Rome, and I'm from Brooklyn. Everybody I hung out with had the same accent." They both laugh and Gino, still suspicious, says, "Thank you for coming, Isabella. It was nice of you."

CHAPTER 33
FRANKIE AND JOHNNY

Richie calls Aldo. "Did you reach out?"

"Yeah, I'm meeting them at two. Where are you staying? We'll come by."

Richie replies, "No, not here. On the way from the airport, I saw a diner called The Lucky Seven. Let's meet there at three. It's just outside of town."

"The Lucky Seven. It's a fucking dive, why there?"

"It's out of the way. I can't take a chance walking around Vegas in the daytime. See you at three, and don't forget the 38."

Aldo is a Vegas low tier gangster that couldn't break through to the big time. He idolizes Richie and wise guys like him, and he always felt he could have been a capo of his own family if things had gone different, but his associates all knew he didn't have the instinct, or the ruthless gene needed to be the head of a crime family. Like Gino Marchetti, he was never able to grab the brass ring. Today, he makes a living selling weed and pills out of a few souvenir shops on the strip. Richie arrives at The Lucky Seven early and parks his car near the back exit and walks around the building to check for fire escapes and any way in or out. He learned a long time ago not to trust anyone. He orders a cup of coffee and sits nearest the exit with a view of the parking lot. At exactly three o'clock, two cars park directly in front. Two men exit one of the cars, and Aldo exits the other. Richie notices that he's driving a new Jaguar f type sports car. The men enter and sit at Richie's booth. "Richie DiNapoli, meet Frankie Gallo and Johnny DelVecchio. These are the guys I was telling you about. I see you're here early. I guess you already cased the joint. You never change, do you Richie?"

"Just making sure. So Frankie, your name's Gallo."

"Yeah, but no relation to crazy Joey."

Richie smiles, looks the men over and extends his hand. "Aldo tells me I can trust you to watch my back. Who did you guys work for in Detroit?"

Frankie looks at Aldo, and he says, "They're from Chicago, not Detroit, Richie."

"That's right, Chicago. I forgot. So, who'd you work for?"

Frankie speaks up. "I was part of the southside crew with Tommy Bello, but he's doing eight years, and nobody stepped up to fill his shoes, so I took off and left town. Let's just say I'm self-employed at the moment."

Richie smiles, looking at Johnny. "And you?"

"Me? With all due respect, Mr. DiNapoli, what difference does it make? I'm here for the twenty-five grand. You pay me, and I'll watch your back. You ain't got to worry."

He looks at the both of them and asks, "You ever kill anybody?"

The men seem annoyed at the question, and Frankie angrily asks, "Why all the fucking questions, Aldo?"

"I'll let Richie answer that."

Richie responds, "I'll tell you why, 'cause if the time should come when I need you to put a bullet in somebody's head, I don't want you to hesitate. No thinking twice about it, 'cause it's my ass."

Frankie nods in the affirmative, "It wouldn't be the first time for me."

Richie looks at Johnny, "Sure, Richie. It goes with the territory."

"So, who do I call when the time comes?"

Johnny looks at Frankie and says, "Me, call me anytime night or day, right Frankie?" Johnny leans back in his chair. "So Richie, I heard a lot about you. You're a big man in this racket. Everybody respects you, but I hear rumors about your past. So, what's the real story?"

Richie seems surprised by the question. "You really want to know, Johnny? Ok, let me give you the short version, and this is the first time I'm telling anybody, but my old man was Tony Diamante."

Frankie sits up in his seat, and he says, "Tony Diamante was your old man? Shit, he's a fucking legend."

"No, he's not. He was a fucking animal. He enjoyed beating on my mother. Sometimes he'd smack me and my brother around just for the hell of it, especially if he was drunk or if one of his pigeons missed a payment, and I was too young to do anything about it. He was a sadistic prick. He liked killing and sometimes, he took me with him and made me watch. But every Sunday, he was in church with the rest of his mob friends, those fucking hypocrites. I grew up surrounded by mob types every day, and they showed me what that world is like. When I was 19, I took off for Florida, and I hooked up with some of the local families, and I started doing some wet work for these mooks. You don't need school when you're taking down 3 or 4 grand a week at age 22. When I was 25, I was banging around mooks who didn't pay up and doing drug deals with the Columbians, and that's when I met Dom and Primo, and I decided to branch out on my own. They were good guys to have around, but they had no business sense. Once I came on the scene, we didn't know what to do with all that fucking money. We came back up north, and you know the rest of the story."

Aldo asks, "What about your old man? How did he fit in?"

"He didn't. I gave Primo the contract."

Johnny puts his cup down and asks, "You put a hit on your old man?"

"Yeah, and right after that, I became Richie DiNapoli."

Aldo stares into space and exclaims, "What the fuck? You had your old man hit?"

Richie looks at Aldo, and the men are silent, and then Frankie asks, "What about your brother, Richie, where is he?" "His name's Joey. It's been years. I have no idea. After that, my mother died in misery, and I never got over it. She couldn't deal with me in the organization and with my old man dead, it killed her, because she loved the piece of shit in spite of what he did to the family. I think about her every day, so that's it fellas. That's my story." He looks around the table menacingly and says, "What I told you doesn't leave this table."

Frankie asks," What happened after that? I heard you went back to Italy and hid out."

Everyone's quiet, and Richie looks around the table, "We were working on a big deal with the Colombians that went south, and I had to get out of town. That's enough questions," and he reaches into his pocket and gives each man an envelope. "There's five grand each as a down payment. When we find the target, I'll give you another five grand, and when the job is done, I'll pay you the rest."

Frankie inquires, "This target must be a big fish."

"Yeah, and he's got a lot of protection." He leans over to Aldo and asks, "Did you bring the piece?"

"Yeah, it's in the car."

"Car, you mean that seventy grand beauty outside? Not for nothing Aldo, but where the fuck did you get the money for that?"

"That beauty is leased to a Dr. Louis Wasserman, a dentist from Reno, and it's closer to eighty grand. You see, I know a guy who knows a guy. Bottom line, the paperwork is all bullshit."

Richie laughs. "Really," and nodding adds, "Nice, just don't hit anything." The men laugh and Richie gets up to leave, "I'll be in touch gentlemen." Aldo follows Richie out the door.

CHAPTER 34
SEARCHING THE STRIP

The sun is setting with a bright red and orange glow and walking on the strip is difficult, as the sun glares off the sidewalk. Richie puts on sunglasses and walks past the tourists and hawkers handing out postcards for strip clubs, Vegas dating sites and wedding chapels. In spite of the commotion and chaos, his eyes are laser focused and looking for one man, Achille Rinaldo. He knows that the man they call the "Vampire" avoids sunlight. He also knows that if he suspects he's being stalked, the "Vampire" will have him executed without hesitation. His eyes dart left and right and to his advantage, Rinaldo has only seen him twice and may not recognize him, but the "Vampire" is hard to forget. He'll have no trouble spotting him, especially if accompanied by his bodyguards. As he walks, he calls Aldo.

"Yeah Richie, what's up?"

"I need a woman for tomorrow night. Who can I talk to?"

"I guess Vegas made you horny, right Richie?" and Aldo lets out an irritating exaggerated laugh.

Richie pulls the phone away from his ear. "Hear me out. The guy I'm looking for eats in five-star restaurants. I want a dining companion so I don't stand out. If she's young enough to be my daughter, even better."

Aldo says, "And if you get laid, it's even better, right?" and he laughs again.

"Come on, Aldo, this is business. Set it up, ok?"

"Sure, Richie. I'll make a few calls. Get back to me in a few hours."

Richie continues to walk the strip, and as the sun sets and the lights become brighter, Vegas comes alive. The restaurants begin to fill, and the casinos are full of action. He knows Rinaldo likes the finer things in life, so he targets the high-end restaurants on the strip and in the casinos. Richie walks in front of The Dove, a five-star establishment serving Italian cuisine. As he walks past, he looks through the window and there sitting at a table in the preferred corner of the room is the "Vampire", Achille Rinaldo, with Isabella. At a nearby table are seated two men, one large and muscular, the other smaller and unassuming, not what a typical bodyguard would look like. Richie knows from experience that the smaller ones are smarter and the most dangerous, because they always feel like they have something to prove. Richie watches from across the Boulevard, formulating a plan. He observes the bigger of the bodyguards walking towards the back of the restaurant. Richie crosses the Boulevard and walks hurriedly into the restaurant past the busy maitre'd and into the men's room. The bodyguard is at the urinal and Richie occupies the one on the end. Faking it he flushes and walks to the sink where he washes his hands. He's joined there by the bodyguard who also begins to wash his hands. Richie looks over and asks, "How's it going?" The bodyguard looks at him suspiciously, not answering. Richie adds, "I'm thinking about eating here. How's the food?"

The bodyguard eyes Richie and replies with an Italian accent, My boss thinks it's great. I don't give a shit. For me, it's a free meal."

"Your boss?"

"Yeah, the guy sitting with the girl. That's my boss."

Richie says, "I might come back tomorrow night. I just wanted to take a piss and check the place out."

The bodyguard replies, "It's good but too expensive. He comes here all the time, every night at the same time, and eats the same thing. I don't give a shit. Like I said, a free meal for me," and he shrugs.

Richie smiles and thinks to himself this guy just broke the first rule of making sure the boss stays alive: never reveal his schedule and keep your mouth shut. Richie dries his hands and turns for the door. "Thanks, see you around." He returns to his vantage point across the Boulevard and waits. Finally, they exit the restaurant and begin walking. Richie follows at a distance weaving in and out of the crowd. They enter the Luxor, and Richie observes them get into the elevator, and it goes to the Penthouse floor. He looks at his watch and makes a mental note of the time. He calls Aldo. "Forget the girl. I don't need her."

Aldo replies, "But I set it up. What do I tell her?"

"Just tell her it's off. I changed my mind. It ain't complicated, Aldo. I got to go."

CHAPTER 35
ANOTHER LOOSE END

The sun is rising as Augustus and Rinaldo's bodyguards drive towards Boulder City. The drive is quiet, then Augustus asks the driver, "Did you ever kill anybody?"

Without taking his eyes off the road he answers, "So, what do you want us to do with this guy?"

"Didn't Mr. Rinaldo tell you?"

"No, he just said to pick you up, and you'll take care of the rest."

"Me?"

The passenger in the back-seat answers, "If you got a problem with that, call him."

Augustus looks out the window and says, "No, I'm good." They arrive at the house and the two men split up. The driver walks to the back of the house with Becker, and the passenger looks through the front window. Manny and his girlfriend are curled up in bed. "Looks like they're sleeping. This'll wake them up." He kicks the door in, startling Manny and his girlfriend, who begins to scream. Augustus and the driver run inside. There's another crash as the front door gets kicked in also. The driver has a gun pointed at Manny, and the passenger has his hand covering his girlfriend's mouth.

The driver turns toward Augustus. "So, now what?"

Augustus looks at Manny, who's trembling with fright. Augustus looks at the bodyguard and back at Manny and in a low voice asks, "So, what does Rodriguez know about our business?"

"Nothing, I swear. He asked me about Andy, and then he came looking for me. I didn't even know Andy was dead until I saw it on the news. He came to the hotel. When I saw him, I hid out, and then I came here. We never talked. I swear. He was after Andy?"

The driver looks at Augustus. "Well, what do we do? It's your call, do you believe him?"

Augustus responds, "Yeah I do."

Manny cries, "I'm telling you the truth. Please don't kill me."

The driver gives his partner a knowing glance and asks Manny, "Is that your car up front?"

Manny answers, "Yeah, that's mine."

"Give me the keys." Manny fumbles through items on the nightstand and finds the keys and hands them to the man. "Thanks Manny." The man raises his gun and shoots Manny once in the head. The bullet goes through and lodges in the wall behind him, a red mist traveling with the bullet and staining the wall. Manny's girlfriend is screaming, but it's a silent scream muffled by the hand covering her mouth and only heard by the people in the room.

Augustus looks down at the body. "What the fuck was that? Why did you shoot him?"

"Rinaldo's orders, Becker. You didn't think he'd trust you with this, did you?" The passenger throws Manny's keys to Augustus. "Here, take his car. We'll finish up here." Manny's girlfriend begins to scream a silent scream again. Augustus quickly walks towards the door and into the car. The screams are louder now, and he hears them above the sound of the engine. He pauses and stares out the windshield before driving away.

It's ten a.m., and Isabella is awakened by Rinaldo. "Wake up. You have a busy day ahead of you, my darling."

Isabella stirs and asks, "What the fuck time is it, Achille?"

"It's time to get to work, Isabella."

She replies sleepily, "Work, what work?"

"The hospital. Remember, we need to dispose of the one person that can bring us all down."

"You mean Amy."

"Of course I mean Amy. You still have the syringe, don't you?"

"Yes I have it. Can I sleep a little more please?"

Rinaldo sits on the edge of the bed leans closer and whispers, "Someone told me once that there's only two things you can do in a bed, and that's sleep and fuck, and you've already slept, so maybe we should try the other thing."

"Alright, alright. I'll get up. May I have some privacy please?"

"Fine, my dear. I'll leave you alone. How about I order us breakfast, and then you can visit our friend Amy? And don't forget the flowers. Now, what would you like?"

"Whatever, I'm too tired to think." They eat breakfast in silence, and then she asks in a subdued voice, "How much do I give her?"

Rinaldo looks at her and takes a sip of tea. "The whole thing. Put it into the IV tube. She does have IV tubes, doesn't she?"

Isabella nods and says, "Yes."

"Splendid, just trace one and make sure it's going into her arm, and it's done." Rinaldo looks at his watch. "Wonderful, by now Manny should be dead and another loose end is tied up." Isabella pushes her plate aside. "What's wrong, my dear? Is the food not to your liking?"

"No, I just lost my appetite."

Rinaldo pushes the plate back in front of her and says, "Eat your breakfast."

CHAPTER 36
I'M SORRY AMY

Isabella arrives at Vegas General Hospital. She's carrying flowers for Amy's room and the staff. She approaches the ICU desk and is recognized by the same nurse that was on duty the first time she visited Amy. She approaches and smiles when she sees her. "Hi Isabella, do you remember me? We met the last time you were here with Gino. I'm Janet, the kids in pediatrics call me Nurse Janet."

"Oh yes, hi Janet. How's our patient doing? Any change?"

"We think so. It looks like she's beginning to recognize voices and reacting especially when Gino talks to her."

Isabella says, "Maybe I can try talking to her. She might recognize my voice. Where's Gino? Doesn't he come around this time?"

"I think he usually gets here about this time, but I haven't seen him today."

"May I go in to see her?"

"Wait here, let me tell the officer you're here." She returns and accompanies her into the room. "Only for half an hour, and don't forget to talk to her. It helps a lot."

"Thank you, Janet. I won't be long."

The officer stands and opens the door for her and tells her, "I'll need to look through your bag."

Isabella pauses and responds, "I'm a friend of Amy's. Janet knows me. I've been here before."

The officer looks at Janet, and she nods.

The officer tells her, "I'll let you know when it's half an hour."

Isabella enters the room and sits next to her and takes her hand. She places her purse on the floor and removes the syringe and places it under the pillow. The officer is walking back and forth, occasionally looking into the room. Isabella has to time it just right. A moment later the officer is called to the desk allowing Isabella to inject the contents of the syringe, sealing Amy's fate. As she injects the deadly serum into one of the IV tubes she whispers, "I'm sorry, Amy." She places the empty syringe back in her bag and sits, continuing to talk to her. She notices a tear running down the side of Amy's face and she gets up to leave, but she sits back down. She hangs her head and cries, and wipes the tears away, so no one notices. She gets up and walks towards the door and doesn't look back.

As she is leaving, Janet notices she's been crying and asks, "Are you ok?"

"I'm ok, it's just so sad. I'll be back tomorrow if I can."

All the way back from the hospital, she was crying. She gets to the Luxor, and Rinaldo notices that her eyes are red and swollen. He takes her by the arm. "Isabella, have you been crying? So, you did the deed I assume." Isabella nods yes. "Why the tears, Isabella? Do you realize how much she could have hurt us? A minimum of twenty years to life in prison, Isabella, for trafficking. Think of what that would do to that beautiful face and that magnificent body. You would be a star in prison, and not in a good way. Now, I need you to massage my neck and shoulders. I've had a stressful day. When you're done, we'll break open a bottle of champagne and celebrate." Isabella notices a knife on a tray from the day's lunch but resists the temptation to pick it up and kill Rinaldo. Rinaldo pops the cork on the bottle of champagne as

Augustus and Justine arrive. "Welcome kids, you're just in time for champagne. I believe all of our loose ends have been, shall we say, tied up, am I right Augustus? Was Manny much of a problem?"

Augustus is angry. "Why the fuck didn't you tell me they were going to kill him and his girlfriend?"

"Don't go soft on me, Augustus. What did you think you went there for? You knew he had to die. It was part of the plan."

"What about raping and killing his girlfriend? Was that part of the plan?"

"We couldn't let her live. She would have gone straight to the police, but rape, that wasn't in the plan. I'll have to talk to them."

"Talk to them? Are you serious? They're fucking animals."

"Watch what you say, Augustus. Those men have been extremely loyal to me. Where are they, and how did you get back?"

"I drove Manny's car. It gave me the creeps. I watched the guy get killed, and then I'm driving his car. How fucked up is that?"

"So, where's the car now, Augustus?"

"It's downstairs in the garage."

"So, you drove the car all the way here where we live, and did you also tell the police where to find it?" Rinaldo raises his voice. "Get that fucking car out of here and dump it somewhere."

CHAPTER 37
I'M SAFE INSIDE

It was nighttime, and Gino was in his element, walking the casinos. His optimism that he and Amy would be together was through the roof. Earlier in the day, Dr. Beasley had told him that she appeared to have turned the corner and was responsive. The doctors were unaware of the slow acting poison administered by Isabella that flowed through her veins. The following morning, their optimism turned to dread when Amy's condition was rapidly deteriorating. A call was placed to Gino, who got home just before sunrise and fell asleep with his phone lying on the nightstand uncharged, and they were unable to inform him of Amy's passing. When he finally awoke, it was late morning and after charging his phone, the voicemail came through loud and clear. Amy had taken a turn for the worse, and he was needed at the hospital. He arrived to find Amy's body covered by a sheet with nurses and doctors gathered around her. Their efforts to revive her were obviously heroic, with the empty vials of medicine and machinery used in an attempt to save her life standing idol, as if witnessing the scene. Janet sees Gino and comes out to try and explain what had happened. Cardiac arrest was the probable cause, but no medical expert there could explain why. At first, there's silence, then Gino lets out a scream, startling doctors and nurses on the floor.

Nurse Janet pulls him into a room and closes the door. "I'm sorry Gino. we tried to save her, but we couldn't do anything."

The guard opens the door and stands watching them. Gino asks, "Why is he here?"

"Just hospital policy, Gino. You see, people handle grief differently and some get violent and attack the doctors and the nurses."

"I'm not violent. Can I see her one last time?"

Nurse Janet looks at the guard. "It's ok, Gino. I'll take you inside, and I'll close the shades, so you can have a few minutes with her." After a few minutes, Gino emerges, wiping his eyes. As he's walking out, Nurse Janet stops him. "Gino, before you go, can you leave information at the desk where you can be reached?"

"Sure, no problem."

Nurse Janet softly touches his arm and says, "I'm sorry Gino."

Captain Steiner calls McMahon. "I cut Dennis McCarthy loose. He made bail his wife posted it a few hours ago."

"Really, one hundred grand just like that."

"Second mortgage, 401's, you know the drill. All I know is I'm happy to get rid of him. He's got a court date, and if he doesn't show, then we can put him back in."

Dennis McCarthy leaves through the front door of Captain Steiner's precinct. He looks around apprehensively and climbs into a car driven by his wife. The ride is very quiet with neither one talking and both staring out the windshield. Her eyes are on the road, and his imagination is racing knowing that Diamond Jack is still out there. Finally he says, "I should have stayed inside. I would be safer. Diamond Jack is still out there."

His wife responds, "Your children want their father. You need to be home for now. When this thing is over, I'm leaving with them, and I don't give a shit what happens to you." They arrive home and the car goes into the garage. From his car across the street, Diamond Jack takes in the scene as Dennis McCarthy and his family arrive home.

CHAPTER 38
LOOK DON'T TOUCH

Achille Rinaldo is planning to leave Las Vegas. He has a meeting in Turkey with his contacts in Istanbul, mostly underworld figures working for a criminal syndicate. He's distracted by something that's been on his mind since Rodriguez escaped the tunnels. The question is who helped him. He phones Augustus. "Come to the Luxor. I need you to do something for me."

"When?"

"Immediately, Becker. Immediately." The men are seated having drinks in silence when Rinaldo says, "You and I are going into the tunnels to the room."

"Why?"

"Do you remember when Rodriguez escaped? You said he may have had help."

"Yes I do, and you ridiculed me."

"It seemed ludicrous at the time, but the more I thought about it, the more it made sense. There must be another way into that room, and I want to find it."

"So what if someone helped him? It was a while ago, and we tied up the loose ends. Rodriguez is chasing his tail. He doesn't know shit, and the police have no clues and nothing to investigate."

"I'm leaving this piece of shit city soon and going to a meeting in Istanbul. Don't you think it best that we be thorough and finish the job?"

"I suppose." Augustus pauses for a while. "So, when do you want to go?"

"Tomorrow morning. We'll take one of my men."

"If we find out that somebody helped him, then what?"

"You'll have to kill them, Augustus. After all, you owe me one for Andy and Manny."

"What if we can't find the person?"

"We'll have to kill somebody to send a message. Besides, nobody cares about those tunnel freaks anyway." Rinaldo smiles. "Goodbye, Augustus. I'll see you at ten am tomorrow. We'll have a nice breakfast together, and then we'll find out who helped him and kill them. Good night." Augustus slowly gets up to leave, and Rinaldo's eyes are on him as he walks to the door. "Oh, and by the way, Augustus, bring some powerful flashlights. I understand the electricity shorted out when your men were fried like two pieces of meat." Achille hears the door slam behind Augustus. He laughs and takes another drink.

Augustus arrives at the Penthouse at ten am. as instructed. Isabella opens the door and greets Augustus dressed in a sheer nightgown with very little underneath. Augustus enters, and he's laughed at by Rinaldo. Isabella attempts to stifle a laugh, but to no avail. Augustus is dressed as if he's going on safari. High waterproof boots tucked into his pants, camouflage jacket and hat and holding two large flashlights. He asks, "What's she doing here?" and aims the flashlight at Isabella."

"Did you forget I live here? And take that fucking light out of my eyes."

Rinaldo interrupts, "Stop and listen, both of you, it's important. Do you remember Mr. Ayad that Isabella dispatched to the afterlife? Well, his associates contacted me, and they're not happy. They suspect that I had something to do with his disappearance. They want to meet with me to discuss a new deal given the circumstances, and I don't know when that will be. So, I'm stuck here in Vegas indefinitely. Meanwhile, my contacts in Istanbul and Russia are getting anxious. What a fucking shit show. Thank you Isabella."

Augustus asks, "Why don't you just leave Vegas?"

"Leave Vegas, do you realize who these people are and what would happen if they found me? When this is over, I want you and Justine to get out of Vegas. Isabella and I are leaving after I straighten this out. There's no sense in hanging around. Perhaps a European vacation would do you both good. I'll be in touch, and we can resume our business when things settle down. What a fucking disaster."

There's a knock on the door and a voice shouts, "Room service."

And Isabella says, "I'll get it." She opens the nightgown just a little and answers the door. The young man on the other side is flustered and Isabella says, "Come in, and place the tray there on the table." The young man enters nervously, trying not to look at Isabella. She bends over to retrieve her purse from the floor, and the young man can't take his eyes off her. She walks him to the door and hands him a twenty-dollar bill. "Thank you so much, young man." Before he walks away, he turns for one more glimpse, and she slowly closes the door. Isabella walks back to the two men, strutting as if on a runway.

Achille looks at her and says," Isn't she fabulous? Now, let's have breakfast."

CHAPTER 39
THE ROOM WITH THE CHAIR

Three men walk through the lobby of The Metropolitan Hotel as the breakfast buffet crowd made up of tourists from all parts of the earth are jockeying for their place on line. They jostle with plates in hand as if it's their last meal. The men push through the crowd as they make their way to the door at the end of the kitchen. They open the door to the tunnels and enter the room with the chair. They go from the aroma of the buffet to the putrid smells of mold and the odor of burnt flesh that still lingers in the air. The police investigators are gone, but evidence of them being there is still visible. Chalk outlines of where the bodies fell are faint but noticeable, as are the blood stains. Augustus and the bodyguard shine their lights around the room, looking for another way out.

Achille says, "Let's try the lights." He flips the switch, and the room is illuminated. The lights reveal a young boy standing by the chair.

He looks at the men and asks, "I heard noises. Who are you guys?"

The men are taken by surprise, and Augustus says, "We're the police, and who are you?"

"My name is Mark. Are you cop friends of Rodriguez?"

The men look at each other, and Rinaldo answers, "Yeah we are. Do you know how he escaped from this room?"

"Sure we helped him," Mark said proudly."

Achille looks at Augustus. "We?"

"Yeah me and my dad."

"And where's your dad now, Mark?"

"He's back there where we live."

Augustus is shocked, and he says, "You live here."

Achille says, "Can you show us where he is? We want to congratulate him."

"Sure, follow me." Mark takes them through the hole hidden behind the chair and down a long dark tunnel and up an incline. "See, it's higher here so when it rains, our place doesn't flood."

Augustus checks his clothes for bugs. A voice comes from inside. "Mark, who are you talking to?"

"Hey dad, it's friends of Rodriguez."

"Who?"

His father comes out of the room with a gun in hand. The bodyguard sees the gun and grabs Mark around the neck and puts a gun to his head. Achille says, "Drop the gun, or I'll tell my man to kill the boy."

"Who are you?"

"No questions. I said drop the gun and you both live."

The man drops his gun and says, "Let my son go. He didn't do anything."

Achille says, "That's quite a brave boy you've got there. I guess he takes after you. What's your name?"

"Charles."

"So, Charles, tell us how you helped Rodriguez escape."

Charles pauses, "If I tell you, let my boy go."

"Tell us, and we won't hurt your son, Mark. Is that right? His name is Mark?"

"Yeah, Mark found him handcuffed to a chair. I always tell him to stay out of that room, but he doesn't listen. I cut the cuffs, and I gave him one of my guns, and then he told us to get out of the room and not come back in. The next thing I know, I heard gunshots, but I didn't see anything. A little while later, the place was crawling with police. That's all I know." Achille looks at Augustus without saying a word, and Augustus draws his gun and points it at the man. "Let my son go. Please, you said you wouldn't hurt him."

Achille says, "Too bad Charles you saw us." Rinaldo nods and Augustus, with hands shaking, pulls the trigger. The first bullet hits Charles, and he falls to the ground. He raises his hand as if to stop the second and fatal bullet. Mark screams and bites the bodyguard's finger, drawing blood, and he loosens his grip. He picks up his father's gun and starts firing randomly at the men as they run for cover. One bullet hits the bodyguard in the leg, and he falls cursing. Achille yells, "Go get him. Don't let him get away." Augustus has his sights on Mark, and he fires the gun randomly as he chases him through the dark maze. Mark is familiar with the tunnels, and he's able to outrun and hide from Augustus. Suddenly, Augustus is alone, having lost sight of Mark.

Augustus screams, "If you tell anybody, I'll come back and kill you." Augustus shines his flashlight into the tunnel and sees nightmarish faces and figures walking around aimlessly. A man is leaning against a graffiti covered wall, shaking and laughing to himself. In the distance, he hears voices, some crying, some laughing. Dim lights are visible in the distance, illuminating makeshift living quarters. Around him are rooms with improvised tables and chairs and beds composed of dirty and stained mattresses stacked on crates or cardboard boxes. To his right, a toothless woman grabs his arm and begs for money, her touch repulsing him. He turns to run but realizes he's lost in this maze. The odor of sewage is nauseating, and he feels imaginary things crawling on him. He begins to swat these imaginary bugs from his face and finally, he screams Achille's name.

The bodyguard is bleeding profusely from his wound, and time is running out. "Please Achille, you have to get me to a hospital."

"I know, I'll help you." Achille looks around, and he sees a discarded plastic bag and walks toward the man. The bodyguard, sensing what's coming, tries to get up, but all he can do is crawl to try and get away. Achille, using his foot, pushes the man back onto the floor. He leans over and whispers, "Sorry, Giorgio." Giorgio begins to beg for his life, but his pleadings are ignored, and Achille slips the bag over his head and pulls it tight. Achille says, "Sorry, but it's better this way. You were going to bleed to death. Ciao, Giorgio." The man struggles, throwing punches wildly into the air, and he tries to rip the bag from his head. As he loses blood, his attempts to save himself get weaker and weaker. Achille continues to hold the bag in place until the man stops moving. As if coming out of a trance, he begins to hear Augustus screaming his name. Achille shouts back, "Follow my voice, Augustus."

Finally he finds the room and sees the bodyguard with the plastic bag still over his head. "What the fuck, Achille. Why did you kill him?"

"What do you suggest we do? Drag him through the lobby trailing blood all over the place? It looks like the bullet hit an artery or a vein or something. What the fuck do I know? I'm not a doctor. He was bleeding to death. He would have never made it to a hospital. Let's get out of here."

"What about them, Achille?"

"Let's drag them back to the room. I'll send my men down tonight. They'll take them to the desert, and they'll be gone."

"What about the boy? What if he goes to the police?"

"The boy is scared. I'm not worried about him. He won't tell anyone." The bodies are left in the room with the chair. He flips the switch again and the room is dark.

CHAPTER 40
TWO LEFT FEET

The news of Amy's death reaches Captain Steiner. He calls McMahon who in turn relates the news to Rodriguez. When he gets the call, he stops his car on the side of the road. "Did the doctors say what the cause was?"

"The preliminary report is cardiac arrest."

Rodriguez responds, "I thought she was getting better. What happened?"

"Nobody knows. Until the autopsy results are in, it's just speculation. Where are you? I hear traffic. Are you on your way in?"

"No, I'm heading to a few souvenir shops just outside of the strip. Just a hunch about Gino."

"Marchetti, what about him?"

"I'm not sure. I'll let you know when I have more information."

He arrives at a small family-owned shop about 5 miles outside of Vegas and he's greeted by the owner. "Can I help you?"

"Yeah, I'm looking for cufflinks. Do you have any?"

"Cufflinks, yeah. I got 'em. Come on back."

"A friend of mine was wearing Jack of Diamonds cufflinks. You have those?"

"I had, but since this Diamond Jack thing, I'm sold out. I'm waiting for an order to come in. The only thing I have is a picture of the ones I used to sell. Some people think they're collector's items, what a bunch of schmucks."

Rodriguez looks at the picture. "How tough would it be to trace the sales of these things?"

"Trace the sales? Are you kidding? There's no way. Why are you asking? Are you a cop or something?"

"Yeah." Rodriguez shows his badge.

"Some of them were online. We may be able to trace those, but the ones I sold in the store, that's almost impossible."

Rodriguez asks, "Do you sell Arista cards?"

"Yeah, I got them, but nobody wants 'em. They're too expensive. Want to see them?"

"No, but thanks for your help."

Rodriguez is sitting with McMahon in Capt. Steiner's office, and he's looking through the file on Amy Styles. "I was thinking, what's the one thing that ties all the victims together?"

McMahon takes a sip of coffee and looks at Rodriguez. "Gambling, prostitutes, winners at the casinos, what else?"

Rodriguez says, "Amy, all of them had a date with what witnesses described as the girl next door type. I'll bet that girl next door was Amy in every case." Rodriguez checks the file and writes down the address. "I'm going to take a ride to her place and check things out. Want to come?"

"Can't, I've got to see Judge Johns in an hour."

"Ok, see you later."

As Rodriguez walks out the door, she shouts, "Hey, Rodriguez, don't break anything.

"I won't, I promise." Rodriguez drives to 86 Highland Place just outside of Vegas. He sees a sign that says Superintendent's Office and rings the bell.

A voice from inside yells, "Hold your horses, I'm coming."

Rodriguez thinks to himself, 'I only rang it once.'

The door opens, and the superintendent Alice says, "Hi, I'm Alice Furlong. What can I do for you? There's a waiting list if you're looking for a place."

Rodriguez shows his badge, "Hi, Ms. Furlong. I'm Sergeant Rodriguez. I'm here about Amy Styles. Mind if I ask you a few questions?"

She says, "Call me Alice," and she looks him up and down. "Sure, come on in. For a minute, I thought you were one of those Vegas dancers looking for a place."

"Really, do I look like a dancer?"

"Well, you look strong if you know what I mean. You want some coffee?"

He looks over at the coffee pot, stained and dusty, and replies, "No thanks, I just had a cup."

"So, Sergeant, how is she doing? Will she be coming home soon?"

"Alice, I have bad news about Amy. She passed away in the hospital."

Alice sits down, "Shit, I didn't realize she was hurt that bad. I read about it, but I didn't think it was that bad. It's so sad. She was such a nice person."

"Sorry to shock you, Alice, but there's a few things I need to ask you."

"No, it's ok. So, what do you want to know, Sergeant?"

"Did you ever meet her fiancé?"

"You mean boyfriend?"

"That's right, boyfriend. Have you met?"

"Sure, he used to come around. She met him on the strip." Alice leans in closer. "I think he's from New York and connected if you know what I mean, but he was always nice to me, but they said Al Capone was a nice guy too but don't cross him," and she gives him a wink.

Rodriguez changes the subject. "You said he came around. How often did he visit her?"

"Not much when they first met, but later he used to come around a lot. She used to complain that he worked too much with his business."

"Business?"

"Yeah, he had a landscaping business, Gino's Garden's, but it went bust recently."

Rodriguez sits up and leans forward. "Would you know if he used a truck for his landscaping business?"

"Sure, he had all the equipment, a few trailers, mowers, you know the usual landscaping stuff. He sold some of it after the business went belly up. Now, he does small jobs for friends mostly. But there's one thing he didn't sell and that's his truck. He loved that truck. He would never sell it."

"Does he keep his truck here?"

"Yeah, it's right downstairs in the garage."

"Mind if I see it?"

"Of course, let's go." They get to the garage and parked in spot 9F is a Ford F150. "That was her spot, same as her apartment 9F."

"Nice truck." Rodriguez takes out his phone and photographs the tires and notices traces of red dust inside the treads and a trace amount on the edge of the rims. He looks inside and it's clean, as if it were recently washed. He looks under the front seat and finds a small bottle full of liquid. He removes it and discreetly puts it in his pocket. "When was the last time he drove the truck, do you know?"

"No, he has a key, so he comes and goes whenever he wants." He looks in the bed of the truck, and it's pristine. He runs his hand between the license plate and the truck, and his fingers are covered in red dust. Alice notices and exclaims, "That red dust gets everywhere."

He rubs his hands together and looks at Alice. "Is there any way I can see her apartment?"

Alice is surprised by the question, and she hesitates. "I suppose it's alright. Come on, I'll get the key." Rodriguez is walking around the apartment and Alice tells him, "All these apartments are furnished, but this is one of the better ones. All the furniture is new. She got lucky 'cause now these apartments have a six-month waiting list. She got in at the right time.

He nods, "yeah, it's a nice place," and walks through the apartment followed by Alice. He notices literature on the coffee table from Gamblers Anonymous. "Alice, can I ask you something? Was Amy in GA? Was she a gambler?"

"No, she hated it 'cause of Gino."

Rodriguez turns and asks, "What about Gino?"

"I don't want to spread rumors, but I think he had a gambling addiction. When they first met, they would argue about it. She blamed gambling for Gino losing his business."

Rodriguez pauses and walks towards the door. "Thank you, Alice. I'm done."

They walk to the street and Alice says, "Thank you for telling me about Amy. It's so sad."

"Yes it is."

Alice looks him up and down again and asks, "Sure you're not a dancer?"

Rodriguez smiles and as he walks away, he shouts back, "Two left feet, Alice. I got two left feet."

Alice shouts, "Bye, Sergeant." He gets to his car and places the bottle in the glove compartment.

CHAPTER 41
DROWNING HIS SORROWS

Rodriguez arrives at Captain Steiner's office, and McMahon calls him in and closes the door. "So, what's this hunch you have about Gino?"

Rodriguez says, "Let me finish before you tell me I'm crazy, ok?"

"Ok, go ahead."

He begins, "The first time I met Gino, we were in the hospital, and I noticed he was wearing Jack of Diamond cufflinks, a gift from Amy. I did a little research, and I found a family-owned shop just outside of Vegas that sells 'em and besides the cufflinks, they have the Arista cards."

McMahon leans forward in her seat, "I hope that's not all you have."

"No, there's more. He had a landscaping business that went belly up. He sold most of his equipment except his truck. It's an F150. I'll bet the tire size matches the tire tracks at the scene of the murders."

"Now you have my attention, Sergeant. Keep going."

"I saw the truck."

McMahon cuts him off, "I hope you didn't break into his garage or some shit."

"No, I didn't. The rental agent showed it to me, a woman by the name of Alice Furlong." Rodriguez takes out his phone and shows her the pictures of the red dust in the tire threads. "I ran my hand behind the rear plate, and I got a handful of red dust. I had a drink with Marchetti last week, and he told me he was a serious gambler at one time, but he doesn't gamble anymore. He said he kicked the habit without Gamblers Anonymous, but I don't believe him. Twelve chips, twelve steps in GA. I found GA literature in Amy's apartment, don't worry I didn't kick the door down. The rental agent let me in."

McMahon sits back in her seat, "You're convinced he's Diamond Jack?"

"It all points to him. Look McMahon, two of the three men that hurt Amy are dead, and I'll bet the earlier victims also hurt her, and he killed them."

"So, what do we do with this information? I don't think there's enough for a warrant."

"If it is Gino, who's the next guy on the list?"

McMahon answers, "Dennis McCarthy."

"Yeah, It's time to put a tail on Gino. If we can't get a warrant, maybe we can keep an eye on him. I hope I'm wrong."

"I'll see if Steiner can put a couple of men outside Amy's house. If he picks up his truck, we'll follow him."

"No, I'll do it. Diamond Jack strikes at night. If he makes a move, I'll be there." Rodriguez gets up and heads for the door. "I'm heading out, McMahon. I'm gonna see if I can find Gino and give him my condolences."

"You think that's a good idea?"

"No, I don't, but it's the right thing to do."

"You don't even know where he is."

"I think I do he likes to do his drinking at The Cosmopolitan." Gino is at the bar drowning his sorrows and Rodriguez approaches. "Hi Gino, is this seat taken?"

"No Sergeant, sit down. What are you drinking?"

"Johnnie Walker Black, a little ice."

"Are you on duty? What happened to the red wine?"

"This feels like a Scotch moment, Gino. I wanted to give you my condolences. I'm sorry I know how you felt about her."

"Thanks, the last few days have been rough." The men make small talk and then Gino asks, "I read about that guy that made bail, what was his name again?"

"Dennis McCarthy."

"Yeah that's it. McCarthy. So, now what happens Sergeant?"

"He's got a court appearance scheduled. If he doesn't show, we issue a warrant, and he goes back in."

"Can I ask you a question, Sergeant? Do you really think Diamond Jack killed his friends?"

Rodriguez is surprised by the question "You know I can't discuss it with you Gino."

"Yeah, I get it, but don't you think it's strange that two out of the three guys you questioned turn up dead?"

Rodriguez finishes the rest of his drink and says, "Yeah, it's strange. I gotta takeoff." He throws money on the bar, "I got the drinks. See you, Gino, and again, I'm sorry."

Rodriguez goes to his car and calls McMahon, "How did it go with Gino?"

"He's torn up which makes what I'm about to ask you even harder."

"Go ahead, ask."

"Didn't we put a gag order on the names of the guys we questioned about Amy?"

"Yeah, we kept it away from the press and as far as I know, it didn't get out. The only thing I saw was a story on McCarthy making bail, but nobody knew that the two guys that were murdered had a connection to the case."

"Are you sure?"

"Yeah, I'm sure."

"Then how did Marchetti know?"

"Marchetti knew?"

"Yeah, he asked me if I was convinced that Diamond Jack killed McCarthy's friends. The question caught me off guard, and I didn't answer. There's only one way he could have known."

CHAPTER 42
THE FIRE WARDEN

Richie contacts Frankie. "I need you guys to meet me in the lobby of The Luxor Hotel. Have a seat. I'll meet you there at 6 tonight." Richie DiNapoli walks into the Luxor Hotel and sits across from the men in the lobby. After a while, Rinaldo gets off the elevator accompanied by one of his bodyguards and Isabella. He tells the men, "I'm going upstairs. If you see that guy come back, call me." Richie waits a while and then calls the front desk, "I'd like to speak to Achille Rinaldo please."

The concierge says, "Please hold. I'll connect you."

Richie remembered there were two bodyguards with Rinaldo a few nights ago, but only one left with him tonight. On the third ring, a voice answers, "Yeah, who is it?"

"Good evening, this is the hotel fire warden. Would you verify your room number for me?"

"Why?"

"I need your room number. Someone on your floor smelled smoke and we may have to evacuate. What's your room number?"

"I don't know, hold on."

The bodyguard returns to the phone. "It's Penthouse 4, but I don't smell no smoke."

"Penthouse 4. I'll be right up. The firemen just got here."

"Firemen? But where the fuck is the fire?"

"Stay in the room. The firemen are gonna check the floor. We're coming up." Richie stands by the elevator, looking through his pockets. A couple gets on the elevator and Richie says, "Do you mind if I ride with you? I can't find my keycard. Luckily my wife is in the suite." The couple look at each other and shrug. He presses the Penthouse, and the couple looks at him. "Business trip. I'm in pharmaceuticals. The company's paying." The couple say something to each other in what sounds like German. They smile at Richie and get out on the 14th floor and Richie says, "Good night." Richie keeps his head down to avoid the cameras. He knocks on the door and announces, "Fire warden, please open the door." The bodyguard opens the door and Richie pushes his way in and points the .38 at the man. He reaches for the gun in his shoulder holster, and Richie says, "Stop, you ain't fast enough. I'll kill you before you get it out." The bodyguard takes his hand away from his weapon and Richie walks over and takes the gun and tucks it into his belt. "Is that the only gun you got on you?" He nods yes but Richie knows he's lying. "I don't believe you. Put them all on the bed, guns, knives, whatever the fuck. Let me see them." The bodyguard puts the weapons on the bed. "Good, now sit down. Put your hands on your knees."

"So, you ain't no fucking fire warden are you?"

"Good guess."

"What's this about? What the fuck do you want?"

Richie looks at the man. "I need to have a few words with your boss." Richie notices a tray of food next to the man and he asks, "Were you having dinner? I'm sorry to interrupt. It must be tough being a working man while your boss is out with a piece of ass living it up."

The bodyguard is staring at Richie. "Wait, ain't you the guy from the bathroom the other night?"

Richie laughs. "That's the first time anybody's ever asked me that. It's kind of weird." The bodyguard attempts to reach for the knife on the tray and is noticed by Richie. "If you think I won't kill you, think again. So, what's your name?"

"Silvano," and then he asks, "What do you want with my boss anyway?" Richie is silent, then the man says, "You know he's going to be here soon, and then you'll be outnumbered, and I'm going to kill you."

"Dream on, asshole. I got no beef with you, just your boss." Richie looks around the suite. "Nice place considering it's the Luxor. What's with all the fake mummies in this joint?"

The bodyguard says, "It's my boss, he likes this Egyptian shit."

"It's all fake. If he likes it that much, why the fuck don't he go see the real one?"

"We been there. He's always traveling. So, what are you going to do, kill all of us?"

"That depends on you and your partner. Don't tell me you like working for this prick?"

"No, not really."

"So just step back and let me do what I got to do. I got nothing against you. So Silvano, what part of Italy are you from?"

"I'm from Malta."

"Malta, no shit. Did you know during World War 2 almost seven thousand bombs were dropped on that island?" Silvano looks at him. "I don't know. I wasn't born yet, so I don't give a shit."

"You should, Silvano. It's your history." There's silence, and then Richie asks, "What do you think this room goes for?" and he looks around the room. He loses focus for a second and the bodyguard takes advantage. He throws the tray at Richie and attacks him. Both men are rolling on the floor and the bodyguard reaches for Richie's gun. The man is bigger and stronger, and Richie is overpowered. He grabs the tray and hits the man in the mouth, and he could hear the crunch of metal hitting teeth. This stuns the man, and he begins to punch at Richie's face. The punches are blocked by the tray, and he hits the man again, this time across the nose drawing blood. He starts to get to his feet, and Richie hits him again in the knee, and he falls to the floor. Richie is on his feet now, and the tray has become his weapon of choice. As the man tries to get up, Richie hits him in the head, bending the tray, and the man goes down again. The tray is useless now, and the man is on his feet, and he throws his full body weight at Richie. They both stumble across the room, and they're fighting near the balcony. The bodyguard is attempting to hit Richie, but most of the punches are blocked. Richie fights back, but his punches don't have the same sting as in the past. The men crash through the balcony doors, and Richie manages to back the bodyguard up onto the balcony. The bodyguard reaches for another gun hidden in his pocket. Richie, seeing this, picks up a chair and pushes the man to the edge of the railing. The man fires a shot at Richie and misses. Richie continues to push the man closer to the edge, and he attempts to fire again, but one final push from Richie dislodges the railing and the man plummets four stories and lands on the roof of one of the hotel's gyms. Richie finds his gun and with the bodyguard's dinner on his jacket, he leaves the suite with his head down. He takes his jacket off and makes his way to the freight elevator.

When Frankie sees him, he asks, "What the fuck happened to you?"

He tells the men, "Split up and get out of here. The shit just hit the fan." Richie fast-walks through the lobby and gets in a cab as police and emergency vehicles arrive.

CHAPTER 43
FAKE COUTURE

A light rain is falling, and fog is settling on the crime scene. Las Vegas PD is there and roping off the area when McMahon and her team arrive. The only access to the roof is a ladder to the rear of the gym. McMahon climbs the 10 steps to the roof, saying under her breath, "Love my job." Rodriguez is right behind her, and he bounds up the ladder and gives her a wink. "Nice, Rodriguez. Show off a little." The first thing they see is the body of the bodyguard face down with a pool of blood around his head, and the section of railing close by. She points to the balcony with the missing rail and says, "Maybe he jumped, or maybe he leaned against the rail, it was loose and next thing, he goes boom."

"Boom, shit, that's cold, McMahon."

"What do you think, Rodriguez?"

He looks up and says, "How many people do you know that lean against balcony railings in the rain? Let's go check the room."

As they prepare to go up, Captain Steiner approaches. "The people next door heard a gunshot coming from the room about a half hour ago. Guess who's room this is."

Rodriguez answers, "Achille Rinaldo."

Steiner says, "Good guess. Come on, let's go up."

They enter the room, and they see the results of the struggle that took place. Rodriguez says, "Still think he leaned against the rail?" As they walk around the suite, Rinaldo comes rushing in, and he and Rodriguez lock eyes. Rodriguez whispers to McMahon, "Well, look who's here. Let's go say hello." Rodriguez and McMahon approach the group. "I'm Sergeant Rodriguez. This is Agent McMahon. We'd like to ask you a few questions."

Rinaldo is looking around the room and he asks, "What happened here, Sergeant?"

"Somebody from this suite went off the balcony, and he's dead. Do you know who he is?"

"That's tragic. One of my security details stayed behind when we went to dinner. It could be him. His name is Silvano Mosconi. He's been with me as part of my security for many years."

Isabella says, "Was it a robbery?"

Rodriguez asks, "And you are?"

"I'm sorry my name is Isabella Joia, I'm Mr. Rinaldo's personal assistant."

Rodriguez says, "Really, and what do you do as a personal assistant?"

"What are you trying to say, Sergeant?"

"We know you visited Amy in the hospital a few days before she died. How do you know her?" Isabella looks at Rinaldo. "Don't look at him, Ms. Joia. I was asking you."

Rinaldo speaks up, "I apologize, Sergeant. Ms. Joia is exactly what you think. We should have been honest with you."

"Thanks, but that still doesn't answer my question about Amy."

Isabella pauses, "Ok, Sergeant. We met through the business we're in."

"Business, what business is that?"

Rinaldo speaks again. "Is this necessary, Sergeant? Yes, she's an escort, and I'm paying for her company."

Rodriguez gets closer to Isabella, "I don't care about your personal business or your relationships, but the next time I ask you a question, don't lie to me."

Rinaldo responds, "It's my fault, Sergeant. I wish to keep our relationship discreet. She was following my wishes."

McMahon interjects, "I'd like to ask you a few questions, Isabella."

"Ok."

"Did Amy ever mention anybody who would want to hurt her? Boyfriend, client, does anything come to mind?"

"No, she never confided in me like that."

Rodriguez looks at the other bodyguard and Rinaldo offers, "This is Paolo. He's also part of my security detail. I'm afraid his English is not very good."

McMahon asks, "Are you here on vacation or business, Mr. Rinaldo?"

"Both, I had a meeting with a business associate some days ago, but now it's a vacation."

Rodriguez asks, "What kind of business are you in?"

"Designer clothing. I import couture fashions to the U.S. from Italy and France."

Rodriguez says sarcastically, "I thought that stuff was made in China."

Rinaldo bristles and glares at Rodriguez. "I don't import knockoffs, Sergeant, if that's what you mean."

"My apologies, do you import women's shoes?"

Isabella looks surprised, turns and looks at Rinaldo, and Rodriguez notices." "No, just clothing."

"You said you had a business meeting. Who was that with?"

"His name is Mansur Ayad."

Rodriguez glances at McMahon, "Is he still in Vegas?"

"No, he flew in for a few days, we had our meeting and he left."

"When was the last time you spoke to him?"

"Why the interest in Mr. Ayad, officers, when one of my employees is dead?"

McMahon says, "Just trying to cover all our bases. It's all routine."

"The night before he left is when we had our meeting. I understand he's traveling abroad presently."

"Do you know where?"

"No, maybe Turkey, but I'm not sure."

"What does he look like, this Mr. Ayad?"

"He's from Saudi Arabia, short and balding. He's an international businessman. He constantly travels."

Rodriguez asks, "Does his wife travel with him," and he looks at Isabella. The forensics team shows up with their equipment in tow. Rodriguez says, "I think you should ask for another room while the forensics team does their thing."

"You're saying I need to leave my suite?"

"I think it's for the best. How much longer will you be in Vegas?"

"I have business in Europe to take care of and another meeting here in Vegas. It's the fashion buying season, probably no more than a week."

"I see and just one more thing. Where was the meeting with Mr. Ayad?"

"It was at The Cosmopolitan. So now what happens, Sergeant?"

"Well, you'll have to identify the body, and I may have a few additional questions for you. So, Mr. Rinaldo, you have no idea who would want to kill a member of your security detail?"

"No, I do not."

"Do you think there's any chance you were the target?"

"No, I don't Sergeant. Perhaps it was a robber."

"Ok, we'll check the cameras. Maybe we can get a handle on what happened."

"Do you have any questions, McMahon?"

"Yes, just one. Did you meet Mr. Ayad's wife when he was here?"

"No, our meeting was brief."

"Ok, I think we're done. They'll let you know when you can identify the body. Do you know if he had any next of kin?"

"Yes. In Italy I think."

"We need whatever information you have on his family." Rodriguez says, "Good night, and thank you for your time. These forensic guys got a long night ahead of them. You may want to talk to the concierge about moving to a different suite."

As they're leaving the suite, McMahon turns and says, "Sorry for your loss." They're waiting for the elevator, and McMahon says, "He tells a good story. He's very convincing, but it's one big lie. Too bad we can't use anything you took out of that room."

Rodriguez interrupts, "That's bullshit, McMahon."

"I wish it was. Do you remember that meeting I had with Judge Johns the other day? Well, I got the word, Rodriguez. It's inadmissible."

Rodriguez rolls his eyes and pushes the button more aggressively. "Isabella has beautiful hair, doesn't she? It reminds me of what I took out of the shower drain in the penthouse at the Cosmopolitan."

"Too bad you can't prove it's hers."

The doors open and they step into the elevator and Rodriguez aggressively presses the button again.

He looks straight ahead and asks, "Did you see her face when I mentioned shoes? I think she'd look hot in stilettos. What do you think, McMahon?"

"Not my cup of tea Rodriguez, but I see where you're going."

CHAPTER 44
TEARS FOR AMY

Gino Marchetti is preparing for his final night as Diamond Jack. His precious Amy is gone, and he has one more score to settle. He prepares the chloroform, 12 chips and the five and seven of diamonds. What he doesn't know is that tonight, unlike other nights Rodriguez, is laying in wait. He's going through different emotions and at moments, he's sad and sobbing, then he's uplifted and giddy, thinking about Dennis McCarthy's demise. He tells himself, "I can't wait to see his face when I tell him who I am." He laughs out loud at the thought, and then he sobs knowing he'll never see his dear Amy again. He's ready to go into the night and finish the work he started. They all hurt Amy, and they paid the ultimate price, but there's one left.

The Las Vegas night is cool, and a fine mist is falling as Sergeant Rodriguez is watching the garage at Amy's apartment building. This is the third night he's been watching the house. He's waiting for Gino Marchetti to show up and drive his truck out of the garage. With Dennis McCarthy out on bail, tonight could be the night that Diamond Jack makes his move. After a while, a taxi stops in front of the garage and a man exits carrying a black bag and disappears into the building. After a while, a black truck drives out of the garage and heads away from the strip. Rodriguez follows close behind, maintaining a safe distance so as not to be detected. The men drive towards Spring Valley, an affluent family-oriented community just 10 miles outside of Vegas. This community is home to Dennis McCarthy. They arrive and the truck takes up a vigil across the street from a beautiful Tudor home on a 1/4 acre of land. Rodriguez drives the rest of the way with his headlights off and stops 100 feet behind the black truck. Time passes when suddenly the front of the house lights up and a man exits the front door. He hurriedly walks to the garage attached to the house. Diamond Jack sits up in his seat and watches as a grey Mercedes leaves the garage and drives towards the strip. The three vehicles drive towards the lights of Vegas, McCarthy followed by Diamond Jack with Rodriguez maintaining a safe distance.

Diamond Jack is waiting for the right time to make his move. He continuously looks in the rearview mirror and realizes he is being followed. He watches as the Mercedes goes through an intersection and as the light changes he speeds through narrowly missing oncoming traffic. Rodriguez attempts to get around stopped traffic but has to go into oncoming lanes to get through the intersection. McCarthy sees the truck and he speeds up, but Gino is on his tail. Rodriguez loses sight of the men, and he drives down a dark street near an industrial park. He looks to the left and sees both cars stopped and the men struggling. He speeds towards the scene and a gunshot rings out and he sees the flash of the muzzle as he approaches. Dennis McCarthy is on the ground as Diamond Jack continues shooting. Diamond Jack speeds off leaving a mortally wounded Dennis McCarthy in the road. Rodriguez reports the shooting and continues following the truck at a high rate of speed. They drive through the streets of Las Vegas, weaving in and out of traffic. Diamond Jack is taking Rodriguez towards the tunnels, hoping he can disappear into the darkness of the underground labyrinth. Rodriguez radios McMahon to inform her of the chase. The tunnels come into view and Diamond Jack breaks through one of the gates and drives into the darkness. Rodriguez follows and finds the truck sitting idle. Diamond Jack is on foot and making his way through the tunnels. Rodriguez draws his weapon and using a flashlight, goes into the tunnels.

He continues into the darkness and as he turns a corner, Diamond Jack is waiting, gun in hand. "Stop, Sergeant. Don't follow me, I don't want to kill you."

Both men are now facing each other with guns in hand. "You're under arrest, Gino. Give it up."

"No, Sergeant. I'll die first. Amy is gone. I have nothing to live for."

"Are you going to kill me, Gino?"

"You don't know what it's like to lose someone you love to these scumbags."

"I get it, Gino, but you can't bring her back."

"Did you know that she was a victim of human trafficking, Sergeant?"

"I suspected Gino, but I don't have enough evidence. Give me names, and I'll track them down."

"I don't have names. She would never tell me who it was. She was afraid of them."

"Put the gun down, Gino and come with me. I understand why you did what you did."

"You don't understand, Sergeant. I loved her, and she was taken."

At that moment, Gino puts the gun to his head and says to Rodriguez "I'm done, I have nothing to live for, Sergeant, and I'm not going to die in jail. Yeah, I killed all of them and put them on Red Rocks, because they hurt my Amy."

"Gino, put the gun down and let's talk. I won't make a move, just put the gun down, please."

Gino pauses and then he lowers the gun and says, "Go, ahead talk."

"The only thing I'm trying to do is save your life until we can sort it all out. How did you know McCarthy was involved?"

"I went to Steve Owens' funeral. They were all there insulting Amy and calling her a slut and a whore. We went out for drinks afterward, and the alcohol loosened them up. They told me everything about that night. I told them my name was Arthur Baker, and they fell for it, the stupid fucks."

"So, Billy Powers on the wheel of misfortune, that was you?"

"Yes, it was. It was brilliant, don't you think, Sergeant?"

"It's not brilliant, Gino. It's murder, and I've gotta take you in. All the victims in Red Rock, are you responsible for them?"

"Yeah, I made those rocks bleed, Sergeant. They were all my kills. They all hurt Amy."

"How did you figure it out, Sergeant?"

"It was a lot of things, Gino. It started with the jack of diamonds cuff-links. It seemed like quite the coincidence."

"Yeah, I bought those after the press named the killer Diamond Jack. It was perfect."

"That was just the beginning, Gino. I found red dust on your truck and all the victims had Amy in common. You knew that the last two victims were suspects and nobody would know that except the killer. You just killed McCarthy, the third suspect."

'You're right, Sergeant. I was going to kill anybody that laid a hand on her. There's only one left. Me. I can't go on without her. I should've done more to save her." Gino puts the gun against his head. "I'm not going to prison. I'll pull the trigger first."

"Don't do it, Gino."

Gino stares at Rodriguez and with tears in his eyes, he says, "Find out who did this to her. Goodbye, Sergeant." Gino fires and the echo of the blast goes through the tunnels. He falls to the ground, mortally wounded. In the distance, Rodriguez hears screams and people talking loudly. He calls for emergency services and runs over to see if there's anything that can be done to save Gino. Diamond Jack dies in the tunnels among the forgotten and the filth.

CHAPTER 45
FINDING RELIGION

The sun is rising in the morning after the deaths of Gino Marchetti and Dennis McCarthy. Rodriguez has filled out the reports and the necessary paperwork, and he's physically and mentally exhausted. As he's driving to his hotel, he passes a church. Anyone who knows him would not call Rodriguez a believer, but this morning there's something he has to do. He turns back and parks in the church's empty parking lot. As he enters the shrine, he remembers going to church with his family as a child. He would dress up on Sunday mornings and would sit through the ritual and as a child with lots of energy, which carried into his adult life, he would find himself bored. This morning was different as he remembers the death of his father almost twenty years ago, and the events of the previous night. Something inside is awakened and a feeling of peace and calm comes over him. He's forgotten the prayers he learned in grammar school, but he attempts to try. His memory fails him, and there are no formal prayers but a one-sided silent conversation with his father. His eyes are heavy, and he rises to leave the church. Before he leaves, he stops and lights a votive candle and says goodbye. He continues the drive to his hotel thinking about his father. His room is filled with light, and he knows he'll never get to sleep.

He calls Agent McMahon, and she answers sleepily. "Yeah ,Rodriguez, are you ok? It's early, you home?"

"Yeah, I just got in."

"It took you a while. Did you stop for a drink or something?"

"No, I actually stopped into a church that happened to have its doors open."

"A church

"Yeah, so I stopped. I was feeling spiritual after what's been going on."

"Welcome to the club, Rodriguez. I've been feeling spiritual almost every day on this job. Which church was it?"

"Not sure. It was on the way back to the hotel."

"So, how do you feel about it, Rodriguez?"

"About what?"

"Church, Rodriguez. How long has it been for you?"

"It's been years. I don't know how many, but it's been a long time. The last time I went, my father was still alive. I tried to pray, but I wound up talking to my father instead."

There's silence and then McMahon says, "So, what do we do now? Go after the trafficking angle?"

"Yeah, Amy was trafficked, and I'm gonna find out who's responsible."

"Are you going solo now Rodriguez or are we still partners?"

Rodriguez laughs. "Partners forever, McMahon."

McMahon says, "Get some rest. We'll talk later, and we'll come up with a plan.

. . .

Rodriguez is on the phone with Detective Spinelli. "Congratulations, Sergeant, on the Diamond Jack case."

"Thanks Marco, it didn't end well, and it was tough on me. I'll explain when I get back. In the meantime, I need you to investigate something for me. Last time we spoke, you told me that Justine Godfrey posted bail with no travel restrictions. Find out if she's still in Oceanview and let me know. How's Detective Jankowski doing? Is he settling into the job?"

"Yeah, he's doing really well."

"Thanks Marco, take care of yourself. Get back to me on Godfrey."

Rodriguez gets to Captain Steiner's office, and McMahon is there. "How are you, Rodriguez? Did you have breakfast?"

"Just coffee."

"Do you want something to eat? I'll buy."

"Thanks, but I'm good. Can I ask both of you a question? Did you ever feel like packing it in and getting the fuck out of Dodge?"

Steiner and McMahon glance at each other, and Steiner says, "Yeah, every day for the last seven years."

McMahon asks, "Why seven years?"

"Seven years ago last month my wife and son died in a car accident on Interstate 15. For the first few years, it was all I could do to keep from putting the gun in my mouth. So, to answer your question, yeah I thought about getting out and leaving Vegas, maybe heading east, but then I thought about it, and it seemed like that would be running away. So, this Marchetti blew his brains out. I understand it's tragic, but think about his victims, Rodriguez. This morning, kids are waking up without their fathers and wives with no husbands. Yeah they were scumbags, but in the end, it's the innocents who pay." There's silence and then Steiner asks, "So, Rodriguez tell us about this human trafficking connection with Amy and Diamond Jack?"

Rodriguez begins, "Before he died, Marchetti said that Amy was under the control of a human trafficking ring, but she never mentioned names. She was afraid." Rodriguez turns to Captain Steiner. "Didn't your men question David Evans? The last man she had a date with?"

"Yeah, but he didn't mention the trafficking thing."

"Did anybody ask him how he met her or who made the introduction?"

"No, he was lawyered up at the hospital and was advised to keep his mouth shut."

"David Evans can break this case wide open. All we need is a name."

"What do you have in mind, Rodriguez?"

"A phone call to Evans. After all, according to witnesses this guy defended her honor. How bad can he be?"

"Be careful what you say, don't put this department in jeopardy."

"Don't worry, Captain. I'll be nice, you know please and thank you and all that shit."

David Evans has a large and professionally decorated office in Silicon Valley. It's a typically hot day in the valley as David Evans strides into the office. With newspapers and magazines in hand, he bids his secretary Ms. Jackson good morning and takes his seat behind his custom-made African Mahogany desk and calls her into the office.

She asks, "Which coffee would you like today, Mr. Evans? The Jamaican Blue or the kopi luwak?"

"The Jamaican Blue, and get me one of those croissants from that French place."

"Yes, Mr. Evans." He turns on his laptop to get the daily stock reports and economic news. Ms. Jackson sends an intern to fetch the croissant and as she returns to her desk, the phone rings the first call of the day. She puts the call on hold and informs Mr. Evans, "There's a policeman named Rodriguez on the phone. He said he needs to speak to you about an urgent matter."

Evans says, "Another detective, really? What do they want from me? I told them everything. Tell him I'm at a meeting."

"I did."

"Then why is he still on the phone? Get rid of him."

"I tried, but he told me to tell you that if you don't take his call, he'll call you every chance he gets until he wears you out."

"Damnit, what's this cop's name again?"

"Sergeant Rodriguez."

"Well, well a Sergeant. Put it through. I'll take it." Evans pauses, motions for his secretary to leave the room and then picks up the phone, "Good morning, Sergeant."

"Good morning, Mr. Evans."

"Look Sergeant, I'll give you my lawyer's number, and you can talk to him, ok?"

"No, it's not ok. Why don't you tell your lawyer to take a walk, and you do the right thing."

"What do you want?"

"Tell me everything about Amy. How you happened to meet her and who was trafficking her."

"Like I said, Mr. Rodriguez, you can talk to my lawyer."

"It's Sergeant, and I want to know who made the introduction."

"This sounds like harassment to me. Perhaps I'll call my lawyer and see what he has to say about it."

"You do that and while you're talking to him, you can tell him that she died three days ago. or would you rather I tell him?" David Evans is silent, and Rodriguez says, "when your conscience has had enough you'll want to call me but don't take too long."

CHAPTER 46
THE NEW SUIT

Richie calls Frankie. "Meet me at the spot tonight around 8."

"What's up, Richie?"

"I'll tell you tonight. Bring Johnny, and I'll call Aldo. There's been a change of plans."

"You got it, Richie. We'll be there."

As usual, Richie is the first to arrive, and he takes the table in the corner facing the door. A while later, Aldo drives up in a brand-new Corvette and walks inside and greets Richie. "Hey, Richie Like my wheels?"

"Let me guess, Aldo, a pediatrician from Las Vegas."

"Close, Richie, a neurologist, but nice try."

"What happened to the Jag?"

"It's a long story, Richie. I see you're here first. I guess you already checked the joint out.

"Yeah, you know me."

At that moment, Frankie and Johnny enter the Diner, and the men sit down. Richie removes two envelopes from his pocket and slides them across the table. "Here hang on to these. Here's the rest of your money, plus 5 grand each. I need you to do something for me."

Frankie replies, "You got our attention."

"The other night at the Luxor, when you guys were in the lobby, I made a move on my target, and the shit went south."

Aldo asks, "Was that the guy I read about on the roof?"

"Yeah, that was him. We seemed to be getting along, and then he took a few shots at me, and I don't like it when people shoot at me. I even told him my beef wasn't with him."

Frankie asks, "So, what's the extra five grand for?"

Richie looks at the two men and waves the waitress over. "Let's get some coffees over here."

Johnny says, "I'll have a double espresso with a lemon rind, and can you sugar the rim of the cup?"

The waitress sighs. Richie looks at him and exclaims, "Sugar the rim? Where the fuck do you think you are, Johnny? At Rao's? It's a diner in Vegas."

Johnny shrugs his shoulders and says, "That's how I like my coffee."

Richie looks at Johnny and shakes his head. The coffees are delivered to the table and Richie leans forward, he stirs in the sugar and takes a sip. "I'm gonna level with you guys. My target is Achille Rinaldo, and the guy that went out the window was one of his bodyguards. Somebody wants Rinaldo dead, and I took the contract, so right about now he might be looking for a new bodyguard." The table is silent, and Johnny sits back in his seat.

Aldo says, "Are you going backwards, Richie? From capo to button man? I'm sure it's been a long time since you did any wet work."

Richie glares at Aldo. "It's been a long time, but I didn't forget how." Aldo puts his head down and continues drinking his coffee.

Johnny says, "Your mark is Achille Rinaldo, that fucking guinea pimp?"

"Yeah, the same. Why?"

"I did some bodyguarding for him when we were in Miami."

"What are you saying, Johnny? You know him?"

"Yeah I do."

"How well?"

"Well, enough that if I ran into him on the strip, he just might give me a job."

"For an extra ten grand, I'll do him, and you won't have to worry about it."

"No way, the contract's mine. I'll see it to the end, whatever that is. I have to get him alone. He's not taking any chances now that his body-guard's dead. I just need you to set him up. I'll tell you when, and I'll take it from there."

"I ain't asking who hired you, but what's a guy like Rinaldo worth to somebody?"

Richie evades the question, "There's a restaurant he likes on the strip called The Dove. It's an Italian joint right across from the Bellagio. Go there tomorrow night around seven, and maybe you'll run into him. I'll be across the street."

Frankie asks, "What about me? How do I fit in?"

"Hang loose, Frankie. Go do some gambling, spend some of that money. If I need you, I'll call."

"So Richie if I run into him, what do I tell him?"

Richie sighs. "You're a bodyguard. Tell him you were bodyguarding or whatever the fuck you guys call it. Listen Johnny, take some of that money I gave you and go buy some clothes. This restaurant is five stars. Look like you belong."

"Why, Richie? What's wrong with this suit?" Johnny's suit looks as if it's been slept in. His white shirt is stained, his belt is old and frayed, and his shoes are in desperate need of a shine.

"You're a good-looking guy, Johnny, but you dress like shit. Spend a couple of grand and get something nice. I'll see you tonight. He won't talk to you if you look like you're homeless."

"I ain't homeless, Richie."

"Don't show up like that. Get some nice clothes."

"What if he don't show, Richie?"

"If he don't show, I'll let you buy me dinner."

Rinaldo and Isabella are dressing for dinner and Isabella asks, "Where are we going for dinner? I'm tired of The Dove. Can we go somewhere else tonight?"

"No Isabella, we'll go there tonight and tomorrow night, you can pick the restaurant. Are you ready? I made reservations for seven.

"It's boring. It's always seven, and it's always The Dove. Can't we change it up, please?"

"Don't be a fucking diva, Isabella. Finish dressing and let's go. Paolo is coming with us."

"What else is new? Paolo is coming with us. Let's go, I'm ready."

From across the street Johnny and Richie are watching the restaurant. Rinaldo and his party enter The Dove, and Johnny begins to exit the car and is stopped by Richie. "Not yet, Johnny. Let them settle in. Give it time, don't jump the gun. I made reservations for you at 7:30. Try the osso bucco. I heard it's the best in town."

"I would but I don't eat meat, just vegetables. Maybe I can get a vegetable dish."

Richie looks at him. "Are you shitting me? You're a vegetarian? No fucking way."

"I am. I gave it up a few years ago. I feel better, you should try it, Richie."

"Yeah, sure. You still drink wine, right? You didn't give that up, did you? You're Italian for Christ sake."

"No, I don't drink nothing anymore, just water with lemon, Pellegrino water, seltzer stuff like that, but no booze."

Richie shakes his head. "What the fuck is this world coming to? Go ahead, Johnny. It's 7:30. Good luck. I'll be here for a little while to make sure it's ok."

Johnny exits the car and walks toward the restaurant, and Richie calls his name. "Hey, Johnny, I see you took my advice, nice suit." Johnny does a twirl and models the suit and continues toward the restaurant. Richie laughs and shakes his head. He enters and is seated a few tables away from Rinaldo's party.

Rinaldo and Isabella are in conversation, and she notices he's distracted as he periodically glances at Johnny's table. "Are you listening to me, Achille? I don't think you're paying attention to me."

"That gentleman over there, seated at the table near the corner, I think I know him."

"You mean the good-looking guy with the nice suit?"

"Yes, him. He was my bodyguard in Miami not too long ago. I believe his name is Johnny. He was quite good. I need a replacement, perhaps he would be interested. I want to speak with him, maybe he's unemployed at the moment. Isabella, use your charms and ask him to join us."

"Right now?"

"Yes, now go."

Isabella goes to the table and as she speaks to Johnny she gestures towards Rinaldo. Johnny peeks around Isabella, and Rinaldo waves him over. Johnny sits and Isabella sits next to him. Rinaldo notices and gives Isabella a look and says, "Isabella, I believe you were sitting here to my right." Isabella unhappily rises and sits to his right opposite Johnny. "There, that's better. Why play musical chairs, my dear? "Your name is Johnny isn't it?" "Yeah, that's me. I worked for you in Miami a while ago." "Yes you did so, Johnny, welcome to Vegas. What brings you to Sin City?"

"I picked up a gig shadowing a high roller, a real big fish, but it's over now."

"Did you hear, Isabella? He picked up a gig. I love the terminology, 'picked up a gig shadowing a high roller.'" Rinaldo is curious and he asks, "This big fish, is it somebody we might know?"

Johnny smiles and says, "The first rule of personal protection is never talk about the client."

"Excellent, Johnny, just as I thought. You see, Paolo? Loose lips sink well, you know the rest." Paolo shrugs and continues eating his roasted brussels sprouts. "So, Johnny, I would like it if you dined with us. Are you alone?"

"Yeah, but I don't want to intrude."

Isabella speaks up, "You wouldn't be intruding, Johnny. Join us."

Rinaldo gives Isabella a look. "Well, it seems you have a fan, Johnny. Try the osso bucco. It's the best in Vegas."

"So I've heard, but I don't eat meat. I'll get some vegetables or something."

Isabella offers, "Good idea, something different."

Rinaldo gives her a sideways glance and distributes the menus. "Here Johnny, whatever you want." Their dinner is served, and there's very little conversation. Halfway through, Rinaldo asks, "So, how long will you be in Vegas, Johnny?"

"Not sure. Depends on whether I can get another gig. I'll probably hang around for a while."

"Well, speaking of gigs, I'm looking for a good man for a short commitment that could become full time employment."

Johnny asks, "Are you offering me a job, Mr. Rinaldo?"

Paolo shoots Rinaldo a surprised look. "Relax, Paolo. I need to replace Silvano. So, when can you start, Johnny? How about tomorrow? Come to the Luxor in the morning around 10. We're in Penthouse 4 and we'll discuss your compensation."

"What happened to Silvano?"

"He had an unfortunate accident a few nights ago. A loose balcony rail I believe."

Johnny plays dumb, "Jesus, is he ok?"

"No, Johnny he's dead, so I'll need to replace him. Are you interested?"

"Sure, Mr. Rinaldo. I'll be there." Isabella smiles at Johnny and it's returned. From across the boulevard, Richie sees the scenario unfold. He gets into his car and drives away.

CHAPTER 47
THE JOB OFFER

Johnny arrives at Penthouse 4 at exactly ten am. Isabella is there as well as Justine and Augustus. He's greeted at the door by Isabella, and she gives him a smile and motions him inside. Rinaldo stands and offers Johnny a seat at the table. "Johnny DelVecchio, I'd like you to meet Augustus Becker and Justine Godfrey, and of course you remember Isabella from last night," he says with a dose of sarcasm.

Justine questions, "You've met before?"

Isabella answers, "Yes, we dined together last night."

Justine extends her hand and says, "It's a pleasure to meet you, Mr. DelVecchio, and by the way, I love your suit." She flashes Isabella a look of disdain that does not go unnoticed by Rinaldo.

Augustus shakes Johnny's hand and asks sarcastically, "Is Johnny another one of your partners, Achille?"

He gives Augustus a look and exclaims, "Where are your manners, Augustus? Johnny is part of my security detail. I needed to replace Silvano. So, now that the formalities are out of the way, how about breakfast? Johnny, what's your pleasure?"

"Just coffee for me. A double espresso with a lemon rind and ask them if they can sugar the rim of the cup."

Rinaldo lets out a laugh "How very Italian, Johnny. I'll make sure they do it exactly that way."

"We'll order a mixed pastry dish and some fresh fruit. Is that ok with everyone? Oh, and fresh juice, orange and tomato. Isabella, would you place the order? Johnny and I have business to discuss. Johnny, let's go into the other room where we can have some privacy." They go into a private room that is being used as an office by Rinaldo, and the men are seated. Rinaldo begins, "So, Johnny, what did I pay you in Miami those few years ago? Do you remember?"

"Yeah, it was 500 a day plus expenses."

"How is 600 a day plus expenses with a caveat."

 "A what?"

"A caveat, Johnny. A caveat, or more simply put, there's a catch, which when the time comes can make you a wealthy man. I remember when we were in Miami you entertained me with stories of how you did special jobs for your boss,' and he runs a finger along his throat."

Rinaldo begins, "I need protection of course, but I may also need someone to do, as you say, a special job for me. My stay in Vegas was supposed to be for a few weeks and no more as I had business in Turkey and Russia to tend to. Unforeseen circumstances have forced me to extend my stay beyond that period, angering my contacts over-seas. I need to show up soon, or the deal is fucked and so am I. I'll lose lots of money and a new trafficking pipeline. I'm surrounded by incompetent fools, and you've just met them."

Johnny smiles and says, "Go on."

"As a result, certain events have drawn the attention of the police and one cop in particular."

Johnny pauses and asks, "Who's this cop?"

"One thing at a time, Johnny. Be patient. If and when the time comes, I'll let you know. It's a last resort. I can't afford to be in Vegas much longer, and if things work out, perhaps you would consider becoming part of my permanent security detail."

"So, this could become a permanent gig?"

"Yes, a permanent gig as you say, and when that happens, you go where I go ,Johnny, and that's when the real money comes in."

There's a knock on the door and Isabella declares, "Breakfast is here."

"Before we go to breakfast, this cop I was telling you about, if we can't get him to back off, I want you to kill him. Johnny, can you do that?"

Johnny thinks and responds, "Yeah, I can. If I do, what's it pay?"

"Johnny, you need to look at the big picture. You'll be paid handsomely if the need should arise, but look to the future, ok?" Rinaldo doesn't give him a chance to answer. "Splendid, now let's have breakfast. I hope the espresso is to your liking."

They return to the dining area, and the table is set with the food beautifully arranged. Rinaldo is impressed and he asks, "Which one of you arranged the food so magnificently, was it you Justine?"

Justine responds angrily, "Why, do you assume that because I'm a woman, I set the table? That's just a little sexist, don't you think?"

Isabella exclaims, "Oh my, it seems someone needs a cup of coffee really bad."

Justine responds, "Fuck you, Isabella."

Rinaldo sternly interrupts, "We have a guest. Let's try to be civil please."

Augustus chimes in, "The guy that brought the food set it up."

"Marvelous, he did a great job. I hope you tipped him well." They settle in to breakfast and partly through the meal, Rinaldo gets everyone's attention and announces, "Johnny will be with us for the next few weeks and possibly permanently."

Paolo, who has been lying on the sofa reading an Italian sports magazine, sits up and looks over at Rinaldo. "What about me, boss?"

Rinaldo says, "Paolo, for someone who doesn't speak English, you understand it fairly well."

Paolo shouts, "Am I out, boss?" and goes back to reading the magazine."

Rinaldo shouts to Paolo, "Don't worry, Paolo. You'll always be with me. You're an old friend, did you understand that?"

Without looking up Paolo shouts back in broken English, "Thank you, boss."

"As to the matter of that nosey cop, Johnny said he would take care of it if the need should arise."

Augustus puts his cup down and asks, "Take care of it? Does that mean what I think it means?"

Rinaldo interrupts, "How's the pastry? It tastes just baked doesn't it."

Justine interrupts, "It means Johnny's gonna kill…"

Rinaldo stops her, "No names, Justine, no names. If and when the time comes, I and only I, will let Johnny know who it is." Rinaldo asks Johnny, "How's the espresso? Is it to your liking?" Johnny nods yes.

Justine smiles and says, "Welcome aboard, Johnny."

CHAPTER 48
MEET THE BARBARIANS

It's late morning, and Isabella awakens and leaves her bedroom. She finds herself alone in an empty penthouse and attempts to call room service, but as she reaches for her phone, it rings and it's Rinaldo. "Good morning, sleeping beauty. Nice to see you finally got out of bed. Remember what I said about what you can do in bed…"

Isabella cuts him off, "Yeah, I know the story. Where are you?"

"Remember those associates of Mansour Ayad I was telling you about? Well, they flew in last night, and they called a meeting for this morning, so here I am with Justine and these fucking cretins. They're barbarians where they come from. They stone people to death for adultery. Imagine that. Johnny is supposed to meet me there, but I'm stuck. See that he's comfortable, buy him breakfast or something. I should be back in a few hours."

Isabella orders her breakfast, and it's taking longer than usual. Finally, there's a knock on the door. Isabella shouts angrily, "It's about time." She pulls the door open and standing there is Johnny.

He asks, "Am I late to the party, or do you always answer the door wearing next to nothing?"

"Hi Johnny, I was waiting for room service and they're late."

"Room service. I'm sorry to disappoint."

"Come in, Johnny. Achille told me you were coming."

"So, he's not here?"

"No, he's not he's at some stupid meeting. I have no idea where. Rinaldo said I should buy you breakfast." She turns to face him and asks, "Would you like some breakfast?" and she opens her robe.

Johnny gets closer and says, "I'd love some." He takes her around the waist and kisses her, and she returns the kiss with more passion. They fall on the couch with Isabella on top. She unzips his pants and mounts him.

There's a knock on the door and a voice shouts, "Room service." The knock is ignored as they're caught up in their love making. The knowledge that Rinaldo could come walking through the door doesn't stop them. The sounds are heard through the door and the server puts the tray down and heads for the elevator. Meanwhile, inside the penthouse, the lovers roll off the couch and onto the floor laughing. Johnny is on top now and they both collapse into each other's arms.

Johnny catches his breath and says, "That was amazing. By the way, your breakfast is here," and they both laugh.

They lie together for a while and then Isabella sits up and says, "Shit, we better get dressed. He may be here any minute."

"Fuck him. Let's get naked. It'll be worth it to see the expression on his fucking pale face."

"Johnny, get dressed please. He can get a little nuts."

"Ok, ok I will."

Isabella runs into her bedroom and Johnny knocks on the door. "If you need some help, I'm here."

"Shut up, Johnny." Isabella returns to the living room, and Johnny tries to kiss her, and she pulls away. "You'll smear my lipstick, Johnny. He'll be here soon. It's been a few hours." They sit across from each other on the couch, she reading a fashion magazine, and Johnny looking at his phone. Occasionally, Johnny looks up and winks at her, and she smiles. The door opens and Rinaldo and Justine walk in, and Rinaldo is carrying a tray. Isabella whispers to Johnny, "Shit, I forgot the tray."

Rinaldo says, "Isabella, here's your breakfast."

"I'm not hungry."

"You're not hungry? You usually eat like a horse at breakfast."

"I said I'm not hungry."

"Johnny, would you like some ice-cold eggs?" Rinaldo looks at the tray, and he says sarcastically, "Sorry to say there's no espresso on this tray, Johnny."

Justine's eyes dart between Johnny and Isabella. Isabella asks, "How was the meeting?"

"It was interesting. They suspect I know more than I'm letting on about Mr. Ayad's disappearance. Apparently, they want to change the deal that we had which means I'm fucked. I was counting on that money to open up a network from Russia to Greece worth millions. Justine, order breakfast for us. Johnny, tell her what you'd like, and for me the usual." Isabella begins to give her order to Justine, and Rinaldo stops her. "Your breakfast is already here if you're hungry."

"But, it's cold."

"Too bad. You should have eaten it while it was hot." Justine looks at her and smiles. Isabella storms into the bedroom and slams the door. Johnny glares at him, and Rinaldo looks at Justine and says," Don't forget Johnny's espresso." Rinaldo goes to the bedroom door and knocks. "Isabella, I want a few words. Open the door."

"Go fuck yourself," is the reply from the room.

Rinaldo looks at the people in the room and says, "She can be emotional at times. Open the door, Isabella. There's no need for hostility." Isabella opens the door a crack. "That's better. We should have a talk." Isabella lets him in, and Rinaldo closes the door and grabs her by the neck. "Don't ever curse at me again, and don't forget you're still alive because of me. Do you realize I just spent 2 hours with fucking assassins? The kind of people who will cut your fucking head off for no reason, so excuse me if I'm a little edgy. They put me in a bad spot, Isabella. No matter which way I turn, I'm fucked."

"Get your hands off me, Rinaldo."

Rinaldo loosens his grip but keeps his hand around her neck, and he confronts her, "So, was he a good fuck?"

"What are you talking about?"

"Don't lie to me, Isabella. It was written all over your face, and you never bothered to have breakfast. You must have been distracted," and he smiles.

She pushes his hand away. "Yeah, I fucked him, and it was great, and I'm gonna do it again. Not because I'm getting paid, but because I want to. Now, tell that bitch to order me breakfast."

Rinaldo smiles, "Well, done Isabella. I love it when you're assertive, and you stand your ground." Rinaldo puts his hand on her breast, and it's swatted away. "So, you got lucky this morning. Go ahead, have your fun, but when I leave Vegas, he comes with me as my head of security, and you…well, I'm not so sure." He pauses and looks into her eyes. "Would you like the usual for breakfast, Isabella?"

She looks at him, "Yeah, the usual."

"Good, I'll let her know please join us." Rinaldo exits the room leaving the door open behind him.

After breakfast, Johnny leaves the penthouse and is walking on the strip. Richie calls. "Hi Johnny, can you talk?"

"Sure, go-ahead Richie."

"How's it going with Rinaldo? Does he trust you? I gotta make a move soon and get out of Vegas."

"Too much drama for me. I was supposed to meet with him this morning, but when I got there, he was gone. His assistant was there, and she gave me the royal treatment, if you know what I mean. Rinaldo wasn't too happy. I don't know what the fuck is up with them. Her name is Isabella, and here's the kicker: he may want me to kill a cop."

"You move fast, Johnny, but killing a cop, that's something you gotta really think about. Did he give you a name?"

"No, he said when and if the time comes, he'll let me know."

"Shit, this fucks up my plans big time. Anything else you can tell me?"

"Yeah, he's got a few people always hanging around. There's this guy Paolo. I think they go back a while, and another bodyguard, a big fucking dude. I think they've been with him a long time. This guy named Augustus, he's kind of Rinaldo's whipping boy, he treats him like shit."

"This guy Augustus, what does he look like?"

"I don't know, he's tall, looks like a Hollywood douchebag."

There's silence, and Richie exclaims, "Becker, is that his last name?"

"Yeah, that's it Richie. It's Becker, the whole bunch of them are into trafficking."

"Yeah I was told, and I know Becker. He's on the Vegas Gaming Commission. I've dealt with those pricks before. They always got their hand out. So, Becker is tied up with Rinaldo, anybody else?"

"Yeah, a broad named Justine Godfrey, acts like some kind of fucking socialite, looks like she don't want to be there."

"What do you mean?"

"Rinaldo treats her like shit too. She looks weak. If anybody in that bunch is gonna break and go to the cops, it'll be her."

"What about your girlfriend? What's her story?"

"I don't know, and I don't care. I think she's in it for the ride. When I worked for him in Miami, I heard stories about him. He's got some weird fetishes, a real fucking strange dude".

"Take my advice, Johnny, don't get involved with this cop thing. It's no good."

"Don't worry, Richie. When I find out who the cop is, I'll let you know, then I'll set up Rinaldo. I ain't killing a cop. I know better, besides I got no beef with this cop."

"Good, Johnny. I think you should stay away for a while. If you keep coming around, Rinaldo might get suspicious. Let him reach out to you when he needs you and don't be too eager."

CHAPTER 49
THE DRINKING CONTEST

Isabella is alone in the penthouse, Rinaldo having gone to another meeting. She's bored, and her efforts to reach Johnny are fruitless, and she paces, not knowing what to do. Rinaldo insisted that she wait in the penthouse for his return. She sits down with the latest Italian fashion magazine and begins to read when the doorbell chimes. She's visibly annoyed, and she slams the magazine on the table. "Yes, who is it?"

"It's Justine. Am I interrupting something?"

"No, come in," and she opens the door. She turns her back to Justine and sits down. Justine enters and looks around the room. "Where's Achille? Are you alone?"

"He's at some stupid fucking meeting with his oversees contacts, the ones he calls barbarians. So, Justine, I was about to have a drink. Would you like one, is vodka ok?"

"I'll have a vodka on the rocks." Isabella hands her the drink and they sit not talking. Finally Justine asks, "How's Johnny?"

Isabella replies, "I don't know. We haven't spoken in 3 or 4 days."

"That long? Is there trouble in paradise?"

"None of your business, Justine. Do you want another vodka?"

"Sure, if you have one with me."

Isabella reaches for a bottle of Vodka and asks, "Are you trying to draw me into a drinking contest, Justine?"

"Pour, Isabella, and don't be cheap."Isabella pours for both of them, and the contest commences. As they drink, the tension between them increases, and the alcohol loosens lips. Justine is feeling the effects, and she says, "You know Isabella, I had my eye on Johnny before you." Isabella looks at her with her eyes half closed, and Justine continues, "How is he in the sack? Is he as good as he looks?" she says, slurring her words.

"Let's just say he can handle himself."

"What about you, Isabella, can you handle yourself?

"There's one way to find out, Justine."

Justine is surprised. "Don't tell me you like girls."

"I like whoever is paying me."

Justine pauses and asks, "What about me, do you like me?"

She replies, "Yeah, you're sexy in a school teacher kind of way, you know the kind that sleeps with her students," and she laughs. Justine makes her way over to where Isabella is sitting. She drops down next to her and slowly moves in to kiss her. Isabella moves her head to make it easier for her. They kiss passionately for a while, and Justine moves her hand to Isabella's thigh when suddenly she's stopped, and Isabella sits up and grabs the bottle. "Come on, let's keep going. We don't have a winner yet. Maybe after a few more drinks, we can pick up where we left off." Justine extends her glass, and Isabella pours but half goes in the glass and half winds up on the rug.

Justine laughs. "You're drunk, you missed my glass."

They continue drinking and Isabella slurring her words asks, "So, what were you saying about Johnny? You had your eye on him or something? Well too bad, Justine. I got him first, maybe he likes them younger."

Justine stares at Isabella. "No, I think he likes them slutty and easy, just like you. I would have made him work for it." Justine is staring at Isabella, and she continues. "He would have bought me nice clothes, some jewelry, but you gave it up right away because you're a whore. That's why Rinaldo wants you around."

"Fuck you, Justine." Isabella starts to lunge at Justine but falls back on the sofa and begins to laugh. "I'd kick your ass, but I'm too drunk," and her head goes back. "Oh shit." The room is spinning, her voice trails off, and she falls asleep.

Justine stands up and walks toward Isabella saying, "I won the contest bitch." She sits down next to her and also falls asleep, her head on Isabella's lap. A few hours later, Justine wakes up to the sound of Rinaldo returning from his meeting. When he walks in, he sees the empty vodka bottle and Isabella still sleeping.

He stops and looks at the scene. "So, Justine, what happened here? Did Isabella get tired of waiting for me?"

Justine replies laughingly, "No, Achille. We had a drinking contest, and I won, and you know what she told me, Achille? She told me she likes girls, and we made out."

She bursts into laughter and Rinaldo says forcefully, "I'm going to bed. Justine, you better leave now. Go, get out."

"Why don't I just sleep here on the couch?"

"No, I would prefer it if you left."

"Ok." Justine slowly gets up and staggers towards the door, turns and says, "Good night, Achille, and by the way, tell Isabella I won the contest."

Rinaldo declares sternly, "Get out, Justine." He walks to the bedroom and slams the door behind him.

The following morning Isabella awakens as sunlight pours through the window. Her eyes slowly open, and there is Rinaldo sitting watching her. She's startled, and she sits up as Rinaldo smiles and hands her a glass of orange juice. She says sleepily, "Thank you, my mouth is so fucking dry," and she takes the juice. "How long were you there watching me?"

"Not long, and by the way, I love those red lace panties you're wearing."

"Son of a bitch. You looked while I was sleeping, you bastard."

He smiles. "It was just a peek. Now, take a shower, get dressed and order breakfast."

"I don't feel like eating. My head hurts from last night. What time did you get in?"

"A little after 1."

"Why didn't you wake me and put me to bed?"

"Consider it a lesson learned. You shouldn't be drinking that much if you can't handle it. Now, order breakfast. I'll have the usual." He gets up and heads towards the office. "Call me when it arrives. Oh and by the way, Justine wants me to tell you that she won the drinking contest."

Isabella snaps back, "The bitch." he laughs as he closes the door to the office.

Breakfast arrives and they sit quietly, and Isabella is picking at her food, and Rinaldo says, "You should eat." He continues eating and looking at her, and he asks, "Have you heard from Johnny?"

"It's funny, but Justine asked me the same question. She told me she had her eye on Johnny, but I beat the bitch to him."

Rinaldo smiles and replies, " So that would explain the drinking contest. It was all about Johnny wasn't it? It's amusing, but don't let Johnny get in the way of our business."

Isabella asks, "And at this point, just what exactly is our business, Achille?"

"It's very simple: a king's ransom will be deposited in several banks scattered throughout the islands and overseas. It's seed money to get our middle east business off the ground, but first we need to find out what the police know, and then we embark on a world tour, recruiting new merchandise, and by next year, we won't know what to do with all the money."

"Who's we, Achille?"

"Me, you and Johnny as my personal bodyguard."

"What about Justine and Augustus? Where do they fit in?"

"I was thinking of sending them to Turkey or Morocco, and letting them fend for themselves. If they survive, we'll reunite."

"You're evil, and what police are you talking about?"

Rinaldo thinks about the question for a while. "The 2 policemen that asked me questions the night Silvano died. What was her name, the female cop, do you remember?"

"Yes, it was McMahon."

"McMahon, that's right." Isabella begins to eat and Rinaldo smiles. "So nice to see your appetite is back. So, you haven't heard from Johnny. I think I'll call him. Would you like to speak to him?"

Isabella replies sternly, "No, I can call him myself."

Rinaldo smiles. "Suit yourself."

CHAPTER 50
THE PRINCE OF THE TUNNELS

The Prince, whose real name is Jason Velez, is holding court in his small corner of the tunnels. He's 25 and grew up on the streets of Las Vegas and has been in and out of the local jail many times. These arrests were mostly for petty crimes and minor drug offenses. Since he was 22, he's been the leader of a ragtag group of young teens who fan out at night along the strip looking for victims. They use knives, pepper spray and intimidation to rob people of their winnings or whatever they happen to have in their pockets. In this army is Tommy, an 18-year-old that grew up in a chaotic home, abused by his alcoholic mother and a drug addicted father. Tommy is a born leader who could lead this group better than The Prince, but he doesn't dare go against him. The Prince knows this, and he keeps him close and uses him as his enforcer. Carlos is another soldier in this army. He's an orphan, abandoned at birth who escaped from an orphanage by stabbing a security guard who luckily survived. Alice is a 16-year-old who looks older than her years, and she uses this to lure men into the parking garages that honeycomb Las Vegas, and she robs them when they are most vulnerable. There's several other "soldiers" that come in and out of The Prince's circle. They sit in waiting for words from their leader, The Prince. He's not happy this morning as he goes through the box where the night's take is placed.

He focuses on the bills, occasionally looking up at his band of soldiers gathered in front of him. He comes across a watch, and he happily holds it up for all to see. "Who got this?"

Alice shyly raises her hand. "Me."

He says, "See this? It's a Rolex. Not a very good one, but it's worth a couple of grand. So, Alice, tell us how you got this watch."

Alice looks around and she begins, "This dude picked me up on the boulevard. He offered me 20 bucks to mess around a little, and I said ok, so he took me to a garage, and when his pants were around his ankles, I put my knife to his balls, and well you know."

The Prince laughs a hearty laugh. "You're a bitch, Alice. So, tell us, did you mess around with him after he gave you the watch?"

"Hell no." Everybody laughs, and the Prince holds up the bills. "I counted 354 dollars. There's seven of you. What the fuck is going on? Alice brings me a watch worth about 2 grand, and the seven of you bring me 354 dollars? Are you holding out on me? Give Tommy all the money you have in your pockets, and don't you hold out on me."

Tommy speaks up, "Maybe it was a slow night, Prince. It ain't their fault."

"Get their money now, Tommy."

"Sure Prince, but it ain't right.

"Do it, Tommy, and shut up."

Since the death of his father at the hands of Rinaldo, Mark has survived on the mercy of the other inhabitants of the tunnels. He hears about The Prince, and that he's always recruiting new soldiers for his army. He finds The Prince's headquarters and as he approaches, he's stopped by a guard who looks down at him and asks, "What do you want?"

Mark answers, "I want to talk to The Prince."

He stares straight ahead and says, "Get lost, there ain't no Prince here."

"Bullshit, I know he's here, they told me."

The guard glares at Mark, "Get the fuck out of here, kid. Don't make me kick you in the ass." Mark reaches behind his back and pulls one of his father's guns and points it at the guard. "What the fuck, kid? Put that away. You ain't scaring me. That shit ain't real."

"Yeah it is, and it's loaded."

The guard stands his ground. "Bullshit. It ain't loaded."

"Tell The Prince I want to talk to him."

The guard looks at the gun and says, "Get lost, you ain't shooting anybody."

The Prince, hearing the commotion, goes outside and sees Mark with the gun pointed at the guard and tells Mark, "Let me see the gun, kid. I'll give it back if you promise not to shoot anybody." He checks the gun and finds that it's loaded. He turns to the guard and says, "It's real, and it's loaded. He could've killed you, asshole. Come on, kid. Walk with me." As they walk, the Prince asks, "What's your name?"

"Mark."

They stop, and the Prince tells Mark, "I'll keep the gun."

"No, it's my father's gun."

"Do as I say or walk back out the way you came in. We don't use guns, and where's your father? Does he know you're threatening people with a gun?"

"He's dead, they killed him."

"They, who's they?"

"They shot him 'cause we helped a cop. It was 2 guys."

"Sounds complicated, kid. So, give me the gun or take a walk." Mark reluctantly gives the Prince the gun. The Prince smiles and nods his head. "You get time added if they catch you with a gun. So, how old are you, kid?"

"I'm 18."

Prince smiles. "Bullshit, I figure you're 15 or 16. Come on, I'll introduce you to the other guys. Maybe you can go out tonight with Tommy, but I'll hold on to the gun."

Mark enters the room with the Prince, and all eyes are upon him.

Carlos speaks up, "Who's this kid, Jason?"

"It's not Jason, it's Prince, and the kid's name is Mark. He's old enough to join us, and tonight he's going out with you, Tommy. I want you to show him what we do."

"Bullshit, Prince. I don't want some kid hanging around slowing me down."

Prince reaches behind his back and takes out the gun and shows it to his gang. "See this? It's Mark's, and it's loaded."

Mark shouts out, "Yeah, and I got 2 more hid away with the bullets."

The Prince looks at Mark. "You got more guns?"

"Yeah, I got bullets for all of 'em."

"You hear that? We got guns now. Take me and Tommy to 'em."

Mark replies, "Sure, come on." They wind their way through the tunnels and at times, Mark seems to be lost, but finally he finds the room he shared with his father. Mark lifts a loose rock off the floor, and the 2 guns and boxes of bullets appear.

Prince says, "Grab 'em, and give them to me."

As he hands him the guns, Mark says, "I shot a guy with that one."

The Prince looks at Tommy, and Tommy smiles, "Sure you did."

"You don't believe me, I'll show you." Mark removes the barricade and takes them into the room with the chair. The chalk marks that outlined the bodies of the men killed by Rodriguez are still barely visible.

The Prince exclaims, "What the fuck is that smell?"

"I don't know, but four people died in this room, and my father was one of them. That cop I told you about killed 2 guys in here. He electro-cuted them."

"Shit, that's what that smell is."

"Yeah and look, here's the bloodstains from the guy I shot. I think I got him in the leg. He was bleeding a lot, and then I ran."

"Why did you shoot him, kid?"

"He was one of the guys that killed my father. The other 2 got away, but I know what they look like."

"Sounds like you've been through some shit, kid. So, who's taking care of you now?"

"My father had some friends. They been feeding me and stuff like that, but I wanna join your gang."

"Yeah, well it ain't that easy, kid. Go out with Tommy tonight. Let's see how you do." The Prince unloads one of the guns and hands it to Tommy. "Maybe this'll help you have a better night."

CHAPTER 51
IT WAS A GOOD NIGHT

The sun is rising in Las Vegas and beams of light penetrate the darkness of the tunnels. Through openings on the surface, the light fills portions of the tunnels. The Prince leaves the comfort of his bed, and the warmth of his lover and begins the daily process of deception. The Prince doesn't live in the tunnels like his army, but he leads them to believe that he's one of them. His life is much different than the life of his soldiers. He lives in the heart of Vegas in a beautiful apartment right off the strip, dines at fine restaurants and drives an expensive car. He finances this lifestyle by selling drugs, mostly cocaine, to tourists. He also has a regular clientele that he services out of his apartment. He puts on his tunnel clothes, ripped jeans, a soiled tee shirt, and a flannel shirt, and goes to work. His army is gathered as he enters the meeting room.

As he walks in, the room becomes quiet. "Good morning my friends. I hope you had a better night last night." Tommy hands the Prince the box and whispers something to him. The Prince shouts, "Listen up, our newest member Mark went out with Tommy last night, and what happened Tommy? Tell us how Mark did." Tommy reaches into his pocket and pulls out a stack of bills and jewelry. He puts the money on the table along with a watch, rings, and necklaces. "Take a look people, that's what you should all be doing." He turns to Tommy. "Did you use the gun?"

"Yeah, he did. He's a natural, Prince. You should have seen him."

Prince removes the other 2 guns from a lockbox hidden away in the room, and he holds them up for all to see. "Who wants these?" He asks, and nobody answers. The Prince says, "Tommy, give this to Carlos."

Carlos says, "I thought we don't use guns. I don't want it, Prince." "Take it. It's not loaded. This way there's no accidents. Use it tonight, Carlos."

Carlos reluctantly takes the gun from the Prince. "What if I get caught, Prince?"

"Don't get caught, and if you do, leave my name the fuck out of it." Carlos just stares at the Prince. "Is there something you want to say?"

"No, Prince, we're cool."

The Prince stares back. "Yeah, we're cool. I'm expecting some big numbers from you tonight. Don't disappoint me." All of you get over here," and his army gathers round him as he hands out envelopes filled with cash. "It might be a little light, but you can blame yourselves for that. The more I get, the more you get. I thought you would have figured it out by now." The group disbands and walks off in different directions. The Prince smiles and shouts, "See you tonight at sundown."

CHAPTER 52
THE RUSSIAN CONNECTION

The Penthouse is quiet as Justine and Isabella sit sipping champagne as classical music from Rinaldo's favorite composer, Gioachino Rossini, plays in the background. Rinaldo is in his office conducting business with his overseas contacts. "This is fucking boring. Let's go out, Isabella, and meet some men. We can lure them to my hotel room and have some fun, and you and I can pick up where we left off the night. I outdrank you. I think they would love it."

Isabella puts down the Italian fashion magazine that she's read cover to cover a dozen times, and she looks at Justine. "Sorry Justine, but that will never happen. I have a date."

"A date? Don't tell me Johnny finally got in touch. Where was he all this time?"

"He was busy, Justine, and it's none of your business."

"Sure, he was busy. He was busy banging showgirls. Do you think guys like Johnny are happy with one woman who just happens to be a hooker? Wake up, Isabella."

"Shut up, Justine. You're jealous that he didn't pick you, because you're a dried-up middle-aged socialite."

"I'm not middle-aged. I'm 37, and I don't fuck for money like you."

"No, you just fuck for jewelry or real estate or whatever is available. We're the same. We just take different forms of payment."

There's silence and then Justine asks, "Did I ever tell you how my parents died, Isabella?"

Isabella shakes her head in the negative, "no."

"They burned to death in a fire. It was at our mansion in Connecticut and one night, something happened with the wiring, and it started a fire."

"Why are you telling me this?"

Justine stares straight ahead. "Do you know how many different ways people can die in a fire, Isabella?" Justine stands and begins walking around the room. "There's smoke inhalation, there's burning to death that's very painful until the fire burns the nerves. Then you don't feel anything and sometimes when they're desperate for oxygen, they inhale, and the heat burns their lungs." As she speaks, there's no emotion and no sadness, considering her parents died that way.

Justine sits down again and stares at Isabella who says, "You're cold as ice, Justine. I wish you would leave now I have to get ready."

"Oh that's right. I forgot. IT'S JOHNNY. Have fun bye" As she gets to the door, she turns and says," Have a good night."

Isabella says to herself, "What a crazy bitch."

Rinaldo comes out of his office and asks, "Was that Justine I just heard leave?"

"Yes, she just left. She's fucking nuts. I'm taking a shower, and I'm going out with Johnny. I'll be away for a few days."

"A few days? So, it's back on?"

"It was never off, Achille."

Rinaldo smiles and asks, "Do you need someone to scrub your back, Isabella?"

"No, thank you." Isabella walks to the bathroom and slams the door.

Rinaldo shouts through the closed door, "I'm also going out. I'm meeting some associates tonight, because one of us has to work."

Isabella steps out of the bathroom and begins to dress for her weekend with Johnny. She finishes packing her bag just as Rinaldo is getting ready to leave. He's putting on his jacket and she asks, "Are you meeting with the barbarians again?"

"Close, they're Russians. Too bad you have other plans, Isabella. These Russian assholes are always boasting how beautiful their women are, and I would love to walk in there with you on my arm to show them what real beauty looks like."

Isabella turns. "Thanks Achille, I didn't think you felt that way about me."

"What way is that? Isabella, you're stunningly beautiful, and you and everybody else knows it. I find Russian women to be demanding, frosty and they smoke and drink too much."

"Well I'm off. I don't want to keep those commie bastards waiting. I want to do business in that part of the world. It could be worth millions."

Rinaldo arrives at a five-star Russian restaurant owned partially by Russian gangsters. He's ushered to a table occupied by 3 men and 2 young girls. One of the men stands and greets him with a hand extended, "I'm Yuri Lebedev. Nice of you to come, Mr. Rinaldo. These are my associates Vladimir and Alexander." The 2 men nod and keep their eyes focused on him. Yuri looks around and says, "You came alone, no bodyguards?"

"I didn't think I'd be needing them, and who are these 2 lovely girls?"

"Oh, how rude of me. This is Svetlana and Irina. They work for me in a manner of speaking."

"Nice to meet you." The 2 girls just stare, and Rinaldo asks, "Do they speak English?"

"No, they are new to your wonderful country."

"How old are they, Yuri? They look very young. If we do business together, no underage trafficking. I had an associate from France who dabbled in it for a very discreet clientele, and now he's in prison and very popular, if you know what I mean."

"That's unfortunate. I brought them along for you if you require some company at the conclusion of our meeting, but as you just stated no underage trafficking."

"I said no underage trafficking. I said nothing about my personal tastes," he says, his eyes darting between the two girls.

"What if I told you they were my daughters?"

"I'd say you were lying."

The bodyguards look at Yuri and he nods. Yuri is serious, and then he laughs a loud belly laugh, "I like you, Achille. At the conclusion of our meeting, they're yours. I heard you're a man who gets to the point, so let's talk business and drink some vodka. I'm hungry. What about you, Mr. Rinaldo?"

"I could eat."

CHAPTER 53
FIRE AND ICE

Isabella is finished packing, and she texts Johnny that she's on her way to the Sunrise Valley Resort, a 5-star resort about 15 miles from Vegas where they'll spend the weekend together. He insists on picking her up, but Isabella always preferred to go on dates with her own means of escape in case the evening took a bad turn. The valet brings her car, and she leaves the garage, driving west.. She drives about five miles on the approach to Highway 159 when the car begins to shake, and the steering wheel pulls to one side and then comes the tell-tale sound of air escaping from one of her tires. "Shit I can't believe this. What perfect timing." She's reaching for her phone to call Johnny when a car comes up behind her. The driver leaves the car and walks toward her, and in her rear-view mirror she sees the figure of a woman. She closes the window and as the figure gets closer, she sees that it's Justine, and the window opens again. "Thank God it's you. I thought it was some serial killer or something."

Justine looks at the tire and says, "Flat tire. That's terrible. I'll help you change it."

"That's ok, I'll just call him. He'll drive out and help me, but thanks anyway. What are you doing out here, Justine?"

"I was following you, Isabella. You see, I cut a small hole in the tire valve stem. You know that little thing where you put the air in. It kind of looks like a woman's nipple."

"What are you talking about? Why the fuck would you do that?"

Justine puts a knife to Isabella's throat. "Do as I say, and I won't kill you."

"Justine, what are you doing? Take that knife away, please."

"Do as I say. I'm not fucking around, bitch. Text Johnny and tell him you can't make it. Tell him Rinaldo is sending you away tonight. Do it and I'll take the knife away."

"Fuck you, I won't do it." Justine presses the knife against her throat and draws blood. Isabella is frightened. "Please take the knife away, Justine. I'll text him, but please promise me you'll take the knife away."

"I promise. Now, text him." Isabella reaches for her phone, and with trembling hands, she texts Johnny. Almost immediately, Johnny texts back.

"Don't answer it, Isabella."

"I have to, Justine." In an instant, Justine grabs Isabella by the hair and slams her face into the steering wheel once, twice, three times until Isabella is dazed. She takes Isabella's phone and purse and runs back to her car and removes a gas can from the trunk. In the distance, she sees a car approaching, and she places the can on the floor and sits Isabella up in her seat.

The car stops, the window goes down and a man's voice yells, "Do you ladies need some help?"

Justine turns and smiles, "No thanks. We're good. Her boyfriend is coming. We'll be ok, thanks."

"You sure? I can change it in a minute."

"Yeah, we're sure thanks again." Isabella begins to stir, and Justine shields her from the man's view with the knife again at her throat and tells her, "Make a sound, and I'll kill you."

The man yells, "Want me to stay with you till he gets here?"

Justine turns and angrily responds, "We're ok. Now, get the fuck out of here."

The man leaves yelling, "I'm just trying to help. No need to curse, bitch."

Isabella begs, "Please stop, Justine. Let me go."

Justine slams her head into the steering wheel one more time. She takes the gas can, empties it into the car, and a half gallon of gas pours over Isabella. She begins to regain consciousness at the same time that Justine ignites the gasoline. Along this isolated stretch of road no one heard her scream.

CHAPTER 54
WHAT IS YOUR EMERGENCY

"911 operator, what is your emergency?"

"There's a car on the approach to Highway 159 and smoke is coming from the driver's side and it looks like there's a body inside behind the wheel." It's at mile marker 132 going west just before the entrance to 159."

"Is the car on fire?"

"No it's just smoke. I don't want to get close, but maybe I should see if the person is still alive."

"No sir, just stay where you are. There's danger. The car may explode. Is the person moving or able to talk?"

"No, she looks dead. There's smoke coming from her body. There's no damage to the car, it looks like somebody set her on fire. I smell gasoline. Is anybody on the way? What's taking so long?"

"I've dispatched units, sir. They're on the way. You said you don't see any signs of an accident, you said there's no damage and you also said there's a woman inside?"

"I think so, but I'm not sure. Looks like she's burned really bad." In the background the sound of emergency vehicles penetrates the quiet. The driver sits mesmerized staring at the wisps of smoke from the passenger side of Isabella's car. He sits waiting for the authorities to arrive.

CHAPTER 55
THE TUNNELS RESPOND

Mark and Tommy are on the strip looking for targets. Tommy is advising Mark on how to pick victims to rob. "See that guy with the boots and the cowboy hat? Avoid dudes that look like that."

Mark asks, "Why?"

"Take a good look at the guy. He's probably from Texas. They all carry in Texas. I guarantee he's packing. You don't want to fuck with him."

"What about that guy over there? He's drunk, and he's dressed nice. He looks like he's got money."

"Wrong, kid. He's a cop. His name is Hector. He's undercover. Definitely don't fuck with him. You'll see him around." Tommy points to a man talking to 2 young girls. He's handsome and well dressed. "Hey, Mark, look at that guy. He's begging to get robbed. See him talking to those 2 girls?"

"Yeah, I see him." Mark stares at the man, and it dawns on him. "Holy shit, Tommy. That's one of the guys that killed my father."

"Get the fuck out of here. Are you sure, kid?"

"Yeah, I'm sure. I'll never forget him."

"Damn, what do you want to do, kill him?"

"No, I don't want to kill nobody. Let's take him to the tunnels. Maybe I'll shoot him in the leg or something and leave him there."

"How do we do that? We got a gun with no bullets." Mark reaches into his pocket and takes out a handful of bullets. "Shit, where did you get these?"

"I had some bullets hidden away. Prince didn't get them all. Keep an eye on him, Tommy. I'm going to load the gun, and we'll take him to the tunnels."

"And how're we going to do that?"

Mark thinks for a minute then says, "Let's get garbage bags and some duct tape. We throw the bag over his head and duct tape the shit, so he can't take it off."

"Yeah, good idea. Watch him, I'm gonna get the shit we need. I'll be right back. Call me if he moves."

Augustus Becker attempts to use his charms to seduce both girls and get them back to his hotel room, but he had a bad night. Alone and feeling sorry for himself, he makes his way back to his car. The boys follow at a safe distance, and as he gets to his car, Mark strikes. He runs from behind the car and points the gun at Becker. "Give me the key."

"Are you trying to carjack me, kid? Get the fuck out of here."

"Give me the fucking key, or I'll shoot you."

Becker is looking at Mark. "Don't I know you ,kid? Where did I see you before?"

"You killed my father, you and the guy that looks like a vampire."

"Oh shit, imagine running into you on the strip. Are you jacking cars now?" It was me or your old man, so what are you going to do? Shoot me with a fake gun?"

"It's not fake, and it's loaded."

"Sure it is. I'm sorry kid, but that guy who looks like a vampire is fucking nuts, so if I didn't shoot, he was gonna kill me. So that's it. Now, get out of the way." At that moment, Tommy comes from behind and as Becker turns his attention to the sound, the bag is placed over his head. He tries to fight them off, and he's successful until Mark hits him with the gun. They put him in the back seat, and Tommy jumps into the driver's seat.

Mark shouts, "Let's get out of here." Mark tapes the bag around Becker's neck and tapes his wrists.

Tommy looks in the rearview mirror and says, "So, what happens now Mark? It's your show." Becker begins to stir, and Mark pulls the bag tighter around his face and applies more duct tape.

Becker is kicking at the car window and struggling against the restraints. "Let's go, Tommy. Can't you drive faster?"

"What the fuck do you want me to do? There's traffic. Let me get off the strip before the cops see us." Becker is mumbling incoherently and is struggling less. Eventually, they get to the tunnels, and they stop the car. "Take the bag off his head, and let's get him inside."

Becker hasn't moved in a while and as Mark tears open the bag, he notices Becker's eyes are closed and his lips have a bluish cast. "Oh shit, Tommy. I think he's dead."

Tommy jumps out of the car and looks at Becker's body. "Shit, I think he suffocated. Why the fuck did you make it so tight? That's a big fucking problem, Mark. What are we going to do now?"

"Let's get him into the tunnels and get rid of the car." They half drag and half carry the body into the tunnels when they come across an abandoned shopping cart and load the body onto the cart. The cart is difficult to maneuver, but they finally find a place to dump the body. Augustus Becker is abandoned in the deepest recesses of the tunnels where no one goes, surrounded by mold and rodents and stripped of his jewelry and money.

CHAPTER 56
BBR

Rodriguez gets the call. "Captain Steiner wanted us to check out a body on the approach to I59 West, burned beyond recognition."

"Any ID?"

"Nothing, Rodriguez. It looks like she was intentionally lit up. It smells like gasoline around here big time."

"I'm on the way."

Rodriguez arrives on the scene and McMahon says, "We just ran the plates, and it's a rental. Guess whose name is on the rental contract?"

Rodriguez walks closer to the car and sees what's left of Isabella's hair in the lights of the emergency vehicles and says to McMahon, "It's Isabella but I can't be sure."

"Good guess. I think it's her too."

"Her hair, McMahon. She had beautiful hair. It's her, I'd bet on it."

"We can't do anything without a positive ID."

"Any theories on who or why."

"Maybe she picked up some psycho fuck ,and he killed her."

"No, Rodriguez. She was too classy to work the streets; she catered to a much different clientele. What about Achille Rinaldo? Do you think he fits in here anywhere?"

"I don't know. I have some thinking to do. I gotta get out of here. Can you finish this up? The smell is getting to me." "Dejavu Rodriguez?" "Yeah something like that."

Tommy and Mark are having breakfast when Mark asks, "What do you know about this Prince dude? Does he live in the tunnels?"

Tommy shrugs. "I guess he lives somewhere down there. He shows up in the morning, collects the stuff and disappears, and once a week he hands us envelopes with cash. Now eat your breakfast before it gets cold."

"What if he don't live in the tunnels?"

"What are you talking about? He's one of us. He lives in the tunnels."

"Where does he stay? You ever seen his place?"

"No, but that don't mean shit. Carlos ain't never seen mine."

Mark just nods and begins eating his breakfast. They're both silent and then Mark says, "I wanna find out where he lives."

"What for? I told you he was one of us."

There's silence and then Mark says, "I just wanna know that's all."

It's almost sunrise and The Prince is walking to the tunnels. He enters his meeting room and finds his army there waiting for him. "Well, for once you're all on time. So, did we have a good night?" Carlos is the first to walk up proudly and hand him a watch and a handful of cash. Immediately, The Prince takes out a jewelers loop and examines the watch. "It's a knock off, but still worth a few hundred bucks." He counts the money out loud. "160, 61, 62, 67, not a great haul but not bad, did you use the gun?"

"Damn right. That shit works. They do whatever you want."

"Nice, what about you Tommy? How did you and the kid make out?"

Mark speaks up, "Stop calling me kid. I ain't a kid."

The room goes silent, and the prince responds, "Ok, kid. Show me what you and Tommy got." Tommy reaches into his backpack and takes out a wad of cash and Becker's very expensive watch and 2 rings. The Prince examines the watch as he did the one before and exclaims, "Shit, this is the real deal."

Mark walks up and drops the key to the car on the table. "It's parked on the corner of Main and 7th, a black Range Rover. It may be a little hot, but I'm sure you can figure out what to do with it." Mark glares at the Prince, "So, am I still a kid?"

The Prince looks at Tommy who says, "He jacked the car. He's a natural." The room goes silent, and all eyes are on Mark.

The Prince is happy with the previous night's bounty. "You did good last night, almost 3 grand in money and jewelry and a fucking car. I guess the guns are working, but remember no bullets. There'll be more money in your envelopes this week." His army nods and talks among themselves and some begin to make their way back to where they live in the tunnels. Mark stays behind waiting for the Prince to leave. The Prince puts the money and the jewelry in a briefcase and tells Mark, "You're doing good, kid. Now take off. I'll see you tomorrow." Mark fakes walking into the tunnels, but his eyes are on the Prince as he leaves the darkness and the stifling air of the tunnels. The Las Vegas sunrise warms the strip, and the heat of the sun replaces the cold night air. The Prince walks, briefcase in hand, towards a large apartment complex off the strip and is let in by the doorman.

The Prince hands him an envelope that he immediately shoves in his pocket. In his apartment, he makes a call to one of his contacts and tells him about the car. "No, I haven't seen it yet. I'm gonna check it out now. I gotta get it off the street. One of my crew picked it up last night. I'll take a look at it. If it's worth it, I'll drive it over. Besides, I got a little something for you. We can talk money when I get there. Check out the car. You can sell it, chop it or do whatever the fuck you want after you pay me." Mark waits across the street with his baseball cap pulled down to hide his face. A short time later, The Prince emerges carrying a small package and heads toward the corner of Main and 7th. Mark knows where he's going, and he dials 911.

CHAPTER 57
SETUP BY A "KID"

"911 operator, what is your emergency?"

"There's some dude. Looks like he's breaking into a car on the corner of Main and 7th.

"What is your name please?"

"It's a black Range Rover. It looks brand new."

"Can you see the plate number?"

"Yeah it's CNTMAN Nevada plate."

"You need to tell me your name."

"Nope ain't happening."

"Are you refusing to tell me your name?"

"You don't need to know my name, just get here. He's about to take off."

"I have units on the way."

"Good, I'm out."

"Sir I need you to stay there, sir …"

Mark hangs up and watches as The Prince drives the Range Rover halfway down the street when 2 units from Las Vegas PD stop him mid-block and officers approach the vehicle with guns drawn. Mark is filming the entire scene on a stolen cell phone. The Prince exits the vehicle with hands raised and the officers begin to question him. For the first time in his short life, The Prince is confused about his next move. If he tells the officers he was set up, it implicates him in the Vegas strip robberies and makes him an accessory to murder. From his vantage point, Mark sees an officer pick up the package from the front seat, then there's a brief discussion, and the Prince is cuffed and put into the back of the officer's car. One vehicle stays behind, and the others drive away with the handcuffed Prince in the back seat. He calls Tommy and explains what just happened and that they no longer need to take orders from the Prince. "We're in charge now, Tommy."

The following morning they all gather to hand in the previous night's bounty, and they're waiting for The Prince to arrive. Mark walks in with Tommy, and they sit at the head of the room where The Prince usually sits. Carlos speaks up. "If The Prince sees you there, he's gonna bust your ass." The rest of the army laugh, jeer and high five each other. Mark takes a gun from his back pocket and fires a round above their heads. The noise echoes through that part of the tunnels.

Carlos let's out a very loud, "What the fuck you doing? The Prince said no bullets. You in trouble now, kid."

Tommy shouts, "Everybody shut up. We got something to say." They begin to quiet down, and then he says, "From now on, you'll be working for me and Mark."

A member of the army shouts, "Bullshit, we work for The Prince, not you two bitches."

Mark yells back, "You work for us, or you can walk away and go on your own."

Alice shouts, "Where's The Prince? Why ain't he here?"

Mark smiles, "'Cause he's in jail, 'cause he got caught with drugs and besides, he was a rat for the cops."

"Bullshit, he wasn't a rat, not the Prince."

Mark takes out the cell phone and holds it up for all to see. "I got it all on this phone, so you can see Prince the rat talking to the cops. Tommy, pass it around." The phone makes the rounds among the 7 gathered there, and they mumble and groan as they pass the phone around. "See, it's like I said, so show me what you got last night and afterwards, I'll show you our new meeting place. It's where me and my father used to live." Mark places the loaded gun on the table and says forcefully, "Bring it up."

Tommy whispers to Mark, "Was he really a rat?"

Mark turns to him, "You think I'm lying?"

There's silence as Tommy turns away.

CHAPTER 58
THE CONFESSION

Rinaldo gets back to the penthouse, and it's early morning. His phone has been ringing throughout his meeting with the Russians. Johnny has been calling, desperately looking for Isabella, but the calls were ignored. Finally, he calls Johnny. "What the fuck is going on, Johnny? You been calling me all night. This better be good."

Johnny replies angrily, "Where's Isabella, you fuck? Where did you send her?"

"Be careful how you talk to me, you guinea prick. I didn't send her anywhere. I thought she was with you."

"She never showed up. She texted me that you told her to leave Vegas."

"That's bullshit, Johnny. I never told her to leave Vegas, why would I?"

"Then where the fuck is she?"

"I don't know, Johnny. She's a hooker. Who knows what the fuck they're thinking?"

"If I don't hear from her soon, I'm going to the cops."

"No cops, Johnny, are you out of your mind? That's the last thing we need. If you think you're in love, you better snap out of it."

"She was on her way to meet me."

"Come on, Johnny, she's a hooker. How reliable do you think they are? I'm done talking about this. I'm going to bed. Remember what I said, Johnny. No cops."

Rinaldo hangs up the phone and pours a drink, sits on the couch and considers his next move when the bell rings. Rinaldo says to himself, "Who the fuck is that now?" He fast-walks to the door and shouts, " Who is it?"

"It's Justine, open up. I have something to tell you."

Rinaldo opens the door. As he does, he says, "It's almost sunup, and I haven't slept so….." His voice trails off when he sees the condition she's in. Usually well-dressed, however dated the wardrobe, Justine is standing in the doorway. Her hair is a mess, her clothes are stained, she's drunk and smelling of gasoline. Rinaldo takes one look and exclaims, "What the fuck happened to you?"

"I need a drink, may I come in?"

"Justine, I was about to go to bed. What do you want?"

Justine walks to the bar and grabs a bottle. She throws herself down on the couch and takes a drink." There's silence, and then she says proudly, "I took care of our Isabella problem."

Rinaldo closes the door and walks over, "Isabella problem? What are you talking about? What did you do?" I followed her tonight. She was going to meet Johnny, so I messed up one of her tires. When she pulled over, I smashed her head into the steering wheel, and I set her on fire. I used gasoline of course." She lets out a sinister laugh and exclaims, " Poof, just like that she's gone." She snaps her finger and continues laughing, but she pauses long enough to drink from the bottle. "Did you know that the reason gasoline burns is not because of the liquid, but the fumes?"

Rinaldo grabs her and shakes her, "You set her on fire? Why the fuck would you do that, you stupid bitch?"

Justine is about to take another drink, when he pulls the bottle out of her hand, and the contents splatter on them and the rug."That's right. I set her on fire. It was easier than I thought. She's dead. If you put on the news maybe…" Justine doesn't have a chance to finish the sentence when Rinaldo puts his hands around her throat and squeezes. Her eyes bulge as she tries to pry his hands from her throat.

"Why did you do it, Justine? I should do the same to you." She scratches his hands and attempts to punch him when he comes to his senses, and he releases his grip.

Justine wheezes and coughs and takes deep breaths, with a raspy voice she says, "You motherfucker. You tried to kill me."

Rinaldo takes a drink and shouts, "Shut up, or I'll finish the job. Where's Becker, do you know?"

"How the fuck would I know where he goes?

"Johnny's been calling all night looking for her. Now what the hell do I tell him?"

Justine laughs again. "I don't think Johnny will have her now. She's quite a mess."

Rinaldo stares at Justine, "Maybe I'll tell johnny what you did to her and let that fucking wop take care of it. Would you like that? Now, call Augustus and tell him to get his ass over here."

Justine is on her phone waiting for Augustus to answer, and she nods in the negative. "He's not picking up."

Rinaldo paces for a while and then orders Justine, "Take off your clothes and put them in a pile and go take a shower."

"No, don't tell me what to do. I'm not Isabella."

Rinaldo stares at her and then he lunges and begins to tear her clothes off. He stops and commands, "You stink of gasoline, and you need to sober up. Now, take them off, or I will."

Justine is in the shower, and Rinaldo collects her clothes and puts them into a garbage bag. He tries to call Augustus and, frustrated, he pounds on the bathroom door. "Did Augustus tell you where he was going?" Justine doesn't answer, and he tries again louder this time. "Did Becker tell you where he was going last night? I need you to think if he said anything. It's important."

Through the door, he hears the shower being turned off. "I told you before, he doesn't tell me what he does or where he goes."

"Hurry up and get out here. We need to talk." Justine comes out of the bathroom, her hair wet and the rest of her wrapped in a towel. She stands in front of him and lets the towel drop to the floor. He's surprised and looks her up and down. "You're drunk, Justine, and besides, I'm sure we have different tastes." He points to a bedroom and tells her, "There's a closet in that bedroom where Isabella has her clothes. Get dressed and get out. I'll keep trying to get Augustus." Justine stomps off to the bedroom and slams the door. After a while, she emerges wearing Isabella's clothes. "Go back to your hotel room and wait for my call. One of my men will get rid of your clothes."

"Are you going to kill me?"

Rinaldo stares at her and ignores the question. "As soon as I hear from Augustus I'll call you. Now, get out."

CHAPTER 59
IT'S JOHNNY'S MOVE

Rinaldo is pacing the penthouse floor, considering what to do next. He knows he can't trust Justine to keep quiet. He thinks to himself that maybe he should have finished the job while he had the chance. He pours a drink and sits. He's about to call Augustus when his phone rings and it's Johnny. He reluctantly answers, "Hello Johnny."

Johnny is breathing heavily with anger. "You motherfucker. Isabella's dead, and don't tell me you don't know anything about it."

Rinaldo pauses and takes a drink, feigning ignorance about Isabella's death, "Calm down, Johnny. How do you know she's dead?"

"Because it's all over the fucking news. Whoever did it set her," Johnny's voice trails off, "poured gasoline on her and set her on fire."

Rinaldo picks up the remote, and the news comes on, and it's dominating the am news cycle. "Come to the penthouse, Johnny. We need to talk."

"Talk, talk about what?"

"Just get here. I'll be waiting." He hangs up and calls Paolo. "I need you at the penthouse. Find Luciano and get over here now."

"What's going on boss?"

"I said find Luciano and get the fuck over here now."

"Yeah, boss. I'm on the way."

Rinaldo goes into his bedroom and unlocks a black case. He removes 2 handguns and tucks one into his belt and hides the other under a sofa cushion, and he sits waiting for Johnny. He pours another bourbon just as there's a pounding at the door. He listens for a while and then shouts, "Yeah, who is it?"

"It's Johnny," and he hears the sound of the door knob turning.

"Don't bother, Johnny. It's locked. I'll let you in." He moves to the side of the door with gun in hand and unlocks the door and slowly turns the knob. Johnny pushes the door open and, also with gun in hand, comes face to face with Rinaldo. The 2 men are now engaged in a stare down with guns pointed at each other. "Well, Johnny, nice of you to come," he says as they circle each other. "We can have a Texas style shootout where we probably both die, or you can join me in a drink, and we can talk like gentlemen."

"Who killed Isabella? She…"

Rinaldo cuts him off, "Said the lovestruck little puppy. Come on, Johnny. She was a hooker, don't act like you were in love with each other. If she told you that, it was all bullshit."

Johnny moves closer. "Who did it?"

Rinaldo replies, "I'm going to have another bourbon. Care to join me? Let's have a drink, and I'll tell you." Rinaldo lowers his weapon and moves towards the bar, fills a glass with ice and pours himself a drink. "You want rocks in yours, Johnny?"

"I could kill you right now, you piece of shit."

"You could, but then you'll never know who killed Isabella."

"And you do?"

"Of course, now how do you like your bourbon?"

Johnny slowly lowers his weapon. He walks toward Rinaldo, who turns, startling Johnny and hands him the drink. "Rocks, just like mine." He sits on the sofa cushion next to where the second gun is hidden. "Put your gun on the bar alongside mine and have a seat." Rinaldo stares at Johnny and takes a sip of his bourbon. "I'm leaving Vegas soon, and the offer is still open if you want the job."

"Fuck the job, I want to know who killed Isabella, and I want to know now."

Johnny is eying the guns on the bar and Rinaldo notices. "Before you make a move for that gun and force me to kill you," and removes the gun from under the cushion. "I suggest you listen to what I have to say."

Johnny realizes he could never move fast enough before Rinaldo fires, and he's resigned to listen. "Go ahead, tell me who it was."

"Not so fast, Johnny. First I need a commitment from you, and then I have a proposition."

"Go ahead."

Rinaldo puts the gun down on the sofa beside him and pauses, "Remember when I asked you to kill a cop who's been prying into my business?"

Johnny nods, "Yeah, I remember."

"I offered you a hundred grand for it, am I right? And part of the deal was that you would be my personal bodyguard, and I would make you a wealthy man. Soon we'll be leaving Vegas and..."

Johnny interrupts, "Come on, get to the bottom line."

Rinaldo glares at him and says, "Patience, Johnny. I'll need you to keep your end of the bargain soon. This cop Rodriguez has to die, or he'll hunt me to the ends of the earth. I know the type. He has a partner, some bitch named McMahon, and I know they're on to me. Ok, Johnny. The bottom line is this. If I tell you who did it, stay cool and don't lose your head, you got it?"

Johnny replies angrily, "Tell me and stop fucking around."

"Do you accept my offer? Think carefully before you decide."

"Yeah, I accept the offer."

"All of it, you'll kill this cop?"

"Yeah, all of it."

Rinaldo smiles. "Ok Johnny, it was Justine." Rinaldo pauses for effect and stares at him.

"Bullshit, it was one of your goons. Do you think I'm stupid?"

Rinaldo smiles, "I can prove it. It's very simple."

"Go ahead, show me, prove it."

Rinaldo points. "See that smelly garbage bag sitting on the cheap hotel rug? Open it and look inside."

"What are you talking about?"

"Go ahead, open it. Your proof is in that bag." Johnny stares at Rinaldo and slowly walks over to the bag. As he gets closer, he smells the gasoline and looks back at Rinaldo. "Go ahead, Johnny, open it." Johnny slowly opens the bag, and the smell of gasoline causes him to step back. "Look at the clothes, Johnny. Do they look like they belong to one of my goons? Those are Justine's."

"Justine, that fucking bitch." Johnny goes to the bar and picks up his gun and heads for the door.

Rinaldo again aims his gun at him. "Stop right there. You work for me, and I call the shots. Don't fly off the handle, or we'll all wind up in prison. Now, go and wait for my call."

Johnny asks," What about Justine?"

"For now, leave her alone. I mean it, Johnny. The last thing we need is another body showing up that can be traced back to us. You can take care of the both of them before we leave Vegas."

"And when is that? When the fuck are we getting out of this joint? I'm tired of Vegas."

"Patience, Johnny. I'm waiting for a rather large sum of money to be transferred from my contacts in Istanbul. I can't leave till then. Is that good enough?"

"Money for what?"

"Let's just say it's a new business venture. My contacts want me to set up operations in Russia and some areas not too friendly to the United States, so we have to be careful. Are you ready for a challenge, Johnny?" Johnny slowly turns and opens the door as Rinaldo shouts, "Wait for my call." Johnny slams the door and heads for the elevator. The doors open and out step the bodyguards Paolo and Luciano. The men eye each other and Johnny steps into the open car of the elevator, his eyes fixed on the men.

Johnny gets to the street and calls Richie. Richie picks up and before Johnny can say anything, he says, "I heard about it this morning. Wasn't that the broad you were banging?"

"Yeah Richie, and how about some respect for the dead? Her name was Isabella."

"Sorry Johnny, bad choice of words. Any news on Rinaldo? What's his next move?"

"He's waiting for some money, then we're out of Vegas. I think he trusts me, so it should be easy to set him up. Before we leave he wants me to kill this cop named Rodriguez."

There's silence and then Richie asks, "What was that name again?"

"He said Rodriguez, just Rodriguez. Why, who cares?"

"I care, did he mention a cop named McMahon?"

Johnny replies, "Yeah, he said that's his partner."

"Shit, Rodriguez is back in Vegas. What the fuck is he doing here?"

"What was that, Richie?"

"Nothing, Johnny. Get out of Vegas, forget Rinaldo. I'll figure it out."

"What are you talking about? You paid me to do a job."

"Forget the job, get Frankie and leave. Rodriguez is off limits. Besides, you'll never get close to him."

"Off limits, what the fuck does that mean?"

"Let's just say we have a history. Let it go.

"What about Rinaldo?"

"What about him? I told you I'll figure it out."

"Why the sudden change of heart, Richie?"

"Listen to me. Get out of Vegas. I don't want to get caught up in this shit."

"Ok Richie, I get it, but there's something I gotta do first."

"What the fuck did I just tell…"

Johnny hangs up before he has a chance to finish the sentence.

CHAPTER 60
ROOM 13

Paolo enters the Penthouse, followed by Luciano. He asks in his trademark broken English, "What did Johnny want? We don't like him, right Luciano?" Luciano just nods in agreement.

Rinaldo speaks up. "This isn't about Johnny. Have a drink, and then I need you to do something for me."

Luciano asks, "What's that boss?"

Rinaldo takes a key out of his pocket and hands it to him. "About two miles east, just outside the strip, there's a dive called the Vegas Motel. In Room 13, you'll find the body of a young girl."

Paolo blurts out, "A body?"

"Yes, a body. It's under the mattress." The men glance back and forth at each other. "Take it to the desert. You know what to do."

Paolo asks, "Who is it, boss?"

Rinaldo gives Paolo a cold stare. "She was a gift from my Russian contact. It's all part of the cost of doing business."

"What happened, boss?"

Rinaldo turns his back on the men and pours another drink. "Things got a little out of hand. Don't ask me stupid questions. Go, do as I say." The men turn to leave and Rinaldo shouts, "Luciano, come back here. I need you to take that bag over there, seal it and dump it in the desert."

Luciano takes the bag and throws it over his shoulder, "Hey boss, it smells like gasoline."

Rinaldo shakes his head. "I'm surrounded by fucking geniuses. I know what it smells like. That's why I asked you to seal it. Go down the service elevator and go out through the garage."

McMahon and Rodriguez are on their way to interview Rinaldo about Isabella's death. "Park in the garage, and let's avoid the front. I don't want anybody to know we're here."

"Yeah, good idea, McMahon." As they drive into the garage, Rinaldo's men are driving out, and they pass each other and lock eyes.

McMahon asks, "Wasn't that one of the guys in the Penthouse that night that guy went out the window?"

"Yeah, his name is Paolo. I'm sure they're up to no good should we follow them?"

"No, we don't have a reason. Let's talk to Rinaldo."

Rinaldo opens the door and exclaims, "Come in, I was expecting you. I assume you're here about Isabella."

Rodriguez looks around and asks, "Has the maid been here this morning?"

"No, why do you ask?"

"Because the place stinks of air freshener. It's a bit much. Seems like somebody's going out of their way to cover up a certain smell."

Rinaldo bristles. "What does that mean?"

Rodriguez continues to walk around the Penthouse. "Were you with Isabella last night before she died?"

"Yes, we were here, but she left around 8, and when I put on the news this morning, I found out what happened.".

"Did she say where she was going?"

"She said she was going on a date."

McMahon inquires, "A date I thought you and her…"

Rinaldo interrupts. "You thought what? That we were together, in love, soulmates? Come on, she was a Vegas call girl or whatever they call them these days. I assure you our relationship was not built on affection. It was business."

"Did she give you a name, a place, any indication where she was going? Did she tell you when she was coming back?"

"No, but she took an overnight bag and a lot of makeup like she was going to be away for a few days. I always wondered why they feel the need to wear so much makeup."

Rodriguez glances at McMahon, "Did she mention a hotel or a place she was staying?"

"No, she didn't. She showered and left in a hurry."

"A hurry?"

"Yes, I suppose she was running late. I didn't ask."

"Were you here all night?"

"Yes, I was, after she left, I had a few drinks, and I retired around 10 and woke up at 8."

"What about your bodyguards, where were they?"

"I don't know. They had the night off. If there's no more questions, I have a busy day ahead."

McMahon looks at Rodriguez. "Are you good?"

"Yeah, for now. When do you plan to leave Vegas, Mr. Rinaldo?"

"I'm not sure. I'm waiting for a shipment."

"Shipment of what?"

"Oh, just some fabric samples, swatches, clothing patterns, things like that."

"Thanks, if anything else comes up, we'll be in touch." As they're walking to the door Rodriguez turns and asks, "You ever been to the Metropolitan Hotel?"

Rinaldo is surprised by the question, "No, the place is a dive. Why would I go there, Sergeant?"

"Just asking. I had a very unpleasant experience in the tunnels directly underneath the hotel."

Rinaldo scowls and they lock eyes, "What does that have to do with me?"

McMahon breaks the tension, "Come, on let's go." As they walk towards the elevator, McMahon says, "What was that Metropolitan thing all about?"

"Nothing, just trying to get a reaction." They pass a maid pushing a cart loaded with cleaning supplies. Rodriguez spots a can of air freshener, and he stops her. "Excuse me, did you clean Penthouse 4 this morning?"

"No, sir. You told me to come back later."

"That wasn't me. Where do you keep the cart when it's not being used?"

"In that closet at the end of the hall," and she points to an open door that says Employees Only.

"Is it always locked?"

"Yes, but I keep it open when I'm working."

"Thank you, sorry to bother you." Rodriguez pushes the button and stares straight ahead. "Did I hear him say he went to bed around 10, and he got up at 8?"

"Yep, that's what he said."

Still staring ahead he exclaims, "10 hours sleep, and he looks like crap."

McMahon finishes, "Like he hasn't slept all night."

CHAPTER 61
THE FIRE IN GREENWICH

Rodriguez is unable to sleep. It's 5am, and he rises and puts on the coffee machine. The morning quiet is broken by a call from Detective Jankowski. "Good morning, Will what time is it there?"

"Good morning, Sergeant. It's 8'o'clock."

"Very good, and that means it's what time in Vegas?"

"Oh shit, I forgot about the time difference. I woke you up, didn't I?"

"It's ok, I couldn't sleep anyway. There's a lot going on here. So, what's on your mind?"

"I did some research like you asked about the Greenwich fire, and it seems that cops in Springfield, Mass. picked up a guy named Julius Baxter for attempted arson on an auto body shop. Looks like an insurance job. Baxter told the cops he met a guy a few months ago named Hector Maldonado who was bragging about a Greenwich fire that he was paid big money for setting a few years ago."

Rodriguez replies, "What is it with these guys that can't keep their mouths shut?"

"Let'em talk. That's good for us. So, we ran a check on this Maldonado character, and it seems he's locked up in New Haven. We're heading up there to interview him tomorrow."

"Great work, Will. what else?"

"Well, rumor has it that Justine Godfrey may be in your neck of the woods."

"Really, and how did this rumor get started?"

"Well, we did a little checking after she bailed herself out, and her name turned up in Reno when she signed a bond note for a guy named Augustus Becker."

Rodriguez adds, "Augustus Becker is with the Nevada Gaming Commission. He's on the board."

"Well, listen to this, it turns out that Becker was arrested for solicitation for the purpose of prostitution."

"He propositioned an undercover, but he didn't stop with the sex for money."

"No, Mr. Becker attempted to recruit her into working for him."

"What was he charged with?"

"Here's the interesting part; he was initially charged with solicitation and attempted human trafficking, but the charges were reduced to solicitation, and he was bailed out with an appearance ticket."

Rodriguez responds sarcastically, "I'm sure he'll show up for that. I think it's time to track down Ms. Godfrey and have a talk. It may sound funny, Will, but I think she has a crystal ball."

"Why do you say that?"

"Because when I busted her at the mansion, she said that we would meet again. I'm wondering how she's connected to Becker."

Rodriguez arrives at the precinct early and calls the Medical Examiner for any information on the death of Amy Stiles. McMahon enters and sits across from him and hands him a coffee. "Did you get anything from the ME on the cause of death?"

"No, the initial report still stands and it's cardiac arrest." Rodriguez leans back in the chair and takes a sip of the coffee. "There's a woman named Justine Godfrey, and I think she's in Vegas or Reno."

"Who is she?"

"She's a socialite from Greenwich, Connecticut who had wealthy parents…"

McMahon cuts him off. "Had?"

"Yeah, they died in a mysterious fire that was ruled an accident."

"Ok, and you don't buy that."

"I don't buy it for a minute. I think she killed them for the money. My detectives are gonna talk to an inmate named Hector Maldonado tomorrow in Connecticut. It seems he was there the night they died. My detectives have a feeling that Godfrey's in Vegas, and I'm beginning to think that this guy Rinaldo, Godfrey and Isabella were involved with Amy Stiles, and she was being trafficked."

"Too bad about Isabella."

"Yeah, there's somebody in Vegas who likes to play with matches. The only question I have about this trafficking thing is the scope of it. Maybe it's international. Remember when Rinaldo said he'll be traveling soon? I wonder what that's about."

McMahon declares, "I keep thinking about Amy. She was doing better, and then suddenly, she takes a turn for the worse and within a few days, she's dead. I'm not waiting for the final Medical Examiner's report. I'm going to the Hospital to have a talk with the nurses on duty."

"Go ahead, McMahon. I'm gonna check the hotels for Godfrey."

"Keep me posted," and then she says sarcastically, "Stay out of the tunnels."

"Yeah, thanks. I'll try."

McMahon arrives at the Vegas general Hospital. She identifies herself and nurse Janet comes out to greet her. McMahon points to a vacant room and asks, "Was that her room?"

"Yes, I read about her fiancé Gino and what happened with this Diamond Jack thing." He seemed like a nice guy, it's sad."

"Yeah it is." What about visitors, did she have many?"

"No, just Gino mostly and a friend of hers."

"Friend? Do you remember this friend's name?"

"Yeah, it was Isabella."

McMahon pauses and walks to the room and turns to Janet. "May I go in and look around?"

"The authorities asked us to leave the room as it is, and we can't put any patients in there till all the autopsy results are verified, you know toxicology and all that."

McMahon replies, "I understand."

"Do you think something happened to her? You don't think she died of natural causes?"

McMahon doesn't answer, she enters the room and looks around. She turns to nurse Janet, "What does Isabella look like?"

"She's young, maybe late twenties, dark hair and light eyes. She had an accent, a slight one."

"How many times did she visit Amy?"

"Just once while I was on duty."

"Just once, how long ago was that?"

"A few days before she died."

McMahon looks at Janet, "How long did she stay?"

"About an hour, maybe a little less."

"Is that the only time?"

Janet thinks for a minute. "Wait, there was a time before that when Gino was here. She visited for a while."

"Did Gino know her?"

"No, that was the first time they met. Gino seemed surprised. She said she was a friend of Amy's for about a year."

"A friend of Amy's for a year, and she never met Gino before? It seems strange doesn't it." McMahon continues to look around the room.

Suddenly, Janet picks up something from the floor. "That's strange."

McMahon replies, "What's strange?"

"This cap. It's for a syringe, but we don't use this type. Our caps are clear."

McMahon finishes the sentence. "And this one's blue. May I have your full name Janet?"

Janet asks, "Do you think somebody..."

McMahon cuts her off. "May I have your full name?" She thanks nurse Janet and leaves. She gets to her car and contacts Rodriguez. "Hey, Rodriguez, how did you make out with this Godfrey character?"

"So far, not so good. I'm heading to the Stratosphere now."

"Oh yeah, your favorite place. Thinking of doing another jump?"

"Very funny, McMahon. How did you make out at the hospital?"

"Better than you. It seems Isabella paid Amy a visit when Gino was there and a few days before she died."

Rodriguez responds, "Did they know each other?"

"I'm not sure. Janet Paterson, the head nurse, said Isabella told her she was a friend of Amy's for about a year. The strange thing is that Gino and Isabella had never met before that visit. Kind of weird."

"I'm sure a woman with Isabella's looks was very busy."

Rodriguez replies, "Yeah, I'm sure."

"The duty nurse, Janet Paterson, found a cap for a type of syringe they don't use."

There's a pause and then Rodriguez asks, "Isabella?"

McMahon answers, "If it was her, I guarantee Rinaldo was behind it."

CHAPTER 62
JUSTINE AND HECTOR

Rodriguez arrives at the Stratosphere Hotel and walks to the main desk. The clerk approaches. "May I help you?"

"Yeah I hope so. I'm looking for somebody. Her name is Justine Godfrey. Is she staying here?"

The clerk looks at him suspiciously. "Why are you looking for her?"

"Your answer tells me she's here, am I right?" Rodriguez shows his badge. "I'm Sergeant Rodriguez. What room is she in?"

When the clerk sees the badge, he exclaims, "I'll get the manager."

The manager gets to the desk and asks, "Sergeant, what can the Stratosphere do for you?"

"I want to know if Justine Godfrey is registered here."

"You do realize that legally I don't have to tell you unless she's suspected of criminal activity."

"Yeah, I know that, but I'm trying to avoid parading her through your lobby handcuffed and being followed by a bunch of uniformed Vegas cops. I think that would freak out your guests, don't you?"

The manager stares at him and says, "She stepped out early this morning, and she hasn't come back. Would you like to leave a note for her, Sergeant?"

"A note, sure I'll leave a note." The manager hands him a note pad and a pen. Rodriguez reaches into his side pocket and removes his own pen. "Thanks, but I'm used to mine." He begins to write and when he's done, he hands the note to the manager and he asks, "What's your name?"

"My name is Ralph Maisonet."

"Ok, Ralph. Read it out loud."

"I can't, I'm not allowed. I could get in trouble."

"Read it, Ralph. I know you're going to read it anyway, so go ahead and read it."

"But I can get fired if I do."

"Don't worry. I'll make sure you don't get fired."

Ralph looks around and asks, "Can we move to the end of the counter, Sergeant? There's less people there."

"Sure, whatever you want."

Ralph removes his glasses from his pocket and begins to read the message. *"Dear Justine, this is Sergeant Rodriguez. I'm sure you remember me from Oceanview. Tomorrow my detectives are traveling to Connecticut to interview Hector Maldonado. We believe he was the fire bug from the Greenwich fire that destroyed the mansion and killed your parents. Give me a call at Captain Steiner's office. He's with Las Vegas PD. Let's have a drink and we can discuss what happened to your parents. Don't wait too long.* Ralph looks at Rodriguez and removes his glasses.

"So, what do you think Ralph? It sounds serious, doesn't it.? "Now put it in an envelope and seal it."

Ralph is silent and then he exclaims, "Wait, I know who you are! You're the guy that went off Sky Jump last year."

Rodriguez doesn't answer but smiles as he walks away. "Make sure she gets the note, Ralph, and let's keep this between us ok." "Thanks for your help."

Detectives Jankowski and Martino arrive at the New Haven Correctional Center. Hector Maldonado is brought into a private office flanked by two correction officers. Hector is a slight man in his thirties with a baby face and as he approaches the officers, he appears nervous and anxious. He sits across from the officers in the pale green painted room, and Detective Jankowski notices the bruises on his face and his swollen lip. "Shit, Hector. What happened to your face?"

Hector replies, "What do you guys want?"

"I'm Detective Jankowski, and this is Detective Martino. We've got some questions for you."

"I don't have to tell you shit."

"You're right, you don't, but judging from your face, I get the feeling you're having a tough time in here."

"Oh yeah? You should see the other guy."

The detectives laugh, and Martino asks, "You ever been to Greenwich, Connecticut Hector?"

Hector sits back and his eyes dart between the men. "No, never."

"Really, that's not what we heard."

"I don't care what you heard. I was never there."

Jankowski says, "Did you know there was a house fire there a few years ago, and two people died?"

Hector smirks and shrugs. "That's got nothing to do with me."

"Really, do you know a guy named Julius Baxter?" Hector is no longer smiling. Jankowski leans forward, "Yeah, I knew that would wipe the smile off your face. It seems that Mr. Baxter overheard you bragging about setting a fire that you got big money for." "You want to tell us about it cause right now you're suspect number one."

Hector becomes agitated and is gesturing wildly, and he raises his voice. "Wait a minute. I can explain what that was about."

"Go ahead, explain it."

"We were in a bar, and I was drunk. I was just bragging, you know, acting tough. I swear I had nothing to do with that shit."

"So, tell us what you know about it."

"All I know is that this guy hired me to do this Greenwich job with him, but when we got to the house, we realized there were people inside. I ain't torching a house with people inside. No fucking way."

The detectives are silent, and Jankowski says, "Who's this guy you're talking about?"

"I only know his first name."

"Well, what is it?"

"It's Sam. He told me his name is Sam."

Martino says, "Sam, that's original. What do you think, Will?"

"I think he's full of shit."

"I swear, he told me it was Sam. That's it. He didn't give me his last name."

"Did he tell you who hired him?"

"No, but he had keys, and he had pictures of the house."

Jankowski glances at Martino. "So, tell us about that night. What happened?"

"I want a lawyer, or I ain't talking."

"Ok, get yourself a lawyer. We'll be back, but we've got Julius Baxter, and he'll testify. He heard you shooting your mouth off. As far as anybody's concerned, you lit the fire, and this Sam guy doesn't exist. So, go ahead. Make the call, but like we said you're all we got."

Jankowski gets up to leave and Hector says, "Wait, wait! Ok, I'll tell you about that night, but what's in it for me?"

"Not much, but maybe I can get you moved to a safer cell block, 'cause I look at your face and damn."

Hector says, "Sit down. I'll tell you what happened."

The men sit down, and Jankowski places a recorder on the table next to Hector. "I hope you don't mind." Hector pauses and nods.

Martino turns on the recorder. "I need you to state that you agreed to have this interview recorded without an attorney being present, do you confirm?" Hector nods. "It's a recorder, Hector. You gotta speak up, say yes that you agree and speak slow, and clear Hector slow, and clear."

Hector begins, "I got a call one night. It was really late. The guy told me his name was Sam, and I was recommended."

"You were recommended, by whom?"

"He wouldn't give me a name, but he offered me 10 grand to help him do this blaze in Connecticut. Like I said, he had keys and pictures of the place."

"So, he's got keys and pictures to the house, but he never told you who hired him, is that right?"

"Yeah, that's right."

"So far Hector, you haven't been very helpful. Is there anything else you can tell us? Like, this guy Sam's address, phone number, is he tall, short anything." Hector is quiet and Jankowski asks, "So, keep going. What happened when you got to the house?"

"He met me on Main and 14th avenue in Stamford. He was in his car, and I was in mine, and we drove to Greenwich."

"Who's idea was it to meet in Stamford?"

"It was his. He said something about it being halfway."

"Halfway between where?"

"I don't know. We parked a few blocks down and walked the rest of the way."

"Did you see anybody?"

"No man, this fucking place is deserted and dark. There's no street lights."

"When we got to the house, we went around the back, and I could hear music, and I could see that a few lights were on."

Jankowski looks at Martino, "It seems strange that you guys didn't trigger an alarm or something."

"Sam said it was gonna be shut off before we got there, but when I realized there were people there, I told him I wanted out. He said he never walks out on a job, and he's not starting now. While he was getting the accelerants ready, I took off to my car and drove out of there. He was gonna make it look like an electrical fire. Next day, I read about it and found out that two people died."

"When he called you, did a number register on your phone?"

"No, just unknown."

Martino asks, "Anything else, Hector?" and he stares at him.

Hector nervously replies, "No, that's it."

"Thanks Hector, we'll be in touch."

"Wait man, you said you were gonna get me transferred."

Jankowski says, "We'll check your story. If it pans out I'll get you moved."

Maldonado watches them as they walk away and then he speaks up. "Wait, I been lying to you guys."

Martino looks at Jankowski. "Well, we're shocked, aren't we Will?"

The men return and sit down, and Jankowski says, "Go ahead, Hector, this is your last chance. Don't fuck with us again." He turns on the recorder. "Go ahead Hector."

"Ok, Sam gave me a name."

"What name Hector? Let's hear it."

"He said the rich bitch that lives there hired him."

"Very good Hector. Was the name Godfrey?"

"Yeah, Godfrey, she's the one. She told him there were expensive paintings in there, insured for some serious bucks, plus the life insurance."

"Thanks Hector, you're back on our good side. We'll do what we can to get you moved."

The men get to their car and Martino says, "Baxter never said he would testify against Maldonado, and he's in custody in Massachusetts."

"I didn't lie. He's in custody, maybe not in Connecticut, but Hector doesn't know that. For now we don't need him, and if we do, we know where to find him, and I think he can be persuaded to talk."

"I see Rodriguez taught you well. Let's fill him in."

"Are you really gonna try and get him moved?"

"Yep, I said I would try. Come on, let's eat. I'm starving."

"I say fuck him."

"Easy Martino, sounds like you need to eat. Come on, I'm buying."

CHAPTER 63
IT'S ME, JUSTINE

Rodriguez is meeting with McMahon at the Las Vegas Police headquarters. Captain Steiner knocks and enters, "Sergeant, there's a call for you in my office. It's Ms Godfrey. She said it's important that she speak to you."

Rodriguez smiles at McMahon, "Looks like I still got it."

She replies, "Don't flatter yourself."

Rodriguez winks and leaves the office. He answers, "Hello, Ms. Godfrey."

"Sergeant, you must miss me. I'm flattered that you followed me all the way to Vegas from Long Island. So, what's this about a drink?"

"Well, I was thinking we can have a drink just before I arrest you."

Justine laughs, "You have a sense of humor. Arrest me for what exactly?"

"For starters, the murder of your parents, accessory to murder and suspicion of human trafficking."

"How did you find me?"

"You bailed Augustus Becker out of jail in Reno. I assumed Vegas would be the next stop and I was right."

Justine is silent. "And I assume you can prove these charges, Sergeant. Of course, you realize that my parents' death was ruled an accident, and the case is closed, and I can't speak to the other charges, since I have no idea what you're talking about."

Rodriguez says, "I've got some time to kill. Let's have that drink, and I'll lay my case out for you."

"Did you say time to kill, Sergeant? No man has ever used that line on me before, so where would you like to meet? I need to be discreet, so somewhere off the strip if that's ok."

Rodriguez suggests, "Sure, do you know a place called Rudy's right off the boulevard?"

"Of course, it's nice and cozy. Let's say 5 'o' clock. I need some time to freshen up ok so see you at 5."

"Yeah, see you at 5."

Rodriguez arrives before 5, sits at the bar and orders a bourbon. Justine is fashionably late, and she walks in overdressed for the occasion as usual. She sits next to him and leans in close, and she notices his drink. "I see that you started without me."

"Yeah, I did. They have a great cocktail hour. What would you like?"

"What is that you're having?"

"Bourbon."

She shakes her head. "I'm afraid it's a bit too strong for me. I'll have a chardonnay."

Rodriguez smiles and says, "There's a surprise."

"Are you mocking my chardonnay, Sergeant?"

"No, it's just that I thought you'd like red."

"So, Sergeant, lay out that case for me. I'm intrigued."

Rodriguez looks around and sees a table in the corner away from the other tables. "Not here. Let's sit down."

He gestures to the corner, picks up their drinks and they walk to the table. They drink in silence and then Justine asks, "So, how are you enjoying Vegas, Sergeant?"

"I'm not here on vacation exactly."

Justine interrupts. "Oh yes, that Diamond Jack case. I read about it. You're a hero."

"Let's just say it was a group effort and everything came together, not happy about the way it turned out."

Justine replies, "Why not? You took a killer off the street, and I like it when things come together," and she flashes a flirtatious look at Rodriguez.

"So, Justine, what brings you to Vegas?"

"Me? I'm just helping out a friend."

Rodriguez takes a sip of his bourbon. "Do you wanna play a game, Justine?"

"A game, what do you have in mind?"

"I'll throw out some names, and you tell me if you know them, and you can't lie to me. I've been a cop too long. I'll know by your facial expression if you're lying."

Justine thinks for a minute. "I assume this little game is off the record."

"Of course, it's just two people having drinks."

"I don't need a lawyer, do I?"

Rodriguez ignores the question. "Ok, here goes the first name. Are you ready? It's Augustus Becker."

"Of course I know Augustus. We were a couple for a while. It wasn't love. Actually, it was mostly lust. We were going to go into business together, but it would have been a conflict of interest since he's on the Gaming Commission."

"So, you and Becker were going into the Casino business?"

"Yes, we were, but besides the fact that he's on the Commission, he can be high maintenance, if you know what I mean."

"No, what do you mean?"

"He's always checking himself out, looking at his reflection in store windows, bragging about his looks, a real vain prick."

"When was the last time you saw him?"

"That's an easy one. When I bailed him out of jail in Reno, but you already knew that. Nice try, Sergeant."

"Ok Justine, are you ready for another one?"

"Gino Marchetti, do you know him?"

"No, but the name is familiar. I believe he was Diamond Jack, wasn't he?"

"How about Amy Stiles, do you know her?"

Justine shifts in her seat and thinks for a minute. "Amy Stiles, no I don't. The name is not familiar."

"Ok, just one more, then I gotta go. Are you ready?"

"Yep, go ahead."

"Sam, do you know him?"

Justine again shifts in her seat and looks at her drink. "Did you say Sam?"

"Yes Sam. Do you know him or not?"

Justine takes a sip of her wine and replies, "Just Sam? No last name?"

"Nope just Sam."

"No."

"Ok, how about Hector Maldonado? Do you know him?"

"You said one more. That's two more. You're not playing fair, and I don't know them."

"That's funny because they know you. They were the guys that burned down the house and killed your parents. You know the house you're living in now. Hector Maldonado is ready to testify that you're the one that hired Sam, and Sam hired him to help burn your parents' house down. I've got more. How about David Evans, Achille Rinaldo, Isabella, do you know any of them?" Justine is agitated and she gets up to leave. "Before you go, I've been in touch with David Evans and with a little persuasion, I think I can get him to come to Vegas and have a talk with me, you know, to clear his conscience."

Justine is glaring at Rodriguez, and she says, "What the fuck do you want from me?"

"Come to Captain Steiner's office, he's at the 15th precinct on Mountainside Avenue, and ask for me around noon tomorrow."

"And what if I don't?"

"If you don't show up, I'll get a warrant."

Justine responds angrily, "This is harassment. I'm bringing my lawyer with me."

"Please do." Justine storms out of the bar. He watches her leave, leans back in the booth and takes a sip of his bourbon.

CHAPTER 64
LAWYERED UP

Justine shows up at the 15th Precinct a little after 12 with her lawyer Attorney William McMaster. They're led to an office where Rodriguez, McMahon and Captain Steiner are waiting. Rodriguez offers, "May I get you anything?"

McMaster answers, "No, let's get it over with. I have a busy day."

McMahon looks at the attorney. "You may want to put some of that on hold. What we have to present is very serious."

McMaster glances at Justine. "First of all, I want to say that my client is here of her own free will, and she's not under arrest and that no warrant for her arrest has been issued. Is that correct?"

McMahon replies, "We appreciate her coming in, and yes that's correct, no arrest and no warrants."

Rodriguez turns to McMaster. "Did Ms. Godfrey tell you why I asked her to come in?"

McMaster replies, "Yes, she stated that you asked her out for a drink, and then you accused her of some outlandish charge of murdering her parents a few years ago. A tragedy that was investigated and ruled an accident, an electrical fire I believe."

"What else did she tell you?"

"She also said that you accused her of being involved in some human trafficking ring, and you named some people that she's supposed to know, and it turns out she has no idea what you're talking about. Sounds like harassment to me, Sergeant, and you should cease all contact. With that, I'm ending this little meeting. Come on, Justine. We're done."

McMahon exclaims, "Sit down. Sergeant Rodriguez isn't finished."

"If there's nothing else, we're leaving."

Rodriguez says, "Sit down. Just because we don't have a warrant doesn't mean we can't get one. What's important is not what she told you, but what she didn't tell you." Rodriguez removes a newspaper clipping from his pocket and he reads, "The date is September 18th, 2018. Mr. and Mrs. Jonathan Godfrey were found by firefighters as they fought a blaze at 421 Seaview Lane in Greenwich, Connecticut. Their bodies were located in a rear bedroom where they took shelter from the heat and the flames. The fire is deemed suspicious until further investigations are carried out. The Connecticut arson unit and the Sheriff's Department are seeking information from the public regarding the blaze." Rodriguez slowly folds the clipping and puts it back in his pocket. He turns to McMaster. "A few days ago, two of my detectives went to New Haven Correctional Institute to interview a guy named Hector Maldonado. This guy was bragging about a fire he started in Greenwich a few years ago where he was paid big bucks. This was overheard by his friend, a guy named Julius Baxter, who's in Springfield Mass. awaiting trial on, you guessed it, arson charges. Julius is trying to make a deal, and he told the authorities about Maldonado. When my detectives interviewed Hector, he told them that a guy named Sam hired him to help with setting the blaze, but at the last minute he, meaning Hector, backed out because he heard activity in the house, and he didn't want to kill anybody. This mystery guy, Sam, told him that this rich bitch, his words not mine, hired him to torch the house for the insurance money."

Justine shouts out, "He called me a bitch? That motherfucker."

McMaster forcefully exclaims, "Shut up, Justine."

"There's more. Maldonado told my detectives that her name was Godfrey."

McMaster sighs, "Is this true, Justine? Did you know any of this before you called me?"

"No, it's all bullshit. He's been after me since that incident in Oceanview."

Rodriguez ignores Justine and exclaims, "One more thing."

McMaster, realizing he's losing the battle, says, "Go ahead, Sergeant."

"You said it yourself, counselor, when we started this conversation. You said it was ruled an electrical fire, is that right?" McMaster is silent. "Maldonado said that Sam was told by Ms. Godfrey to make it look like an accident, an electrical fire. It's very possible with a house that old, but If Maldonado wasn't there, how would he know that?"

McMaster leans forward, "So, is my client under arrest?"

Rodriguez responds, "No."

"So, what do you want, Sergeant?"

"Besides the arson in Greenwich, we believe that your client is involved or may know people involved in a human trafficking ring that might be tied to a larger international ring."

Justine exclaims, "That's bullshit."

McMaster states, "Justine, please let me handle this. Don't keep digging. That's a serious charge. What proof is there?"

McMahon answers, "Mansour Ayad might be able to answer that if we can find him." Justine fidgets in her seat and looks at McMahon.

McMaster asks, "Who is he, and what does he have to do with my client?" He turns to Justine and asks, "Have you ever met this Ayad?"

"No, never."

McMahon says, "Mr. Ayad checked into Penthouse #1, but nobody saw him check out. They just assume he did. Supposedly, his assistant took care of everything, but we don't believe that. We think Mr. Ayad never left Penthouse #1, at least not alive."

Rodriguez reaches into a bag by the side of the desk and says, "You know, for the life of me I can't figure out what happened to the other shoe." He places a red stiletto shoe on the desk. "It's a size five, and I'm looking for Cinderella?"

Justine jumps up and says to her attorney. "Get me out of here."

McMaster asks, "What's this all about? Why the theatrics, Sergeant? If my client is not under arrest, we're leaving."

Rodriguez protests, "Not yet, sit down. There's one more thing."

"You've harassed my client long enough, what do you want?"

"You can leave, but tomorrow I want you both here at noon just like today. I'll tell you what I want then. If you don't show up, I'll get a warrant for Ms. Godfrey's arrest for the Greenwich fire, so I guess I'll see you both tomorrow."

Godfrey and her attorney leave the office as Rodriguez takes the shoe off the table and returns it to the bag. McMahon, obviously upset, asks, "So, what was that all about?"

"What, the shoe?"

"Yes, the shoe. Where did you find it, and why didn't you tell me?"

"First of all, I didn't find it. I bought the pair at some sex shop on the strip for $59.99, not a bad deal."

Captain Steiner smiles. "Did they come with a matching G-string?"

McMahon looks at Captain Steiner and exclaims, "Really, Captain?" Rodriguez is suppressing laughter as she continues to question him. "Like her attorney said, why the theatrics?"

Rodriguez leans closer. "Did you see her reaction when she saw them? She knows what went on in Penthouse #1, which means she met Mansour Ayad, and she knows what happened to him."

McMahon answers, "I think all this ties in with Amy Stiles and Isabella, and I think the key to Rinaldo is Godfrey. So, we need to decide on what we do next."

Rodriguez reaches into his bag and takes out the recorder with Hector Maldonado's confession. "I know what to do." He plays the recording. "Ain't FedEx grand? It arrived yesterday. It's Maldonado on the tape. I want to wire Justine tomorrow. We can use her to get to Rinaldo."

McMahon says, "Good idea, but the honorable Mr. McMaster might not want you to wire his client."

"Well, I'm thinking this recording might persuade him."

McMahon exclaims, "If they show up."

Rodriguez looks at his watch. "Any minute now McMahon."

"Any minute what?"

"You'll see. Want a coffee?"

"Sure, what's going on Rodriguez? I know that look."

Rodriguez returns with the coffee just as a courier appears at the office door and declares, "I have an envelope for a Sergeant Rodriguez."

Rodriguez glances at McMahon, her eyes fixed on him. He says, "'I'll take it," and he shows his identification. The courier leaves and he holds up the envelope and waves it back and forth.

"Ok, Sergeant. The suspense is killing me. What's inside?"

"It's an arrest warrant all the way from Connecticut for Ms. Justine Godfrey, and now I'm going to serve it. Once she's in our custody, we'll have a stronger bargaining position."

"Nice, but I'm coming with you."

"No McMahon, I'm doing this alone. It's kind of personal. Right about now, she's packing her bags. She wasn't coming in tomorrow. I guarantee it."

"I'm assuming you don't want back up."

"For Ms. Godfrey? I don't think so. See you later, McMahon."

"Damn you, Rodriguez."

He laughs and flashes the peace sign as he walks out the door.

CHAPTER 65
ARE WE SQUARE?

Johnny is walking the strip after doing some serious drinking, considering his next move. He's standing outside Justine's hotel, and he calls Rinaldo. "It's been a few days since Isabella died. Are we any closer to getting the fuck out of Vegas? I've been a good soldier. I did everything you asked."

"Give me a few more days. All the transfers will be complete, and then we can get out of Vegas. You ever been to Istanbul, Johnny?"

"No, why?"

Rinaldo laughs. "'Cause that's our first stop. Then from there, Morocco and then to Moscow where my contacts and I will set up shop. Trust me, Johnny. You'll forget about that whore Isabella between Istanbul and Morocco. By the time we get to Moscow, we'll be rolling in money, and that whore will be a distant memory. Did you ever sleep with a Russian woman? She'll help you forget. They're very obliging, Johnny, if you know what I mean. Isabella's got nothing on them. A guy with your looks, you'll be fighting them off. Are you still on-board, Johnny? Don't disappoint me." Johnny is quiet. "I want your answer."

"Yeah, I'm still on board."

"Great, let's have dinner tonight. Come to the penthouse at seven. We have plans to make."

"Yeah, sure." Johnny begins to walk back to his hotel with Rinaldo's words about Isabella echoing through his head. He stops into a bar, and he continues drinking. As he drinks, his anger reaches its peak. He throws his money down and walks on the strip. Eventually, he stops and says, "Fuck this."

He dials Rinaldo. "Yes, Johnny."

"Guess what, asshole? I'm on my way to kill that bitch, and you can't do shit about it. Fuck you, and fuck your plans. I'm gonna kill Godfrey, and then I'm out of here."

"Johnny, wait. Don't be an idiot. You're gonna bring the cops down on us. Do you remember our talk?"

"Yeah, I do, and you can forget about that cop. I ain't killing a cop."

"Johnny, calm down, ok? Forget about killing the cop, and I'll take care of Justine before we leave Vegas. Come to the penthouse now. We need to talk."

"Yeah, you think I'm stupid? If I come back there, those fucking goons of yours will kill me." Johnny is screaming loudly, and he's heard by Paolo standing nearby who shakes his head in the affirmative as Rinaldo waves him off. "I'm gonna take care of business and then I'm tipping off this cop Rodriguez. So long, douchebag," he shouts into the phone.

"Johnny, Johnny? Fuck." Rinaldo is panicked, and he barks orders at Paolo and Luciano. "Luciano, call Massimo. Tell him to have the plane fueled and ready in an hour."

"We leaving, boss?"

"Of course we're leaving. Johnny just fucked everything up. Both of you, pack your shit. I'll call down and have them come for our bags."

Luciano asks, "you want me to find him and shut him up boss?"

314

Rinaldo answers angrily, "there's no time for that you idiot I told you to pack your shit and hurry up."

Johnny enters the lobby of the Stratosphere and sees a bellhop standing in front of the elevators. He looks down and reads his name tag. "Hello, Tobias. Busy day."

Tobias is taken by surprise by the question, and he takes a step away from him. "Not too bad."

Johnny moves closer "Well Tobias, it's about to get bad really quick. In my pocket, I have a gun pointed at your back, and if you say or do something stupid, I'll shoot. Do you understand? Just nod."

Tobias nods yes. "What do you want? "Are you robbing the hotel?"

Johnny smiles,"No, I want you to take me to Justine Godfrey's room and let me in."

"I don't know what room she's in." The elevator doors open and they get in. Tobias is scared and with a shaky voice he asks, "Are you going to kill me?"

Johnny sighs. "How old are you, Tobias?"

"I'm 19."

"Do you go to college?"

"Yes, I do."

"What are you studying?"

"I wanna be a veterinarian."

"You love animals?

"Yes."

"Me too, so stay in school you're going to make a great animal doctor don't turn out like me. Now, look up her room number." The doors open on the ninth floor and as people get on Johnny says, "This is going up."

"Yeah, we know. We're going to Sky Jump."

"Sky Jump, are you going to do that?"

"Yeah, that's one of the best things about Vegas."

Johnny shakes his head, "Why do people risk their lives like that?" Johnny looks at Tobias, "How are you doing with that room number?"

Tobias says, "Press thirty-seven, please."

"I was just telling my friend Tobias here that you should never do silly things that can get you hurt, right Tobias?"

Tobias reluctantly responds, "Right."

"I guess it's the adrenaline rush." The elevator stops at thirty-seven. "Well, this is us." They walk down the long corridor

Tobias says, "Thirty-seven-o-three is at the end of the hall."

"When we get inside, I want you to lock yourself in the bathroom, and do not come out no matter what you hear. Got it?"

"What are you going to do?"

"Just do as I say."

They get to the room, and Tobias says, "I don't want to do this."

"I know you don't, but you have no choice. None of this is your fault. Now, open the door."

Rodriguez parks in the Stratosphere garage and fast walks to the front desk. The clerk approaches. "May I help you, sir?"

He identifies himself, "Has Justine Godfrey checked out yet?"

"No, she hasn't but she called for a limousine going to the airport. It should be here any minute."

"I need the key card to the room."

"But Sergeant, I can't do that. Guest Confidentiality. It's the law in Vegas. You need a court order."

Rodriguez looks at his name tag. "Give me the key card, John. it's important."

"But, Sergeant."

"Now John."

John sighs. "I'll have to call the manager…"

Rodriguez raises his voice. "Give me the key, or I'll go up and kick the door in, and you can explain that to the manager."

John finds it and nervously hands him the card." "Thanks."

Tobias opens the door, and they enter the suite. Johnny pushes Tobias into the bathroom on the right and closes the door. Justine has her back to the door and she's startled. "You're early. I'm still packing and aren't you supposed to knock first?"

Johnny walks toward her. "I'm not here for your bags, Justine."

She recognizes the voice and turns around, "Johnny."

"Don't act surprised, Justine. Rinaldo told me all about how you killed Isabella."

"Rinaldo's lying to you. His goons did it."

"No, it was you. He showed me your clothes stinking of gasoline. You never liked her, and you always had it in for her. You thought you were better than her." Johnny continues walking towards her. As he gets closer., he puts the gun back in his pocket.

Justine, seeing this, relaxes and says, "So Johnny, you're not going to shoot me after all?" He gets closer and grabs her by the neck with one hand and pushes her down on the bed. She slowly takes a knife from her open travel bag and attacks him. The knife makes contact before Johnny disarms her. He looks down and sees the blood coming from his side. She tries to fight him off but Johnny now has the knife and plunges it into her chest.

"How do you like it?" and he continues to stab her.

The elevator doors open and Rodriguez steps out just as Johnny staggers out of the suite. Rodriguez shouts, "Police! Stop!" Johnny turns and fires as Rodriguez takes cover. He fires again and begins to run for the exit. Rodriguez steps out and shouts again, "Stop!" Johnny turns and is about to fire again, but Rodriguez fires first, hitting Johnny, and he falls. He checks the suite and sees Justine bloodied and lying across her luggage, the knife still protruding from her chest. He feels for a pulse, but she's dead. Tobias opens the bathroom door and as he emerges. Rodriguez commands, "Step out with your hands on top of your head. Do it now." Tobias is shaking and Rodriguez asks, "Who are you?"

"My name is Tobias. I work here and this guy…" His voice trails off as he sees Justine's bloody body.

Rodriguez calls for assistance and tells Tobias, "Get back in the bathroom. I'll tell you when to come out." He grabs a towel and checks on Johnny. He puts pressure on the gunshot wound. "Hang on, I radioed for an ambulance."

Johnny asks, "Is she dead?"

"Yeah, she's dead."

Johnny says, "Good. She should go to hell, the fucking bitch." He coughs. "Good shooting. cop." He pauses. "What color is the blood?"

Rodriguez evades the question. "Why did you kill her?"

"She killed someone close to me. She burned her to death. Her name was Isabella. She set her on fire."

Rodriguez replies, "I know all about Isabella. How did you get involved in all this?"

"Me, I made the mistake of falling hard for her. She worked for this guy named Rinaldo, a real piece of shit. He was gonna give me a job bodyguarding him, and he promised me all kinds of money. The only catch was I had to kill a cop that's been dogging him."

"Does this cop have a name?"

"Yeah Rodriguez, just Rodriguez." There's silence and then Johnny says, "Shit, don't tell me that's you."

"Yeah, that's me."

"Just my fucking luck. I'm Johnny DelVecchio from Detroit. Nice to meet you. I was supposed to kill you."

"So Johnny, how'd that work out?"

He's quiet then he says, "You didn't answer me. What color is the blood?"

"It's dark red, almost brown."

"Cancel that ambulance. I ain't making it. I've seen guys shot through the liver. It bleeds brown. It's only minutes before they check out. Just my luck all these years I'm dealing with fucking wise guys, and I get fooled by some broad. It's my fault. I let my guard down. Rinaldo's your man. He's behind it all: the trafficking, that hooker Amy and the rest. It's all on him. He's at the Luxor penthouse 4."

"I know where he is, Johnny."

The elevator doors open and emergency personnel arrive. Johnny says, "He's always got these fucking goons with him, so be care…"

Captain Steiner arrives with the first responders. "Rodriguez, what the hell is going on?"

"There's a homicide victim in 3703. Her name is Justine Godfrey. This guy is Johnny DelVecchio and he killed her. I gotta go. You'll get my report tomorrow. Oh, and before I forget, there's a guy in the bathroom. Tell him he can come out. He's ok. He works here."

Rodriguez trots to the elevator. Captain Steiner calls, "Rodriguez, "Rodriguez! What the hell is going on?"

The doors open and more officers pour out of the open car. Rodriguez turns to Steiner. "Tomorrow, Captain."

The doors close and Steiner angrily says, "Goddammit."

Rodriguez is driving to The Luxor when his cell phone rings. "This is Rodriguez."

"Congratulations on catching Diamond Jack."

"Who's this?"

"It's Richie DiNapoli."

"DiNapoli, how the fuck did you get my number? It's been almost a year. Are you ready to turn yourself in?"

"Very funny. I got your number from a mutual friend, and after this call, I'm gonna forget it. So, how bad do you want that fucking pimp Rinaldo?"

Rodriguez pauses. "Go ahead, I'm listening."

"I had a guy on the inside posing as his bodyguard to set him up."

"Set him up?"

"Yeah, an associate of mine hired me to kill Rinaldo, and Rinaldo wants my guy to kill you. I tried to get him once, but his bodyguard got in the way."

"So, that night when he went off the balcony, that was you in the hallway camera."

"Yeah, I'm still in Vegas, in case you're wondering. I told my man to back off and get out of town. Bottom line, Rinaldo wants you dead asap. If it ain't my guy, it'll be somebody else."

Rodriguez asks, "Your guy wouldn't happen to be Johnny from Detroit?"

"Yeah."

"Well, you're a little late, DiNapoli. He's dead."

"Shit, I told him not to fuck with you, but he didn't listen, the dumb wop."

"Why are you telling me this, DiNapoli? I thought you wanted me dead."

"Wrong, I don't want you dead. I want you out of my business. I never backed out of a contract, but I'm sitting this one out. This prick Rinaldo's all yours."

"Why are you after him?"

"Nothing personal. It's just that I've had my eye on this castle," Richie pauses, "it's a long story. Consider this call pay back for Maxie. I know what you been doing for him."

"And what am I doing for him?"

"Come on, Sergeant. I'm in hiding. I'm not dead. How long do you think he would have lasted in that joint? I had a few guys watching his back to make sure he didn't get hurt, but you know how it goes in there. He's not like us. He doesn't have the instincts. Maxie's always been a loyal friend, and by moving him, you saved his life, and I'm paying his debt by warning you. Next time you see him, tell him. The slate is clean now. I'm getting out of Vegas. Are we square?"

"What do you think?"

"Yeah, that's what I thought. So, I guess the chase is on."

"Maybe, but thanks for the warning."

"Yeah sure, Rodriguez. See you around."

CHAPTER 66
AB

With lights flashing and sirens blaring, the ambulance races through the Vegas night as the driver radios ahead. "This is unit 82. We have a John Doe on board. He was found in the tunnels. Looks like a concussion and oxygen deprivation. He's severely dehydrated and has multiple lesions,especially around the face and arms. Looks like insect and rodent bites. Some of the wounds are open and appear to be infected, please advise."

The answer comes from Vegas General, "Start an IV, administer oxygen and monitor vital signs. Is John Doe conscious?"

"Not entirely. He's Incoherent at times and comatose at others."

"Thank you, 82. We have a triage team waiting. Do we have any way of confirming identity?"

"No, just a monogram on his shirt. It looks like the initials AB. It's hard to see, but it looks like AB."

"You picked him up in the tunnels?"

"Yeah, somebody found him wandering around and called it in, but he doesn't look like a resident. Gucci shoes, Armani belt, no wallet, no watch or jewelry, this guy looks like he's a victim."

"Ok, come in. There's a team waiting."

Augustus Becker is moved on to a hospital gurney muttering and incoherent as he's being wheeled into Vegas General.

CHAPTER 67
DESERT DEMISE

Rodriguez speeds to The Luxor and parks in the underground garage. He removes the bottle he found in Gino's truck from the glove compartment and puts it in his pocket. He walks through the service entrance and past the kitchen and hotel staff. He sees a waiter wheeling a room service cart onto the elevator. He flashes his badge. "I need to go to the Penthouse floor. I'm gonna ride up with you."

The waiter is surprised seeing him with blood on his shirt and jacket, and he asks, "Don't you have to check with the concierge?"

"No, let's go."

He pushes the button and as they ride up the waiter asks, "What happened.?"

He looks down. "You mean the blood? It's a long story." Rodriguez asks, "What's your name?"

"My name is Tomas."

"I'm Rodriguez, the guy that went off Sky Jump last year."

Tomas' eyes brighten up. "Oh man, that was you? What happened? Did you try again and miss?" and he motions towards the bloody shirt and jacket.

Rodriguez smiles. "No, Tomas. It's not mine." The doors open on the 25th floor and Tomas exits the elevator. He turns and, Rodriguez says, "Good night, Tomas." He arrives at the penthouse and listens by the door. There's activity coming from inside, and Rinaldo's voice can be heard above all the commotion. He draws his gun and knocks on the door. The knock surprises the men inside, and the suite goes silent.

He overhears Rinaldo. "Tell them to come back in half an hour. We're not packed yet."

Luciano opens the door, and Rodriguez, with gun drawn, says, "Get back inside." He attempts to reach for his gun, but Rodriguez hits him on the side of the head, and he falls unconscious. Rodriguez is moving his gun between Rinaldo and the bodyguard Paolo. He takes Luciano's gun from its holster, and now he has one gun trained on Rinaldo and the other on Paolo. He focuses his attention on Paolo. "Your name's Paolo, right." Paolo nods. "Ok, take out your gun with two fingers, and put it on the sofa, and stand by the door with your hands up." Paolo does as he's told.

Rinaldo says, "What the fuck do you want? I'm leaving Vegas. Is that against the law? "

Luciano begins to stir and tries to get on his feet. Rodriguez shouts, "Stay down. Don't make me hit you again."

Rinaldo orders, "Luciano, shoot this fucking cop now."

Paolo recognizes him and asks, "You were here the night Silvano was killed. That was you with that lady cop, right?"

"Yeah, that was me."

Luciano gets to his feet and attempts to attack Rodriguez, but he's hit again and he goes down. Rinaldo shouts, "Get the gun and shoot him, Paolo. What the fuck is wrong with you? Kill him."

Rodriguez shouts, "Shut up, Rinaldo." He turns his attention again to Paolo. "Hey Paolo, it's your lucky night. I'm letting you go. Leave tonight. If I catch you anywhere in Vegas, I'll lock you up."

Paolo looks at Rinaldo who says, "You work for me. Don't listen to this cop."

He answers in his usual broken English, "Sorry, boss. I don't want to go to jail."

Rinaldo shouts again, "Is that the only gun you have? What kind of fucking bodyguard are you?"

"I'm leaving, boss," and he picks up one of the suitcases.

Rodriguez asks, "Is there another gun?"

"No, I swear just one," and he opens the door."

Rinaldo shouts again, "Get back here, you fucking stupid guinea."

He pauses and puts down the suitcase "I'm not a stupid guinea." He picks up the suitcase and opens the door, but he stops and turns to Rodriguez. "Mr. policeman, can I tell you something?"

"Yeah, make it quick."

"There's a girl…"

Rinaldo interrupts, "Shut up! Shut your fucking mouth."

Rodriguez orders, "Shut up, let him talk."

Paolo continues, "This girl, he killed her in a Motel close to Vegas. Me and Luciano buried her in the desert. He told us to do it."

Rinaldo looks at Rodriguez, "Don't listen to him. It's bullshit. I didn't kill anybody. Shut up, Paolo."

Paolo puts his head down. "She was young, maybe fifteen or sixteen. I'm sorry."

Rodriguez is staring at Paolo, and he tells him, "I'll count to five. If you're not out of this room, I'll put a bullet in your fucking head. One, two, three," and the door slams behind him. "Let's go, Rinaldo."

"Am I under arrest? Where's the cuffs?"

"Shut up and move."

Rinaldo exclaims, "Don't forget to read me my rights," and he laughs.

Rodriguez gives him a shove. "Move. My car is in the garage. We're going down the back through the kitchen and out the service entrance." The men get in the elevator, and Rinaldo says, "All that blood, what happened to you?"

"The guy you hired to kill me wasn't up to the task. He told me all about Amy and Isabella."

"Who's Amy? I don't know anybody named Amy."

"Don't play stupid. It's over. Get in the car."

"Why are you arresting me? You don't have a body. It's all a waste of time."

"I don't need a body or witnesses."

"Let me go and save yourself the embarrassment. You have no evidence."

Rinaldo attempts to get in the back, and Rodriguez stops him. "Put your hands behind your back," and he handcuffs him. "Get in the front."

"The front? But don't prisoners usually ride in the backseat?"

"I said get in the front." Rinaldo sits and stares straight ahead. Rodriguez walks to the back of the car and pours the liquid on to his handkerchief. When he gets in, he places it over Rinaldo's face. He struggles briefly, but then he stops moving. Rodriguez drives the state road through the Mojave Desert. He travels approx. 7 miles and turns onto a mining trail, and he travels an additional 3 miles.

Rinaldo begins to awaken, and he's confused and disoriented. He looks around and asks, "Where are we?"

Rodriguez says, "Turn around." He removes the cuffs, draws his gun and orders, "Get out."

Rinaldo looks at him in disbelief. "Get out here? You can't leave me here. It's the middle of the desert."

"I drove in about ten miles. You can walk back. Just look for the lights."

"You're a cop, cops don't do shit like this."

"Get out and start walking."

"Fuck you, I'm not getting out."

"I know you had Amy killed, and you promised Johnny a lot of money to kill me. What about Andy, did you kill him?"

"No, it wasn't me. It was Becker. Augustus Becker. I can take you to him."

"I'll find him on my own, but thanks anyway. What about your business associate Mansur Ayad? I have the feeling he never left Vegas, am I right?"

"I didn't kill him. It was Isabella, I swear," Rinaldo responds frantically. "Is that what you want? A confession? Alright, I'll confess. Just take me back."

"Too late, get out."

Rinaldo says, "No."

Rodriguez puts the barrel of his gun against Rinaldo's knee. "You can walk back to Vegas, or you can crawl. Now, get out." He reaches across and opens the door. "Out."

Rinaldo's demeanor changes and he begins to grovel. "I won't survive in the desert. I'll never make it back to town. You can't do this. You're a cop for Christ's sake."

"Did you kill that girl in the motel?"

"No, no Paolo was lying. He was lying."

"Why would he lie? You killed that girl, didn't you?" Rinaldo is silent. Rodriguez says, "Give me your phone, and get out."

"No, please. I'll go to jail but…"

Rodriguez yells, "Out!"

Rinaldo shouts, "Fuck you! Goddam cop!" He gets out and slams the door. Rodriguez drives away, leaving him standing in the middle of the trail.

CHAPTER 68
CRISS CROSS
(DEATH BY THE VINEYARD)

Richie is aboard a private plane to New York. He stares out the window and thinks of the early days when he was coming up through the ranks. He never failed to fulfill a contract, and he wonders if there's something he could have done differently to get Rinaldo. He contemplates going back to finish the job, but he's resigned to the fact that in this instance, abandoning Vegas was the smart move. Maybe Rinaldo will spend the rest of his life in prison and justice, in some way, will be served. He sits, sipping champagne, and one of the attendants asks if he'd like a newspaper. The paper is delivered and anticipating a long and boring flight, he begins to read. As he goes through the paper, the article on page two gets his immediate attention. "ITALIAN BUSINESSMAN FOUND DEAD IN THE DESERT. Achille Rinaldo, a well-known international apparel businessman from Malta, was found dead in the desert approximately 6 miles outside of the Las Vegas strip. Authorities are investigating the mysterious death and have no leads at this point."

He stares at the headline for a while and finishes the champagne in his glass. He continues reading and pours himself another glass and folds the newspaper. He smiles and puts his seat back and looks out the window. He thinks to himself, "You're more like me than you think, Rodriguez."

The jet lands in New York, and Richie connects for a flight to Sicily. It's just before sunrise when he arrives in Catania. The drive to Carazzo's villa is along the shorefront with beautiful baroque mansions and white washed villas reflecting the rising sun. He's exhausted from the flights and the lack of sleep and considers stopping and resting, but his desire for vengeance pushes him on. He arrives at the road leading to the villa. He hides the car and goes the rest of the way on foot. In the early days of his rise in organized crime, he was known for his ability to kill silently, and he carries his trademark tools, ice pick, straight edge razor, and garrote made of piano wire. He knows that Lorenzo Carazzo is a man of habit, and he enjoys his morning coffee watching the sunrise on his vineyard. This morning is exactly that type of morning with the scent of jasmine permeating the Sicilian air and the mist on the eastern side of Mt. Aetna glistening in the sun. He slowly makes his way from the rear of the villa on the opposite side of the vineyard. He knows that Carazzo will have extra men patrolling the grounds, and he needs to get in and out as quickly as possible, and he knows there's no room for error. The sun is over the horizon, and the villa is now well lit. The sun is skimming the vineyard, casting long shadows in the aisles between the rows of vines. A cool breeze coming from the seaside of the villa invigorates him, and he cautiously moves on.

Carazzo sits on the veranda, admiring his vineyard with the newspaper neatly folded, ready for his morning ritual. His personal bodyguard, Guido Sarconi, has always been there in the morning with his espresso, fresh fruit, and breakfast pastry, but this morning is different, and something doesn't feel right. He calls to Guido, and there's no answer.

He calls again, "Guido, dov'e la mia colazione?" {Guido, where's my breakfast?}

A voice from behind him exclaims, "Guido non può sentirti." {Guido can't hear you.}

Carazzo recognizes the voice, and he makes the sign of the cross. Carazzo is silent and then he says, "Did you kill Guido?"

"No, Lorenzo. I didn't come here for Guido."

"Please, Ricardo. Think of my family."

"Your family is not my responsibility Lorenzo, you made the sign of the cross. I'll give you a chance to pray."

"Ricardo, it was Santino, not me, that set you up."

"Not true. That's a lie. How did he know what flight I was on?"

Carazzo pauses, searching for something to say, "He checked the airlines going to Vegas. That's how he found out, Ricardo."

"No, that's another lie. I told you I was flying under my real name, and it's not DiNapoli, it's Diamante, and now you'll go to hell with that lie on your lips."

Carazzo, in shock, asks, "Diamante, Tony Diamante."

"Yeah, I'm his son."

Carazzo attempts to reach for a gun that he keeps under the table, but Richie says, "Don't do it," and he slips the garrote around his neck Carazzo is weeping as Richie says, "Goodbye, Lorenzo." Lorenzo folds his hands to pray as Richie tightens the wire. He cries out ,and he kicks, knocking over the table and the dishes crash to the floor as Carazzo tries to pull the garrot from his neck, but it's beyond that now. His death is inevitable. Carazzo's fingers are bleeding as he fights with the wire. Richie can feel the life leaving Carazzo's body and eventually the struggle ends with one last gasp from Carazzo. Richie leaves the garrote around his neck, and he says, "Deliver the message to Santino."

Sensing someone behind him, he turns and Guido, who was unconscious a few minutes ago, is running towards him, aiming to fire. Richie falls to the floor and takes the gun from under the table, and as Guido gets closer, Richie fires twice, killing him. The sounds of gunfire bring more of Carazzo's bodyguards running towards the vineyard. Richie runs back the way he came, opposite the vineyards. He hides in the gardens surrounding the villa as Carazzo's bodyguards search for him. He slowly makes his way to the car, and as he drives away from the villa, shots ring out and a bullet shatters the back window. Driving at a high rate of speed, he's being chased by a car with three of Carazzo's bodyguards inside. They're traveling on the narrow road with the cliffs on one side and a rock wall on the other. Another shot rings out, and Richie knows that there's no place to hide on the narrow roadway.

Up ahead, he sees his opportunity to bring the chase to an end. In the right lane, he sees a truck slowly making its way around a curve, and he speeds up and moves into position in front of the truck and slows down. The pursuit car reaches the curve, and Richie's car is not in sight, and they speed up, thinking Richie is still ahead of them on the road. As they drive by the truck, Richie is ready with gun drawn. He empties the gun through the passenger window, bullets and bits of glass find their mark. The driver is wounded, and he loses control of the car as Richie speeds off. The pursuit car caroms off the rock wall and is hit by the truck. The car is vaulted over the guard rail and plunges down an embankment. Richie accelerates and exits at a sign that reads Messina-Traghetto per San Giovanni (Messina Ferry to San Giovanni)

A week has passed and Rodriguez is back in Oceanview. He's in his office booking a flight to Paris for a long overdue vacation. Jankowski enters his office. "Agent McMahon called earlier. She wants you to call her back." Rodriguez dials and sits back in his chair.

"Hello Sergeant, how's Oceanview? Are you settling back in?"

"I'm taking a vacation, McMahon. Just booked a flight to Paris. I need to get away for a few weeks."

"Paris, how nice. Do you know anybody there?"

'Yeah, but I haven't seen her in a while."

"Great, you need a vacation. How's Bogie doing? I'll bet he missed you."

"Yes, he did, but Jankowski's a good foster parent. He did a good job. What about you, McMahon,?"

"Me? I'm closing this case, and then I'm going back to L.A. Captain Steiner and I were just having a cup of coffee, discussing how much we miss you. Ain't that right, Captain?"

Captain Steiner takes a sip of his coffee, smiles and nods. "That's right."

McMahon says, "We finally saw the surveillance footage from the penthouse floor a few days ago." The hotel didn't want to give it up."

There's silence and then he says, "And what did you see?"

"There was a lot of activity on that floor. First, this guy leaves carrying a piece of luggage. We have no idea who he is, maybe one of his body-guards. A little while later, two men leave and one of the men is Rinaldo, but the other looks a lot like you."

"Me, really?"

"Yeah, but when I went back to look at it again, it was gone."

"What do you mean gone?"

"That part of the tape was gone, like it was erased. It's strange. I don't know what happened. It disappeared. In the suite, we found three phones with mostly international numbers. Interpol is involved now. Should be interesting to see who they belong to. So, when are you going to Paris?"

"I'm leaving Friday night."

"Enjoy the vacation, and don't forget to keep in touch"

"I will, McMahon. Too bad the security footage wasn't more help."

"Yeah, it's a real shame."

"Thanks for everything, McMahon."

Augustus Becker is anxiously sitting up in his hospital bed, his face bandaged, waiting for the plastic surgery team. In a conference room,

Dr. Lucas is briefing her team. "Augustus Becker was a John Doe brought in a few weeks ago, incoherent and disoriented, and was identified by his fingerprints. The authorities believe he was a victim of a robbery and assault and left in the tunnels. He suffered severe rodent and insect bites, which became infected. With treatment, the infections have subsided, but further reconstructive surgery will be needed. Let's check on his progress, shall we?" Dr. Lucas enters the room with her assistants. "Good morning, Mr. Becker. How are you feeling this morning?"

He responds, "How the fuck do you think I'm feeling?"

Dr. Lucas nods at one of her assistants, and he prepares a syringe. "How much, Doctor?"

"I think 5 ccs should be enough."

"What are you talking about? 5 ccs of what?"

"It's just a mild sedative, Mr. Becker. If you should need it. The infection is under control, and the wounds are closing; however, this is the first step in the recovery process and…"

Becker interrupts, "I want a mirror. Where's the mirror?"

"We have a mirror, but when we take off the bandages, we'll see the progress. Please keep in mind that the wounds to your face and arms were severe. Are you ready, Mr. Becker?" Doctor Lucas begins to slowly remove the fabric from Becker's face.

Becker is wide eyed and anxious, and he exclaims, "What's taking so long? Hurry up."

"This can't be rushed, Mr. Becker."

The last section of fabric is removed and he demands, "Give me the mirror. Give it to me."

Dr. Lucas is examining his face. "Some of the wounds are still open, Mr. Becker. Perhaps when they have healed further, you can have a look."

Becker is agitated and he says, "Give me the fucking mirror," and he wrestles the mirror from the assistant's hands.

Dr. Lucas tells her assistant, "Go ahead."

The sedative is administered and the room is suddenly quiet and then a voice echoes through the Intensive Care Unit. "THAT'S NOT MY FACE. THAT'S NOT MY FACE. THAT'S NOT ME."

EPILOGUE

Achille Rinaldo an international human trafficker and members of his organization met their match in Sergeant Rodriguez and Agent McMahon. From the Wheel of Misfortune to the tunnels under the Vegas strip, Rodriguez and McMahon confronted the serial killer Diamond Jack and also uncovered a human trafficking ring.

Watch for the next riveting crime novel from George Marzocchi and Red Penguin Books!

ABOUT THE AUTHOR

Red Rock Bleeds completes the Detective Rodriguez series which started with Stained Glass and continued with Cyclist Club. George has also written several short stories in the crime/mystery genre also published by the Red Penguin Collection. Although the Detective Rodriguez series has come to an end there are currently other works underway in the crime and mystery genre.

George is an avid fan of cinematography and classic/nouveau film noir. He has a visual eye and has spent many years as a professional photography and is currently working in the large graphics field.

www.ingramcontent.com/pod-product-compliance
Lightning Source LLC
Chambersburg PA
CBHW060228100726
47907CB00003B/550